THE CRIES OF MONSTERS

HER CURSED PROTECTORS

THE CRIES
OF
MONSTERS

HER CURSED PROTECTORS BOOK 2

MIA HARTSON

ISBN: 978-0-6457298-1-8

First printing edition 2023 in United States

Cover design by Trif Book Design

Copyedited by Lyss Em Editing

Mia Hartson

PO BOX 1052, Golden Grove Village, SA 5125

www.miahartson.com

For you, dear reader. I hope this book makes your mind whirl, your cheeks ache (from laughing, I mean), and your heart race.

Mia x

CHAPTER 1

~ Locke ~

I flew high over the city, my wings cutting through the frigid air as I soared over sprawling mansions and cobbled streets filled with monsters who were only just beginning their night. Lanterns around the city burned steadily, the thousands of small blue fires resembling a smattering of stars, but I didn't see the beauty of it. I never did anymore. Katakin was a place ruled by power and greed, and for me, it was the hell that never ended.

I wondered then whether Raine would appreciate the sight, and my lips unwillingly twitched upward into a half smile. *I look forward to it, asshole.* The last words she said to me repeated in my mind, accompanied by the image of her face, her pink lips pursed and her amber-eyes brimming with hatred. I had a feeling she'd see Katakin much as she saw me. She would tell herself that she despised everything about the city, but deep down she'd be enthralled by it.

Captivated by its darkness and beauty like a moth drawn to a flame. I didn't doubt parts of her loathed us monsters, but it wasn't all hate. Her being with Kade was proof of that.

My thoughts went to the delicious moans I heard coming from Kade's bedroom while I'd been trying to read in the common room. It was obvious what they were up to and as my mind conjured images of the two of them together, my pants had become tight. Kade and I had shared a few females in the past, mostly so we could keep one another in check, and the urge to join them had made it impossible to focus on the words on the page in front of me.

Fuck. Just thinking about it again had me grinding my teeth. My thoughts then went to my father who had visited my personal rooms not too long ago, and the fury I'd been trying to contain reignited. I knew Warrick's fucking games. He hadn't just gone out of his curiosity to see Raine. He'd visited my rooms to remind me that I couldn't keep any secrets from him, and he could take everything from me if he wanted, including the spirited little human.

I'd told him Raine was a shifter newblood, and I could only assume he believed it. But for how long? If Warrick figured out she was still human, he'd drag her to his lab, where he'd pull her apart if it meant finding out more about the curse that tormented us. The vampire had the power of the Taratun council behind him, and if he put forward the case that he needed her, the council would order me to hand her over. But I wasn't going to let him fucking have her. And I suspected my brothers wouldn't either.

Red flashed before my eyes as I thought of Warrick trying to take Raine away, and I flapped my wings harder, breathing in deep through my nose and hoping in vain that the chill air would cool my temper. It's why I was out there. When Warrick had left our rooms, I knew I had to get out of the mountain before my anger made me do something stupid.

The moment Warrick's coal-black eyes had landed on Raine, the urge I had to kill him had been unlike anything I'd ever experienced. Rage made my body shake, and it had taken all my willpower to stop myself from launching forward and twisting my father's head from his body. If it were any other female, I don't think I would have felt such outrage. I'd wanted to kill my father more than once, but never that badly. The bond between Raine and me made the need to protect her so strong that it was a constant battle for me not to pull her to me and hide her away, but I couldn't blame the bond entirely. There was something about her from the moment I'd seen her in that clearing on the island. Those amber eyes burned to my soul, and that body screamed for me to touch her.

I tried to focus on the cold wind that traveled from my cheeks through my limbs and to the tips of my wings. It was a pleasant sensation that usually worked to loosen my muscles, but this time it did nothing to douse my rage.

Angling my body, I curved around one of the gray stone guard towers that rose into the sky, when a voice sounded in my head. *Locke. You need to see this*, said a gruff voice, and a watery image of the statue of the Devil Rondsolen appeared in my mind along with a sense of urgency.

Carved from black stone mined from deep beneath the earth, the large statue was situated on the western end of the city, near the extravagant House of Thorem, the high house of demons.

I didn't hesitate to change my direction, heading toward the location the image had indicated. Before long, my feet were again on solid ground, my wings folded neatly behind my back, and my boots gliding over the cobblestones in the western district. I strode forward purposefully, passing tall stone buildings that lined both sides of the street. With every step, the feeling of dread inside me intensified. I knew Garan wouldn't have contacted me unless it was serious and being so close to the high house of demons didn't bode well.

I smelt the blood before I saw the carnage. The coppery tang became stronger as I neared the communal square at the end of the street, the smell mixing with the scents of freshly baked bread and wood smoke. My steps didn't falter as I continued forward, but darkness settled over me as the statue of the Devil Rondsolen came into view. The huge mass of black stone had been erected in the center of the square atop a platform that was three feet high, and it stood illuminated by four blue-fire torches that were positioned at each corner of the platform.

The statue had been carved to depict a male who was taller than any of the monsters in Katakin, with bulging muscles lined with protruding veins and a proud expression etched on a handsome square face. Large, pointed horns speared out of a head covered with black locks, and a thick tail with a spiked end curved around hooved feet. Black blood trailed down the large statue, sliding over Rondsolen's bare shoulders and broad arms to drip from his clawed fingers.

I peered up at where a headless demon's body was speared atop Rondsolen's horns, as if the poor soul had been thrown there. Around the statue, multiple bodies were also strewn around the square. Most of them were demons I recognized as occupants of the House of Thorem, but some of the victims were undistinguishable. The bodies rested at awkward, unnatural angles and many had missing limbs.

My face hardened at the gruesome sight, and I cursed under my breath. Moving forward, I stopped beside a gray-skinned gargoyle who was frowning up at the huge statue of the devil. Garan's pale, white gaze remained fixed on the victim speared atop Rondsolen's horns. Large, membranous stone wings remained folded behind

Garan's back, and pointed white horns protruded from his ash-gray hair. If I hadn't known him better, I would have thought Garan hadn't noticed I was there, but instead, I knew he would have heard me the moment my feet touched the cobblestones.

Garan didn't speak in my mind this time, but he turned to me, his movements jerky and stiff, just like all the gargoyles'. Gargoyles could only pass small messages and images to one another's minds, which was how they communicated with one another when they watched over the city, and it was only because Garan and I had become close during our childhood that we'd forged enough of a bond that he was able to send snippets to my mind as well. Unfortunately, I couldn't send anything in return, but his ability had allowed us to stay in contact during times when it mattered most.

"Two of my team spotted the outlier from above, but we weren't able to stop the creature in time to save them," Garan said, not bothering with a greeting. His voice was a deep rasp as though it had been some time since he'd last spoken.

I didn't need to ask to know he was talking about his inability to save the victims around us. "A single outlier did this?" The fae curse that turned all the humans in Katakin to monsters had lately started affecting our animals as well. Except, when the animals turned, they became monsters unlike those we'd seen before—great beasts with no conscience or desire other than to destroy and maim those around them. We called these monsters the outliers.

Garan nodded and gestured his head to a shadowed spot far across the square where a large mass rested in a pool of blood.

Other gargoyles, members of Garan's team, were spread around the area, observing the scene. Chaol, Garan's second-in-command, a gargoyle with a scar across his left eye, strode over to us. "General, I found another body halfway down the next street. That makes fifteen in total."

Garan gave him a grim, jerky nod. "Start documenting their names. We'll have to notify Borren within the hour. He will not be happy."

Borren. Normally, my lip would have curled at hearing the name of the alpha of the House of Thorem, but not then. Right then, I pitied the arrogant demon, because while the gargoyles would inform him of the dead, as alpha, Borren was the one who would have to break the news to the kin of the deceased. It was yet another reminder of why I didn't need the responsibility of being alpha for the House of Nesarin, the high house of vampires, no matter how much my parents wanted me to.

Chaol ducked his head, indicating that he'd heard the order, and then he was striding away, beckoning another gargoyle to him as he went.

"Chaol was one of the ones who first spotted the outlier, and he dealt the fatal blow," Garan commented as he stared after his second-in-command. "I can tell he blames himself for not getting here sooner, but if it weren't for him, more would have been lost." Letting out a heavy sigh, Garan gestured with his head to the massive body across the square. "Come. Let me show you why I brought you here."

At that, he began walking and I followed after him, skirting around the statue of Rondsolen and past the mutilated bodies until we reached a dead outlier. The beast of a monster was the size of a small building, with three heads flopped onto the ground, spines trailing down its bony back, and four wickedly clawed feet. Its mouth was open, revealing long, pointed fangs covered in what appeared to be a steaming yellow slime.

"Poison," Garan said gruffly, confirming my suspicion.

I squatted to get a closer look at the creature. "We haven't seen anything like this. Warrick will want to inspect the body."

"A messenger has already been sent to him," Garan said, and I frowned, confused as to why the gargoyle would have called for me then.

In answer to my silent question, Garan indicated to the monster's tail, where a small tuft of brown hair sprouted from the tip. "I thought you'd want to see this."

Leaning closer, I peered at the outlier's tail. There was no hair on any other part of the monster, and the silky fibers seemed at odds with the thick leathery skin that covered the rest of the creature's body. At first, I didn't understand what Garan was implying, but then my gaze flicked sharply back to him as realization settled in. "It's from the herd?"

Garan's expression darkened. "It appears so."

"Fuck," I cursed. The city's livestock was under guard day and night, and yet one of our domesticated animals had been turned into an outlier. The brown hair resembled that of one of our herd of cattle. If our domesticated animals were now turning into outliers, it would severely impact our food supply. Not to mention, we had hundreds of livestock just beyond the city. If they all turned into outliers at once, it would be as though an army of outliers had descended upon us.

"I'll head over to the farms next," I said, shoving to my feet. "Maybe someone out there saw something. Thanks for the heads-up." I didn't have as much power now that I was no longer a part of the House of Nesarin, but I was still respected enough that the farmers would answer my questions. The citizens of Katakin knew very little about the outliers, and even though the Taratun council and alphas of the high houses knew more, they still chose to ignore the threat. Warrick was the only one studying the outliers in his efforts to try to understand why the curse was changing, and it was the one thing we agreed on. Finding a cure for the curse.

Garan gave me a slow nod that was probably the warmest gesture the gargoyle could manage, and I moved away from the scene before stretching out my wings and launching into the air. I was grateful for the relationship Garan and I had. General to the gargoyles who watched the city from the sky, he was a powerful ally, and had remained so even after I had cut ties with my house.

We weren't the warmest of friends, but more so, we had a mutual understanding that we would help each other out from time to time. This strange understanding had forged between us when we were surviving our childhoods. When you save another from death enough times, at some point, a bond is formed that transcends time and any socially acceptable confines of even our world. What I had with Garan wasn't the same as the friendships I had with Kade, Asher, and Darian, but I was thankful for it, nonetheless.

My blood went cold then as I thought of Raine back in the mountain. I'd left her with Kade and the others, so I knew I shouldn't have worried for her safety, but the protective bond in my chest urged me to go to her. It took all my effort to keep flying toward the edge of the city, rather than to the mountain and where I knew she was.

Two fucking nights. My own words echoed in my ears. That was what I'd given them. My brothers had two nights to get Raine to change into a monster using methods other than fear, and then it would be my turn. But as the eastern edge of the city came into view, the endless buildings giving way to farms boasting fields of green, yellow, and red, I couldn't help but think about how it wasn't only Raine who was in danger. If we didn't figure out why our animals were turning into outliers soon, there was no telling how many nights Katakin had left.

CHAPTER 2

~ Raine ~

I ran through the forest, my breathing ragged as I leaped over fallen logs and dodged past bushes and trees, not caring when the twisted ends of branches scratched my arms and face. The pounding of heavy footsteps sounded behind me, thudding loudly on the forest floor, but I didn't dare turn my head to try and glimpse my pursuers.

Gasping for breath, I broke through a layer of trees and burst into a clearing. The open space was shrouded in darkness and as indecision went through me, I took a shaky step backward. An animalistic cry pierced the air behind me, and a crashing sounded in the forest, the impact shaking leaves from the trees. It was enough to spur me into action again.

I launched forward, my heart pounding in my chest as panic heightened my senses. On the second step my bare feet slipped on the slick grass, the ground wet as though it had only just rained, but I managed to stay upright and pushed myself forward.

I was halfway across the clearing when a tree fell to the ground behind me, but I didn't stop. If I stopped, I knew I would die.

I had to keep...

A sweet song filled the air, the sound leaking through the trees ahead of me, and I abruptly halted, my muscles locking up. I frowned, dazed for only a moment before a slow smile spread across my face, all thoughts of monsters and running instantly forgotten.

The music wound around me, sinking into my skin and warming me until my chest felt light and my body loosened. I blinked and Darian was before me, a soft smile curving his lips and an arrogant expression on his face.

Moonlight had broken through the clouds above, and the male was shirtless, the pale skin of his bare chest gleaming under the light. The forest was quiet around us, and the clearing sparkled as if the grass was a sea of silver. Gems hung from the branches of the trees and even the air seemed to glitter.

Music continued to wrap around me, an almost tangible thing that slid through my fingers. The melody called to me, and I began moving toward Darian, my bare feet gliding over the soft grass.

The siren was like a god before me, his regal face watching as I approached, and satisfaction went through me at the *idea that he was looking at me and only me. I needed his skin on mine, his body...*

I paused midstep and frowned, tilting my head to the side. God? *No, I knew this male wasn't a god. He was a monster. Wasn't he? I peered at where Darian was before me, but his image shimmered and almost disappeared before solidifying again.* No, this isn't...

· · · · ● · ● · · ·

I jolted awake, my arms and legs flailing in the water. For a moment, I struggled to recall where I was, but then I remembered Kade taking me to the washroom after our training session and me blissfully sinking into the warm water. After Locke's father, Warrick, had visited the common room hours earlier, Locke had stormed from the room. Kade was tense, and he'd been quick to load us both up with weapons. Leaving Asher and Darian, he'd taken me to a small unoccupied cavern, and we'd trained for hours until blisters had formed on my hands and my legs shook from the strain. But I still didn't change into a monster.

I wanted to know what it was about Warrick that had Locke and Kade so on edge, but I didn't ask. I had other problems. Like you know, still being the only human in a land filled with monsters. I'd deal with Locke's cruel father if it came to it. Until then, I just hoped he'd leave me alone.

Dropping my feet, relief went through me as I found purchase on the cool stone at the bottom of the pool, and I stood, my top half springing out of the water.

Scowling, I glared at the silver-haired male who watched me from the side of the pool with only his fingertips in the water. No sound was coming from him now, but an amused smirk twisted his lips, and I knew what he'd done. His song, his power, had infiltrated my dream. Sure, I'd been having a nightmare, but he still didn't have any right.

"I could have drowned," I groused.

"That you could have, Raine lovely. Hasn't anyone warned you that sleeping in water is not a good idea? Not unless you're a water monster, that is," he responded.

For a startling moment, I peered down at my body, frantic that I'd find a tail, or gills, or worse...*tentacles*. When nothing appeared out of the ordinary, I let out a sigh. *Thank the Mother Falia.* Now that I realized having monster abilities would help me find my sister, Cara, I wanted to turn, but I was hoping to become something useful like a vampire with wings or a demon with instant healing abilities. Gaining a fishtail wasn't high on my list. "Still human," I said more to myself than to him.

Darian's grin grew wider. "Then you should be thanking me for saving your life. When I found you, your head was almost submerged."

"And wouldn't it be such a shame if I died," I deadpanned.

"Indeed," he replied, his eyes sparkling. "Wouldn't want us to all die just when life is starting to get interesting."

Goddess, he was infuriating. I mean, sure, there was this weird bond between us, linking our lives, and they had the theory that if I died, they would die as well, but did he have to make this about him? "Why are you here?" I asked, narrowing my eyes. "And where's Kade?"

Darian's expression sobered then, the smile falling from his face and his features hardening. "Kade, Locke, and Ash are preoccupied with another matter."

A strange feeling that couldn't possibly have been worry slithered through me, but I kept the emotion from showing on my face. I tried to tell myself I was only worried for Kade, but I knew it was a lie. The idea that Asher and Locke were involved as well bothered me. I thought of Asher, the bulky demon with short violet horns and a violet forked tail, and Locke, the vampire with eyes as dark as night. I could tell from Darian's face that whatever they were doing, it wasn't something to be taken lightly. I wanted to ask him for more information, but I kept my lips pressed together.

As quickly as it had appeared, the concern left Darian's eyes, and his lips molded back into a smile. He lifted to stand and shook off the water from his fingers. "But that's enough about them. You've been sleeping in there for a good hour, and I trust you're feeling more like yourself.

Day has broken over the city, and it's my turn to try to get you to change. Once you're dressed, we'll be on our way."

· · · ● ● · ● · · ·

Minutes later, Darian led me from the rooms and up a tunnel that wound higher into the mountain. My hour-long soak hadn't done much to ease my aching muscles, but it was enough that I was able to walk at a reasonable pace.

"Where are you taking me?" I eventually asked, mostly just to break the silence between us.

"You shall see" was his only response, and I didn't push the matter. First, because knowing wouldn't change anything, and second, because I was so exhausted I was too busy focusing on putting one foot in front of the other.

It wasn't long after when Darian slowed to stop beside a long stretch of bare wall. Blue torches flickered close by, revealing nothing out of the ordinary, and I pivoted toward the siren to find he was staring at the wall with a look of concentration on his face. *All righty, then.*

"If you're lost, we can just go back to the rooms," I suggested hopefully. I'd become accustomed to sleeping during the day, and after my training session with Kade, I needed some serious shut-eye.

When Darian ignored me, I was about to open my mouth and repeat myself when the wall began to shift. I blinked in surprise as the rock appeared to melt away until it revealed a thin iron door with a large symbol of a tree carved into the center. *Whoa.*

In hindsight, I should have guessed there was a secret door. I'd seen doors disappear into the walls when the monsters had put me through my earlier trials, but it was still a bewildering sight.

Reaching out toward the door, I ran my fingers along the cool iron. "How did you do that?" I'd wanted to know from the first moment I'd seen one of the doors disappear nights ago.

Darian lifted his chin and gave me a smug smile before peering back at the door. "When the fae queen cursed our king, she unleashed her magic into the very bones of this mountain. It's believed she intended to only curse the king, but somehow her curse and her power spread far beyond. All those in Katakin were cursed, yes, but they were also given a small portion of her magic. Remnants of her power also remain within the mountain itself and the land beyond. Combining the magic within us with the power that seeped into the land, all monsters are able to perform small acts such as creating blue fire and, to a small extent, reshaping the mountain."

I thought of when I'd glimpsed the monster city beyond the mountain and the rivers of blue winding between the houses. "The water?"

He nodded, somehow understanding what I was asking. "The rivers have glowed blue ever since they were touched by the queen's magic. The concentration of the magic in the water does little to affect us, but it is spectacular to look at."

I wanted to question Darian more, but he pushed the iron door open and gestured for me to walk through the doorway. When I stepped forward and peered into the space beyond, my jaw almost hit the floor. I had assumed he was taking me to another cavern that only held more rocks and sand, but as I moved past him, I was utterly speechless.

Darian hadn't taken me to some sparse cavern where I would be chased by a wolf or crushed by a stone ceiling; instead, it was a freaking paradise. Rather than the blue fire torches and dim lighting I'd become accustomed to, sunlight streamed from an open section high above, bathing the area in natural light. I stared in awe at the blanket of grass that covered the floor and the thick vines which climbed up the sides of the small cavern, twisting over colored crystals that jutted from the walls and creeping over lush layers of moss and lichen. Flowers shaped like bells and blossoms spread across the glistening green, sprouting between cracks in the walls and from tufts of greenery on the ground.

In the back half of the cavern, a small lake sparkled an iridescent blue, the surface dotted with lily pads and the sides crowded with reeds and long grasses. Glowing blue water rushed down the far wall, splashing onto algae-covered rocks in the lake, and droplets of water misted the air, making it pleasantly cool. I breathed in deeply, taking in the scents of vegetation, soil, and the sweet fragrance of flowers.

"It's breathtaking," I whispered, still struggling to believe what I was seeing. The space was too beautiful to be in a mountain of monsters.

Pulling off my boots, I left them near the door and stepped further into the cavern. The grass was soft as it brushed against my ankles, and I ran my fingertips over the furry leaves of ferns and the soft petals of dewy flowers.

"What is this place?" I asked in wonder as I stopped before the lake, finally turning to peer back at Darian.

He had followed behind me, and his lips were curved upward as he watched me with interest, like he intended to savor my reaction to everything I saw.

"Do you like it?" he asked, and the hint of uncertainty in his tone made me think this wasn't a place many had seen.

"It's incredible," I admitted with a smile, turning back to the lake. "How is this even here?"

"You'd be amazed at the secrets this mountain holds," he answered cryptically, then added, "A friend made this haven for me."

I frowned. "A friend?" As far as I knew, neither Kade, Locke, or Asher had indicated that they had a way with plants, so I knew he had to be talking about someone else. I turned back toward him and sucked in a breath when I found he was only an arm's length away. The bond between us urged me to get closer to him, but I fought against it and forced myself to remember why he had brought me there. It wasn't just so I could enjoy the view.

Clearing my throat, I asked, "How will this get me to turn into a monster?"

His only response was to give me a sensual smile, and then he was pulling his shirt over his head. *What the—?* He dropped it to the ground near his feet, and then his fingers trailed to the front of his silky pants.

Oh, hell no. I'm not letting him near the water so he can use his power to turn me into a mindless love-sick female again. Just earlier, he'd used his power when only his fingertips were touching the water, so my safest option seemed to be to keep him away from the lake. I wanted to turn into a monster, but I didn't see how him making me think he was some sort of sex god was going to help that.

Before I could stop him, his pants dropped to his ankles, and I turned my head to the side to keep from accidentally catching a glimpse of him down below. *Shit.* Determined to get him to dress again, I bent forward, intent on grabbing his clothes so I could shove them at him and order him to put them back on, but he was too close. As I swung down, something hard smacked into my eye, sending pain shooting into my head and making my eye water. It was huge and warm and fleshy, and...

Oh. My. Fucking. Goddess.

With a curse, I recoiled and tried to stand again, my fingers abandoning the clothing I'd been trying to grasp. My body flung backward, and I teetered, unbalanced, before falling into the shallows of the lake, the cool water not doing much to stop my ass from thudding to the ground.

I quickly lifted myself back upright and stood, only to find a still-naked Darian clasping his very defined belly as he roared with laughter. "If I'd known you were that eager, lovely, I would have showed you earlier," he said when his laughter finally died down.

Scowling, I tried to ignore the warmth in my cheeks, and placed a hand over my injured eye. "I was *trying* to get you to put your clothes back on. You're the one who assaulted my eye." I couldn't help myself then. My gaze lowered to stare at the offending member between his legs.

Ho-ly Goddess. It was huge. Maybe even bigger than Kade's. It was no wonder that the bloody thing had almost blinded me. In its erect state, it was like a freaking weapon ready to spear someone.

My core heated at the thought of Darian putting his very large cock to good use, but I dug my nails into my palms and lifted my gaze back to his face. Thankfully, the siren was busy wiping tears of laughter from his eyes to notice.

"What the hell are you doing?" I snapped, and his expression finally became serious.

"I like these clothes. The last thing I want is for them to get ruined when I transform. I assure you, Katakin silk is not as easily procured as you might think."

Goddess, I wished I had a dagger so I could stab him. "That's not what I meant, and you know it," I gritted out.

He frowned and peered down at his still-very-erect cock, then added, "Oh, that. Well, now, that's not my fault. It seems to have a mind of its own when I'm around you."

I groaned and rubbed my hands over my face, pausing to flick stray strands of wet hair out of my eyes. "I meant, why are you planning to transform?" I clarified. "You've already tried to get me to turn with your power. It didn't work."

"Oh, yes. Well, I want to attempt something different this time. Unless, of course, you'd rather I stick to torture to try to get you to change?"

I didn't answer. At this stage, having to continue to stare at him while his beast of a cock was standing on end as if it was pointing right at me almost was a form of torture.

He obviously took my silence to mean that I preferred his (what he deemed to be) nontorturous methods, and he stepped into the water passing by me and moving forward until he was submerged up to his waist. Before my eyes, his legs transformed, molding together to form a fishtail that shimmered with blue-and-silver scales. His tail flicked out of the water, spraying droplets into the air, and Darian stared at me with a self-satisfied smile.

"And here we go again," I muttered under my breath.

CHAPTER 3

~ **Darian** ~

"Are you coming, lovely?" I called out to where Raine stood in the shallows of the lake with her arms crossed and an unimpressed expression on her face.

Her amber eyes watched me warily, but she let out an exasperated sigh and stripped out of her leather outfit until she was standing almost naked. Something pulled in my gut as my gaze trailed from where her long red hair had fallen over her shoulders and covered her breasts, to her curved body in the black lace panties. The female was perfect in every way, and the fact she didn't seem to care just drew me closer to her.

Ignoring my stare, she threw her leather outfit onto the bank and waded through the water. She stopped a short distance away from me, but I glided toward her, my tail wrapping around her legs and my cool scales sliding against her skin as I pulled her closer.

"Hey!" she protested, her arms flying up defensively, but I quickly slid my hands behind her back.

"Just wait and listen," I said, my gaze locking onto hers, and to my surprise and delight, she stopped squirming and stilled.

The steady beating of her heart sounded in my ears as we waited, a rapid thudding that beat in time to my own, and I cocked my head. Normally, being with females didn't leave me so affected, but with Raine so close to me, a thrill of excitement zinged through my body. I enjoyed the company of other females as much as they enjoyed mine, but having Raine in my arms was making me feel things I hadn't felt in a long time. It wasn't just sexual, though my hands certainly longed to slide lower on her body and grip her curved ass, and it wasn't just because of the bond between us that made me want to protect her with my entire being. But...something else. I found my grip tightening, as though I was afraid that if I loosened my hold on her, she would slip through my fingers and leave something empty inside of me in her wake.

"I don't hear anything," Raine said softly, her adorable brow wrinkled, and her head tilted as she listened to the world around us.

"Patience," I said with a chuckle.

I had barely finished speaking when the faintest song kissed my ears, the notes high and sweet. At first, Raine didn't seem to hear it, her human ears not as sensitive as my own, but then, as the song became louder, the single voice joined by another deeper, soulful one, her eyes widened, and her gaze flicked to mine. Within a matter of moments, countless voices filled the garden, all singing the same tune in perfect harmony, the sound spiraling down from above.

I watched Raine's face, pride going through me at the awe I saw shining in her features. "Where is it coming from?" she whispered, as if she was afraid that if she spoke any louder, she would disrupt the song.

"Every morning, while most of the monsters are sleeping, the sirens watch the sunrise and sing this same song. The notes speak of past times and new beginnings that we hope will come to pass. There are many things I detest about the sirens, but this..."

"You miss being a part of it," she finished for me, and I nodded as a sadness overcame me.

"Why did you leave your house?" she asked softly.

I stared down at the human who had begun to haunt my thoughts. I was used to monsters asking me the question because they wanted to try to exploit or ridicule me, but I didn't get that feeling from Raine. It was as if she genuinely wanted to know the answer simply to satisfy her own curiosity. She wasn't planning on using the information to her benefit but was merely interested in *me*. Not in my power, not because of my looks, but because she wanted to know my story. That knowledge was equally as alluring as her pouty pink lips and fiery amber eyes.

My chest fell as I let out a sigh. "Different monsters have their strengths and weaknesses, and for sirens, they covet beauty and power above all else. Honesty and love are things long forgotten, as is loyalty. On the eve of the night I was to take my place as alpha for the House of Saceris, I was betrayed by the female who was to be my second and, I had hoped, my mate." I tried to keep my face neutral, to not let the hurt I always buried deep inside me show, but Raine was able to see it.

"You really loved her," she said.

Swallowing back my anger, I lifted my head higher and shrugged a muscled shoulder. "I thought they all loved me as much as I loved them, and Cordelia, my second-to-be, most of all." The image of the siren's delicate face drifted across my mind, but I forced it away. "But I soon learned that the high house of water monsters is truly a house of lies. Going behind my back, Cordelia gained the favor of many of those within the house in an effort to make herself alpha. None of my so-called friends told me of this, though some had been part of the plans.

"Everything came to light when I caught Cordelia conspiring with another male, Hersondal. Only the strongest of the house can be the alpha, but from what I gathered, she had hoped to drug me and let the siren Hersondal take care of the rest. It was a laughable plan, and one I could have easily squashed, but from that moment, I wanted nothing more to do with that house or its inhabitants. From then, I spent weeks drifting through the city, content to drink myself into a stupor, and it was on one of those fateful nights that I met Asher."

My gaze finally went back to Raine then, and I could see the apology on the tip of her tongue. Before she could speak it, I added, "I come here when I want to feel connected to that world again. I enjoy being with Asher and the others, but at times, I do feel as though something is missing." I paused then, and as I stared at the female in my arms, I started to wonder whether it was not a thing but a "who" that was missing.

A slight flush pulled across Raine's cheeks as I stared at her, the red tinge spreading all the way to her slender neck.

"But, as to why you're here," I continued, "I believe all music has a form of magic weaved between the notes. A siren's power has no effect unless it is directed at a specific individual, so listening to their song will have no detriment to you. I thought after you'd endured Kade's barbaric methods of training to try to get you to change, we could try a different approach. One more emotional rather than physical."

"Emotional?"

"Dance with me, my lovely Raine. And let the music fill you."

"What? I-I can't dance," she responded, her face paling, and I chuckled. It was perhaps the most frightened I'd seen her.

"To the contrary, I see you dance every time you fight," I said as I pulled her effortlessly through the water.

"That's different," she said, but she didn't try to move away from me as we glided around the lake, the voices of a hundred sirens filling the air around us. I leaned closer to her, and the bond between us hummed as the side of her face brushed against mine.

"I don't believe it is" was my only reply. Raine's body was stiff as I pulled her along, but as time passed, her muscles relaxed and it was as if she molded against me, the pair of us becoming a single entity as the water seemed to part for us. I tipped her backward, and her back curved as her head kissed the water. Her red hair drifted in the water above her head, and then I was lifting her back to me, pressing her chest against mine.

Sweet Toros, she was stunning. But even with the music and the power of the sirens warming the air around us, she remained human. I had hoped this different approach would unlock something inside her, but her body stayed the same.

"You know you broke free from my power when I enchanted you the other night," I said against the shell of her ear, delight going through me when bumps prickled along her arms at the touch of my lips against her skin. "No one has ever broken free from a siren's power, let alone *my* power. You are the most curious thing to happen in two hundred years."

"I hadn't meant to break free," she said, and I could tell she was thinking back to when I'd entranced her nights ago. Apparently, she'd needed to pee so badly that she'd fought her way out of the trance, but I didn't think that was the only reason. There was power within her. We'd already seen it when she'd turned the ceiling into sand during another trial. Whether the power was because she was already turning into a monster or due to another reason, I wasn't sure, but she was stronger than she believed herself to be.

I wasn't confident that trying this would get her to turn, but I figured it wouldn't hurt to give it another go. "I'm going to add my song to that of the other sirens' now, and I'm going to use my power on you."

At my words, her jaw hardened and her muscles tightened, but she nodded. "All right."

Keeping my gaze fixed on her, I parted my lips and my song began filling the cavern, my power like a bubble that surrounded her, being absorbed into every fiber of her being. Her eyes glazed slightly, and she smiled, desire evident on her face as she began to grind against my body, her nails digging into my arms as she became desperate to be even closer to me.

When she'd been like this the other night, I'd enjoyed the way my power affected her, but this time, it made me feel ill. I'd always told myself that I enjoyed the look of adoration in their eyes as my song gripped them, but not now. Now I'd give anything to see Raine's eyes light up as they had when I'd tipped her head back to touch the water. I didn't care if she was a monster or not. The female was already perfect.

Her tongue licked at my bottom lip, her breasts rubbing against my chest, and while I couldn't deny my own desire that ignited from having her against me, her hard nipples dragging against my skin, it wasn't what I wanted. I wanted *her*. The real her. But I kept singing, my song an endless stream of sound as it filled every part of her mind.

Jumping, she wrapped her legs around me, and I held her as my power drove her mad. As time went on, I began to doubt whether she would be able to break free again. Had her physical need to relieve herself truly been the only reason she'd been strong enough? I didn't want to believe it. *You can do this, Raine.* I wasn't sure why I was so desperate for her to resist me. Maybe because no one else could. Or maybe because I wanted to know that Raine was different from all the others. Different from Cordelia. When I'd found Cordelia conspiring against me, I had used my power until she was again fawning over me, but I'd known then that it wasn't real. I didn't want the little human to be like that.

The slightest spark lit Raine's eyes for the briefest moment, and hope shot through me. She blinked, and I continued to sing, not sure if I'd been imagining things.

Flicking out her tongue, she wet her lips, still under my spell. *No, there.* Another spark. Another blink.

Come back to me..

She shook her head, and then, as though it was a miracle from when we used to believe in the gods, her eyes cleared, the amber a vivid golden red. Those eyes were the most beautiful things I'd seen in a century.

"Please tell me I didn't try to do nasty things to your tail," she said, quickly untangling her body from mine.

Coldness spread through me as she moved away, but I couldn't stop the smile that dominated my face. No one else had ever broken free from my power, and now she had done it twice. My magic was strong enough that I could even overpower other sirens if I wanted to, but not Raine. She was real, and that idea was more intoxicating than anything I'd tasted before.

I watched as her face contorted with a mixture of relief and disappointment as she realized she was still human.

"Don't you like my tail?" I asked.

She didn't answer my question. Instead, she said, "Why are you smiling so hard even though I didn't change?"

The song of the sirens had all but finished now, and the cavern was silent once again, but I couldn't stop grinning. The human might not have changed, but I realized now that she was changing the rest of us. Locke didn't see it, but I did. And so did Kade. It wasn't just the bond. This female was like a missing piece, the fifth point of our star. Raine was ours, whether we had a house or not, and I didn't want to let her go. If it weren't for the fact that she was more vulnerable as a human, I wouldn't have cared if she ever turned into a monster.

"Because, my lovely Raine, I'm starting to see what you truly are."

Her brows lowered in confusion. "You already knew I was a human."

I moved closer to her, my fingers gently lifting her chin higher so she was peering at me. "You're precious."

Shock flashed in her eyes, and her lips trembled imperceptibly, the movement so small I almost missed it. "You and the others aren't what I expected."

"Neither are you, little human," I said, and without thinking, I pressed my lips against hers. Before she had the chance to react, I pulled away, the hand that gripped her chin falling to my side. I half expected her to curse at me, but she looked as surprised as I felt, her cheeks flushed and her arms dangling awkwardly at her sides. Slowly, her hands curled into fists as she seemed to regain herself, and I smiled, loving the effect I'd had on her.

· · · ● · ● · · ·

~ Raine ~

Darian and I walked back from the garden in relative silence, only the sounds of our footsteps echoing along the tunnel. My mind whirled as I thought of his cool lips pressed against mine, and how badly I had wanted more. *Precious.* That's what he'd called me. Goddess, what was happening?

Swallowing, I forced myself to forget how sweet he had tasted and instead focused on what I'd learned about the siren. Cordelia was a fool for breaking his heart. When Darian had spoken about her, the pain in his eyes had been real. He'd loved her, and she'd betrayed him.

When we entered the common room, disappointment went through me when we found no one else was there. I didn't know if the others were in their rooms or not, but I hoped they were. I hadn't forgotten the worry that had been in Darian's eyes when he'd told me they were preoccupied with another matter. My gaze snagged on Kade's closed door, and I felt Darian's presence as he stopped behind me.

"If you wish to stay with him, go ahead, but you should know that Kade doesn't have to be your only ally."

My head twisted as I turned to peer at him. *Ally?* Was that what Kade was to me? I could still feel the smoothness of Darian's tail and the dampness of the water from back at the garden. I realized what he was really saying was "I don't have to be your enemy," and the thought made my head spin.

"You're welcome to stay in my room," he added when I didn't respond. "Despite what you may think, taking a female against her will isn't my way. I have a spare couch, and you're welcome to it."

My heart pounded hard at the thought of staying in his room. I didn't doubt he was being honest. Of the many things I'd just learned about the siren, it was that he valued honesty. Craved it, even. But I hadn't seen Kade all day, and a part of me wanted to make sure he was all right. Plus, exhaustion still made my body feel heavy, and if I went to Darian's room, I wasn't sure if I'd be able to sleep.

"I'll think about it," I said, giving him a small smile, and disappeared into Kade's room.

CHAPTER 4

~ Kade ~

I closed my eyes and inhaled, my nose wrinkling when I detected the faint scents of death and decay lingering among the smells of pine and earth. Wherever there was an outlier, the scent of death remained, and my face hardened as I thought of how I'd left Raine back in the washroom. My Mahare. The outlier that had once been here was dead, brought down by the gargoyles in the city, and Darian was there to watch Raine, but I still hated the thought of being so far away from her.

I stepped over to Locke's side, not at all liking the entire situation we were in. The Taratun council should have been dealing with this shit, but as usual, the bastards were ignoring the problem and hoping the threat would somehow resolve on its own. The whole bunch of them were useless.

Warrick was the only one who showed an interest, but from what Locke had told me, his experiments hadn't revealed any answers. I scowled as I thought of all the outliers we'd captured and brought to him in the past.

"Deer is the strongest fresh animal scent I can identify," I said to Locke with a soft growl. My wolf side didn't care about the outliers. That animalistic part of me only cared that I was too far away from Raine, and the urge to shift so my paws could eat up the distance between us was making my skin itch. I tried to ignore the feeling and said, "It's likely it was a deer that was turned into an outlier."

"Well, that's better than it bein' a buffalo, right?" Asher asked from where he stood with his arms folded over his broad chest.

"Yes," Locke said, not looking away from where he was staring at a set of heart-shaped deer tracks on the ground.

Lifting himself, Locke straightened and brushed leaves from his black leather coat as he turned toward us. "The last outlier attack was mere hours ago. The two scaled monsters were larger than the tallest ogres and trolls in Katakin. Then there's also the incident of the outlier that took out over a dozen members of the House of Thorem just yesterday night. Borren was not happy to hear so many of his demons had been killed. The occurrences of outliers are becoming more frequent, and we need to find out why."

"I say let the Taratun deal with this. Who cares 'bout a few dead demons," Asher commented, his tone devoid of emotion.

But I knew him better than that. When we'd been striding into the forest and Locke had told us of the attack near Asher's old house, the House of Thorem, I'd seen the way Asher's face had pulled tight. There was a part of him that still cared, no matter how hard he tried to deny it. Borren, the alpha of the House of Thorem, deserved death for leaving Asher to deal with his crazed mother by himself until it was too late, but many of the other demons hadn't played any part in the events that transpired. Asher didn't want them all dead. His heart was too soft for that.

"This world is already falling apart," Locke said coldly. "If outliers overrun the city, it will be the lower houses who suffer most, and the city will fall into chaos. No matter how much we hate this place, none of us can leave. The curse won't let us. And if the city falls, so do all of us."

He didn't need to say any more than that. I was already thinking about the human back in our rooms. This world was already dangerous for her, and Locke was right. We needed to figure it out.

"Could the fae be takin' our animals and sending them back through portals after corruptin' them?" Asher asked thoughtfully as he began pacing and rubbing his chin.

I ground my teeth at the thought of the fae visiting our kingdom to corrupt our animals, but then I reminded myself that it wouldn't entirely be a bad thing. If the fae arrived in Katakin, I'd finally have the opportunity to tear them limb from limb and get vengeance for my family. When the fae had attacked my old house, the House of Worzel, all those years ago, they'd slaughtered a dozen wolves, including my mother and sister. Raine had pulled me out of the depths of my grief and my guilt, but I was still angry. There hadn't been a fae attack since then, but I knew they would be back. And I'd be ready for them.

Locke's lips thinned. "It's possible, but nothing so far has indicated the fae. I visited the farms, and aside from learning that at least three other buffalo were unaccounted for, none of the farmers had noticed anything unusual. Until I forced them to count, they weren't even aware that any were missing."

Locke began walking around the clearing, inspecting the trees and foliage, and Asher and I did the same. As Locke ran his fingertips over the bark of an old oak tree, he said, "If the fae are turning our animals into weapons against us, then this is much worse than I thought."

"Though, if that's the track of the poor animal that changed, doesn't that mean the beast was normal here before it turned?" Asher said, pointing back in the direction of the deer tracks. "So, if the fae were involved, either they came here and hit the animal with magic, or maybe it wasn't the fae at all?"

Locke turned his attention away from the tree he'd been inspecting and stepped to another, carefully moving from one shadow in the forest to another. Sunlight wouldn't kill him, but it wasn't pleasant either. "It may truly just be that the curse has somehow changed and it's now affecting animals. Either way, I'd hoped we might find clues out here to help us figure out this mess, but once again, there's not much here to go by. I'll let you know when Garan informs me of the next attack. If the trend continues, we can expect more outliers over the coming nights."

"If it's the fae, then let them come," I said gruffly, rolling my neck as I resisted the urge to shift. *I'll make them fucking pay.*

CHAPTER 5

~ Raine ~

I awoke to find Kade's arm wrapped around me and his rough chin resting against the side of my face as he slept. He hadn't been there when I'd entered his room hours earlier after Darian had taken me to the garden, and I wondered when he'd joined me.

The wolf shifter's breathing was heavy, his short russet-colored hair shading his eyes, and I smiled as I ran my fingers over his arm. Realizing what I was doing, I dropped my hand as my smile fell away. Waking in his arms had felt too right. It had made me feel safe and warm, and that was dangerous. I couldn't get used to feeling like that because it wouldn't last. I'd be gone soon. Wouldn't I?

I tried to imagine where my sister, Cara, might be, and for the first time, I wondered whether she would even want to leave. It had been a decade since she'd been taken, and Kade had said newbloods were often treated like queens when they joined a house. *What if when I finally find her, she doesn't want to leave?*

When I arrived in Katakin, I'd been so focused on the idea of saving her that I hadn't even considered the possibility she might be happy. Hope bloomed in my chest as I questioned whether my fear for her might be misguided, but it disappeared quickly. It was just as likely that she was stuck with monsters she despised and was being treated poorly. Either way, I had to find her and make sure she was all right. If I could apologize to her, maybe I could start to heal some of the damage between us.

Leaving Kade still sleeping, I dressed and exited the room to find Asher lying on his back on the settee closest to the fire and tossing grapes into the air to catch them in his mouth. He grinned when he saw me and tossed a grape so high into the air it almost touched the ceiling.

As it fell, I darted forward, catching it in midair and popping it into my mouth with a grin.

"Well damn, Sharachi, way to ruin a monster's fun," he said, but the crooked smile he gave me was downright panty-dropping, and I quickly moved away to grab my own plate of food. *What the fuck am I doing?* I scolded myself. He was a monster, and I was acting as if we were...*friends*. I was losing my mind. Somehow managing to contain my horrified expression, I plucked some cheese and fruit from the platter on the low table.

Turning, I looked for a place to sit, and my gaze landed on Locke who was standing at one of the higher tables against the far wall. He was scowling as he bent over a piece of aged parchment, and from the expression on his face, I could tell something was bothering him. My stomach dropped, though I couldn't really explain why.

Before I knew what I was doing, I was moving closer to him and coming to a halt beside his table. His gaze tracked over the inked map, a long finger tracing along different routes through the city and moving out to a space marked as forest. *A map.* My heart leaped at the sight of it. I had no idea where Cara was, but I knew that map could help.

Though Locke must have noticed my arrival, it was only now that he turned to peer at me, his black gaze fixing on my face. My throat went dry as he stared at me, my gaze lifting to meet his.

"Something wrong?" I asked.

At the sight of the map, I'd almost forgotten the whole reason I'd moved closer to him, but now I remembered the concern in his intense features as he had stared at the parchment.

He opened his mouth to speak, and all he said was, "One night left, *beautiful.* You'd better hope Asher and Darian can get that pretty little body of yours to turn. If not, then you're mine." Without waiting for a reaction, he completely dismissed me and turned his attention to Asher. Tipping his head up, he gestured to the washroom door. "Kade and I will be heading into the city tonight, so you and Darian will be on your own. When Kade wakes, tell him to meet me at our usual spot."

I narrowed my eyes at the vampire. I liked Kade, and even Darian was growing on me, but Locke was still the same ass who'd chosen me back in the clearing on my island.

"Will do, brother," Asher said before tossing another grape into his mouth.

Holding my tongue, I watched as Locke snatched the map from the table, folded it, and slid it into a pocket on the inside of his coat. I thought of the tunnels that wound through the mountain and the sprawling city beyond. I would find a way to get my hands on that damn map.

Biting the inside of my cheek, I watched as Locke strode from the room and shut the door behind him. Even after he was gone, I stood staring at the door, my stomach still feeling hollow, and it took me a startling moment to realize that it was once again worry that twisted inside me. But I couldn't be worried for that asshole Locke, could I?

I thought of his serious face, his furrowed brows and set jaw. Something bad was happening. I'd known it when his father had surprised us with a visit not too long ago, but now I was doubly sure. Was Locke in trouble? Perhaps we all were.

"You're goin' to wanna actually eat that," Asher said from where he still lounged on the settee, his gaze fixed on the plate in my hands, and I gave myself a mental shake before turning to him. Without even bothering to ask him why I grabbed a piece of squishy red fruit and shoved it into my mouth. These monsters were many things, but so far, they'd proven they weren't liars.

· · · ● · ● · ● · · ·

"Take a seat, Sharachi," Asher said. He was sitting up now, and he patted the empty space beside him on the red-velvet settee, a roguish expression on his handsome face. I frowned at the nickname but didn't comment. It didn't bother me as much now that I knew what it meant. *Sharachi.* The name of one of the seven devils they believed in—the one who was most known for seduction and war. I wasn't trying to seduce anyone, but war? Well, I was all right with that.

Asher had waited until I'd finished my plate of food and used the washroom, and for Darian to join us before he'd called me over, the male looking way too eager for my liking. The demon was the largest of the four of them, with thick muscle covering his wide body, but somehow, he always seemed the least imposing. Well, except for the time when I'd touched his tail. I could still picture the fury and pain in his eyes when I'd held it in my hands, and a shudder went through me. That was *not* a mistake I was going to make again anytime soon.

Short violet horns poked out of Asher's shaggy coffee-colored hair, and his forked violet tail rested beside him, draped over the edge of the chair. I eyed the area beside him and thought about refusing, but I wanted to turn into a monster, didn't I? Becoming a monster would make it so much easier to survive this brutal world.

Steeling myself, I dropped next to him, my ass sinking into the soft velvet. Immediately, Asher lifted his broad arm, draping it across the seat behind me, his huge body closing in on my personal space. I wiggled in my seat but pretended not to notice.

Lifting a hand, he held up a small clear bag holding a silver powder and gave me a mischievous smile. "Thought we could have some fun tonight."

Fun? What the fuck does that mean? Frowning, I turned to Darian to find he was leaning forward on the settee across from us, an unreadable glint in his eyes. I thought of what the siren had said to me not too long ago: *Kade doesn't have to be your only ally.* Given what he'd said, the fact he didn't seem too concerned about what was happening right then gave me a small sense of comfort.

Kade had exited his room a short while ago, and when Asher had given him the message about him needing to meet Locke, he'd simply kissed me on the head and loaded himself up with weaponry before heading out the door. He didn't seem worried at the idea of leaving me with

Asher and Darian, but there was no way of knowing whether he knew what they had planned for me.

I stared back at the seemingly harmless powder Asher was holding, the bag dwarfed by the demon's large hand. "How is this going to get me to change?" I asked dubiously.

"It's Silver Sand," Asher said as if he thought saying the name of the powder should have been enough information. After a pause, he elaborated, "The drug makes you lose your inhibitions. It loosens up your body and your mind."

My face scrunched in disapproval. "So...you want to drug me? And how exactly is that going to help?"

Darian answered this time, his eloquent voice steady and almost clinical. "The drug raises your heartbeat. While your mind and body are relaxed, your internal systems go into overdrive. It might be just what your body needs to allow the change and turn into a monster." Despite his even voice, I could tell he didn't really think it would work, but it was clear he thought it was worth a shot.

I eyed the bag of Silver Sand, not liking my situation. Everything inside of me was telling me that taking the stuff was a bad idea. There was a plant back on my island that caused similar symptoms, and some of the villagers would chew the leaves so they could forget the world for a few hours. I'd been tempted to try it once, but I'd known I had to keep my head clear. That I had to keep training and pushing myself so that when it was time to find my sister, I was ready.

"Look, I don't blame you for not wantin' to take it, and no one is going to force you, but we're runnin' out of ideas here," Asher said, obviously sensing my reluctance. "If this doesn't work, I don't know what will."

Letting out a long breath through my nose, I peered at the demon and siren. I didn't trust either of them, but I didn't think they would try to kill me. Time was running out, and I knew this was likely my last chance to turn into a monster before Locke was going to put me through hell.

Squaring my shoulders, I sat up straighter. I mean, how bad could it be? "How long does it last?" I asked.

Asher rubbed his chin, thoughtful for a moment. "Depends on the dose."

"Cryptic," I said, giving him a level look.

"With the amount we're thinking, you'll be at our mercy for most of the night," Darian said, his clever blue eyes watching me intently. "That's what you really wanted to know, isn't it, Raine lovely?"

I clenched my jaw. It *was* what I wanted to know but not what I wanted to hear. I'd be vulnerable around them for hours if I took the drug. I hated it. Hated the thought of giving them so much power over me, but it was worth it if it would help me turn into a monster.

"Fine," I finally said. "But just remember that it'll be easier for me to kick your ass when I turn into a monster. Don't make me regret this."

Asher let out a hearty chuckle, and Darian's lips pulled into a smile as he leaned back, folding one leg over the other.

"Oh, we already know," Darian said.

With that, Asher passed the small bag of silver powder to me, and I weighed it in my hand.

"We won't let anything bad happen. You have my word," Darian added, and I'd never seen his expression so sincere before. It almost had me believing him.

I looked at Asher, half expecting him to have a strange tool in his grasp. "How do I take it?" I asked.

"Swallow it and chase it down with this," Darian said and reached across to grab a goblet of liquid I hadn't noticed and slide it closer to me.

I nodded. Not letting myself hesitate any longer, I opened the bag and lifted it to my lips, tipping the entire contents into my mouth. The Silver Sand was grainy and tasteless on my tongue, but I choked it down. Asher lifted the goblet for me, and I grabbed it and gulped down the pink liquid I'd come to nickname "pink poison."

When I'd finished swallowing, I wiped my mouth with my hand. "How long until it takes effect?" I didn't feel any different aside from noticing the gritty taste that lingered on my tongue.

"Not long" was Asher's response, and as he said it, the demon's right leg brushed against mine. The small contact had my heart racing, the bond between us humming, and I frowned, unsure if the drug was already affecting me.

Pulling my focus away from his leg, I closed my eyes and tried to think only of my body and how I felt. Seconds passed, and I felt ridiculous sitting there while I knew Asher and Darian were staring at me. Nothing was happening. *Maybe the drug doesn't work on humans.* The thought seemed farfetched, but it was worth hoping. I wanted to turn into a monster, but being at the complete mercy of the two monsters didn't sound like a party. Neither did the idea of loosening up my mind.

Bored of waiting, I snapped my eyes open. "Well, this isn't so bad," I said with a triumphant smile before bursting into maniacal laughter. The room had begun to spin, and I leaned my head back, not caring that I was resting on Asher's thick arm. A wave of pure happiness went through me as if someone had poured liquid sunlight into me, and it was warming me from the inside out.

"It's all right, Sharachi," said a calm, casual voice. "We've got you."

Got me? I lifted my head again and peered at the male still beside me. His violet horns looked longer than normal, or were they shooting stars bursting out of his hair?

I waggled my finger at him and slurred, "For now, buddy. Believe me when I say I'm here by choice. I could have escaped nights ago if I wanted to." In the dark recesses of my mind, some part of me knew I wasn't behaving normally, but right then, I didn't care. Nothing that I'd worried about in the past mattered anymore. *Goddess, maybe I should have taken that drug back on the island.*

"Do you think we let her take too much?" Darian's silky voice was faint, and another giggle jumped out of me.

"It was only the standard dose. The drug affects everyone differently."

"The standard dose for a monster. She's a human."

"Well, I don't know how much they used to take when we were human. Besides, we want her to change, don't we?"

"We also want her alive." A shadow dropped down before me, and Darian's face came into view, slightly blurred but still distinguishable. "Raine lovely, how are you feeling?"

"Never been better," I said, my eyes struggling to focus on him.

"Listen to my voice. Try to search inside yourself. Do you feel anything unusual?"

"What're you doin'?" I could hear Asher's voice this time.

Unusual? I thought of the warmth that was heating in my belly at the idea of Darian crouched before me and Asher at my side. Was that unusual? "Nope, nothing," I said.

"Why don't you close your eyes again and picture yourself? What does that image look like?"

There was a beat of silence as I did as he suggested and tried to picture myself. But I wasn't alone in the image. Instead, a naked Kade walked into view, followed by a butt-naked Darian. They were both standing there in all their glory, sporting huge erections. My mouth burst open, and I snorted as laughter poured out of me.

"You need to focus, Raine," Darian said. "Listen to the sound of my voice."

Uh-huh. His voice. In my head, my image of Darian was the one who was speaking, but I cleared my throat exaggeratedly and tried to banish him from my mind.

"Picture yourself in a room," came Darian's voice.

"What kind of room?" I asked as I kept my eyes shut.

There was a long sigh. "Whatever comes to mind."

I did as he said and let my mind wander, thinking of a room. At first, I thought of the room we were in. A cavern with finely crafted furniture, blue fire crackling in the fireplace, and splashes of red and brown from the tapestries hanging on the walls and the carpet beneath our feet. I even thought of the massive weapons shelf near the front door. But then, as if my mind had a will of its own, the setting changed, and I found myself in my wooden cottage from back on the island, the rich carpets and furniture replaced with dull wooden walls.

I was in the main room of the cottage, a small, round table with three chairs sat to my left, and on my right, there was a tiny kitchen with a few battered iron pots hanging from the wall. Strangely, the front door to the cottage was nowhere to be seen, but the shutters on the windows at the front of the cottage were open, and warm island air filtered into the room, ruffling my hair. I could almost smell the coconuts and scent of the sea, and for the briefest moment, a sense of contentedness and familiarity went through me. My lips tipped upward into a soft smile.

"Now imagine there is a door to that room. All you have to do is walk over and open the door so you can step through." Darian's voice came to me as if booming from above now.

All right, just open a door. Sounds simple enough.

I focused on the front of the cottage, where a door would have been if it was my real home from back on the island. Concentrating hard, I imagined a door appearing in the middle of the wooden slats at the front between the two windows. The shifting and banging of wood sounded in my ears, and then a door appeared, just as I remembered it. *Easy.* But when I stepped toward the door, more banging and shifting sounded around me, and I whirled to find two more doors had also materialized—one on my left side and another behind me.

"Which door do I go through?" I asked, hardly able to hear my voice over the steady pounding of blood in my ears.

"What?" Darian asked, but it was difficult to hear him over my thudding pulse.

"Which door?" I repeated, but this time, there was no answer. A shadow moved in my peripheral vision, and I whipped my head to the side as a ghostly image of my father appeared. He was sitting at the small table, his shoulders hunched, torn clothing hanging loose on his thin frame, and lines crossing his gaunt face.

"Father?" I moved closer to him as all the happiness drained from me, and a familiar ache bloomed in my chest instead, but even when I was right beside him, he seemed not to notice me. Staring straight ahead, his gaze remained fixed on the wooden cup before him as if he thought if he stared at it for long enough, it would make his troubles disappear. It was the same expression I'd seen on his face countless times during the years after Cara had been taken.

We'd both grieved in different ways in the wake of her absence, and my father's method had involved him trying to drown out the world with copious amounts of coconut wine.

"Just try pickin' one," Asher's voice finally sounded through the windows of the cottage, cutting through the thudding in my ears, but I kept staring at my father. At the image that had become burned into my mind.

I wanted to grip his shoulders and shake some life back into him. To once again tell him that I was going to find his daughter and bring her home, but I knew he wouldn't believe me. Just like he hadn't the dozens of times I'd tried to tell him that in the past. After Cara had been taken, my father hardly spoke to me at all. He never said it, but I was sure he blamed me for her being chosen, which made sense because it was my damn fault.

"Raine?" said Darian, and the soothing tone of his voice was enough that I managed to pull my gaze away from my father and turn my attention back to the three doors. In the real cottage back on my island, there were actually four doors. The front door, then three doors at the back—one to my father's room, one to the washroom, and one to the room Cara and I had shared. But now there was only the one at the front, one at the back, and the last one to the side near where my father sat. *This isn't real,* I reminded myself. *Just get to the door.*

Clenching and unclenching my fists, I moved away from my father, taking another step toward the front door, but as I shifted, the world turned to darkness through the windows, as if night had fallen over the island. The silence of the cottage was broken as the door began rattling violently, the metal hinges shaking as if something from the outside was trying to get in.

I changed direction, instead taking a step toward the door that was close to my father's image, but when I moved, this door changed, seeming to grow smaller and then larger again as though it was a mirage. *All righty, not that one either*, I thought grimly.

Pivoting, I turned toward the door at the back of the room, changing course to make my way toward that one instead. Nothing happened as my steps creaked over the floorboards, but as I reached for the wooden knob, black tendrils of smoke began seeping through the cracks around the door as though they were snakes trying to wiggle their way through. I recoiled, pulling my fingers away. *What the hell?* It was then that I heard her. Cara's voice came from the other side of the door, only just distinguishable against the rattling and banging still coming from the front of the cottage.

"Cara?" I croaked, my throat suddenly as dry as sandpaper.

Seconds passed with no reply, but then, "I-I'm here, Rainie. I'm here."

My heart crashed against my rib cage, and I shot forward as a mixture of horror and hope rushed through me. She was there behind the door. I grasped the doorknob in both hands, not caring when black tendrils slid over my fingers, ice-cold against my skin. The black smoke climbed up my skin and slid up my arms, but I didn't pull back. When the door still wouldn't open, I cursed and released the doorknob, only to begin bashing my shoulder against the door.

Pain ricocheted down my arm at the impact. "Cara!" my voice rasped as a sob worked its way up my throat.

Thud. More pain jarred my arm as my shoulder dug into the wood again. Tears watered from my eyes, blurring my vision, but I gritted my teeth.

Moving further into the room, I ran at the door, but as I braced myself for the impact of my body hitting wood, a thousand voices exploded in my mind, the endless screams like needles plunging into my head. With a cry, I slammed to my knees, my hands clapping over my ears in a desperate attempt to keep the voices out.

Not a single voice was speaking coherent words, but I knew they weren't human. I could make out the hisses, growls, bellows, and snarls. These were the screams of monsters, and they were clawing at my mind.

"Stop," I rasped, rocking my head from side to side. They had to get out. All of them had to get the *fuck* out of my head.

Somehow through the din of voices, Cara's whimper sounded from the other side of the door, and I pulled my hands from my head and forced myself onto shaky legs. Staggering forward, I launched myself back at the door with a desperate cry.

My side impacted painfully with the wood, but the door still wouldn't move. Leaning my head on the door, I slid to a crumpled heap on the floor. The front door rattled harder, and I peered at the other side of the room to see my father staring at me with fury in his wide brown eyes. The door behind him had morphed into a black vortex that swirled angrily, and more voices and screams spewed from its depths as though I was looking at a portal to hell.

The front door rattled harder, and one of the hinges tore from the doorframe. The voices in my mind became louder, and the screaming and wailing had me gripping at my head again. I struggled again to my feet, my back sliding up Cara's door, and the black smoke leaking around the door's edges wrapped around my torso like thick bands of rope.

"Raine!" There was the faintest sound of someone calling my name, but I couldn't tell who it was. Energy sparked in my chest as the pain in my head intensified to the point that nausea made me gag.

There was the sensation of fire shooting through my veins, and then my eyes flew open. Energy poured out of me, magic crackling in the air and leaving a metallic taste on my tongue. Spears of icy wind shot through the windows at the front of the cottage, making the entire building shudder and creak. The shutters on the windows flapped furiously, and the furniture was tossed around the room, the image of my father nowhere to be seen. The pots from the kitchen clanged as they flew from their hooks and banged against one another as they joined the swirling tornado inside the cottage.

Monsters kept screaming in my head as the wind raged around me, and energy continued to stream out of me. My feet remained rooted to the floor, my back still pressed against the door holding Cara captive. Reaching out, I lifted my arm until my hand rested on the doorknob.

I twisted my wrist, but the knob still wouldn't move. *Why won't it fucking budge!* I wanted to rage at it, but a deep, soothing song slid past all the other voices in my mind, and as the song became louder, it drowned out the cries and screams, taking the edge off my pain and anger.

A longing filled me, so intense that I almost stepped away from Cara's door, but I frowned and pressed harder against the wood, not releasing the doorknob. I couldn't go.

The song became louder, the music gripping my heart and squeezing, but I wouldn't let it stop me from doing what I needed to. "No," I croaked, my voice barely audible over the howling wind, music, and voices in my head.

But then goosebumps washed over my skin as four warm hands grabbed me, sliding up my arms and bracing on my legs, and the cottage disappeared.

CHAPTER 6

~ Raine ~

Two faces came into view, and it took me a moment to recognize Asher and Darian. They were gripping onto me tightly, their faces pinched with concern. Around us, an unnatural wind circled the common room. Wickedly sharp weapons flew through the air along with the furniture and dinnerware. The tapestries on the walls flapped, threatening to tear from the walls, and the only piece of furniture that remained on the ground was the settee I was sitting on. Blue flames in the torches on the walls crackled and fizzed, the fire licking at the air. But I hardly registered what I was looking at.

The soothing song still sounded in my ears, and I peered at where Darian crouched, his lips parted, and his brow furrowed in concentration. Weariness shone in his eyes, and I stared at his hands on my body. Asher was in a similar position, and his lips were also moving, but I couldn't hear any of the words he was saying.

A wooden jug that swirled through the air smashed against a table and veered toward us, colliding with the back of Darian's head. The siren swayed, the glow in his crystal-blue eyes dulling before his eyes shuttered, and he collapsed to the floor, his hands falling from me.

Panic went through me, startling me back to reality as I watched the siren fall, and the room came into sharp focus. I blinked and sucked in a huge, gasping breath, my lungs expanding painfully as I stared around me as if I was finally seeing clearly. *What?* I blinked again and shook my head as I tried to remember what had happened before I found myself in the cottage. *The Silver Sand.* The memory of me tipping the powder into my mouth came to the forefront of my mind. *It's not real. Fuck, none of it was real.* Cara's whimpers still haunted my mind, but I realized what it was now. A hallucination and a side-effect of the drug. As I had the realization, the wind died, the voices in my head disappearing, and the energy no longer pulsing in my chest.

"Fuck! Watch out!" Asher shouted before he stretched out, his body flattening over Darian and me and sheltering us as furniture, weapons, and the contents of the room clattered and smashed to the floor. When the room was silent again, Asher peeled himself from us, his violet eyes flicking over my face with concern.

"You all right, Sharachi?" he asked.

"I—I think so," I answered, still not quite understanding why the room looked like it had been torn apart.

"Goddess, Darian!" I exclaimed as my gaze went to the siren's crumpled form prone on the floor. "Please tell me I didn't kill him."

Asher gave me an amused grin, but there was a seriousness in his eyes. "Don't worry. It'll take more than that to kill one of us." Bending down, he lifted Darian's limp body into his arms. "He was pushin' the limits of his power to try to get you back, though. You probably did him a favor by knockin' him out."

Get me back?

Before I could ask what he meant, Asher walked away, taking Darian to his room. When he returned a short while later, I asked, "What do you mean he was trying to get me back?"

I thought of the cottage with the three doors and the song I'd heard. Before Asher had even answered me, I knew then that it had been Darian's song that dulled the screams of the monsters in my mind.

Asher rubbed at his chest with his palm. "Whatever you were experiencin', the pain in our chests told us you were in trouble. Darian was tryin' to pull you back before you hurt yourself, mentally or physically."

I felt even guiltier then about what had happened to Darian. If he hadn't been trying to help me, he probably would have noticed the jug and would have been able to deflect it before it smashed against his skull.

"Fuck, I'm sorry, Sharachi," Asher said as he rubbed the back of his neck and sat beside me, his weight making the settee groan. "Silver Sand can be a bit unpredictable dependin' on the one who takes it. In most cases, it helps people forget about the past and leaves them in a giddy, happy state. But for some, it has the opposite effect. What happened?"

What had *happened?* It was a good question and one I'd been asking myself. How could I tell him about the room, and Cara, and the voices? It was bad enough that I was coming to realize that I was going crazy. He sure as hell didn't need to know.

"I saw someone. Someone I lost a long time ago," I said, my voice cracking at the omission. It was as much as I was willing to tell him.

His violet eyes softened at the emotion in my voice. "It was the Silver Sand playin' tricks on your mind. The drug can make you see things that aren't real. If I'd known you had ghosts, I wouldn't have suggested you take it. It's why I usually refuse to touch the stuff."

I nodded, not wanting to tell him anything more, but he kept staring at me. Exhaustion made my eyes want to flutter closed, but I forced myself to stay awake.

"I need to know what happened, Raine," he prodded again. "What was that wind?"

I sighed heavily and thought of the wind that had howled around the cottage. A wind that was still raging when I found myself back in the monsters' common room. *It can't have been me, can it?* Deep down, I knew there wasn't any other rational explanation for it, but I shook my head in disbelief. Acknowledging that I could turn rock to sand was one thing but creating gale-force winds in the middle of a damn mountain was too much.

It was then that I noticed the dagger poking out from under one of Asher's shoulder blades. The small blade was in deep, with only the silver hilt still visible. "Your back!" I gasped, covering my mouth with my hand.

He turned his head to the side. "Well, how 'bout that," he commented with as little concern as if a mosquito had bitten him. Twisting an arm around, he pulled out the weapon without so much as a grunt. Black blood dripped from the blade onto the chair's armrest, and he flicked his hand, throwing the dagger to the ground.

I wasn't sure if it was the Silver Sand still messing with my emotions, but even though the wound closed over instantly, tears welled in my eyes at the sight.

"Hey now, I'll be all right, Sharachi. Demons are expert healers," he said with a wink and reached around to position an arm across my shoulders. "This isn't the first time I've been stabbed," he added with a grin, and I knew he was referring to when I'd surprised him and stabbed him in the shoulder nights ago. Laughter squeezed out of me then, and I sniffed, blinking rapidly to banish away the tears.

With his arm around me, the bond between us urged me to move closer to him, and this time I didn't fight it. He'd just saved me by sheltering me from the falling contents of the room, and I convinced myself it wouldn't really matter if my walls were down for a short while. Leaning into his warmth, I pulled my knees up to my shoulders. For so long, I'd maintained a barrier around my heart, but it felt so good to be near him. Asher barely hesitated before wrapping his arms tighter around me. It was as though he knew just how badly I needed to be near someone right then. No, not *someone*. Him. I needed to be near *him*. His scents of musk and leather surrounded me, and even though rationally I knew he was a monster, a sense of safety went through me, making my body sag into him. It was similar to how I felt when I was curled against Kade and a feeling much more addictive than any drug I could consume.

Neither of us spoke, and we sat there for a long while with only the crackle from the burning logs in the fireplace breaking the silence.

I thought of what Asher had said about ghosts. The male always seemed so lighthearted that I would never have guessed he had any sort of dark past, but then again, even

Darian had proved he was more than my first impression of him.

Finally, my curiosity got the better of me, and I said, "You don't seem like you have any ghosts."

He shrugged casually, his massive body shifting against me. "Refusin' to take Silver Sand helps."

I nodded, completely understanding his resolve to stay away from the stuff. There was no way I was ever going to try the powder again. Someone should have named the drug Silver Death instead because Silver Sand sounded way too innocent for what it was.

I hadn't expected him to say anymore, but I was surprised when he continued speaking. "I was five when the curse spread throughout Katakin, and my mother and I were turned into demons. As a child, I didn't understand what was happenin', and I thought it was incredible. I looked like one of the make-believe monsters my mother had spoken to me about at bedtime.

We moved into the House of Thorem, and I was so excited. Borren, the demon alpha, talked about us bein' part of their new family, and I didn't have any siblings, so I loved the idea of livin' in a house where I could make new friends."

Asher's body tensed, and I knew what was coming next wouldn't be good.

"But my mother didn't deal well with the change. She became crazed and obsessed with the idea that she had to find a way to turn us human again, to the point she began mutilatin' her own body. And when she talked about doin' it to me, I ran."

I couldn't hide my horror. "Didn't anyone from your house do anything to help her?"

When I peered at Asher's violet eyes, they were dark, haunted by whatever memory he was reliving. "Oh, Borren helped her all right by puttin' her out of her misery. As for me, well, no one bothered to go after the offspring of the crazy female who stained the name of the House of Thorem."

I tried to hide my shock, not sure if he'd hate the idea of me pitying him. My life hadn't been all sunshine and roses, but I hadn't been through anything like that, and I found myself hurting for him. I remembered the pain and fury that had been in his gaze when I'd grabbed his tail just nights ago, and cold dread swept over me. *Holy Mother Falia.* Had his mother done something to cause the trauma? I couldn't bring myself to ask, and in any case, it wasn't my place.

I fumbled as I tried to think of something appropriate to say. "I'm sorry" didn't seem like it would cut it. My thoughts then went to the voices I'd heard in my head. Of the thousands of howls and screams. It occurred to me then that I could be going crazy like Asher's mother. *Oh, Goddess.*

"Maybe you shouldn't have shielded me," I said, swallowing. I didn't want to die, but I couldn't stop thinking about those voices. About their screams and wails. That couldn't be normal. "You're only guessing that you'll die when I die. I could be turning into something truly horrific," I said quietly. I could still feel the Silver Sand loosening my tongue, but I meant what I'd said.

My response had Asher's gaze sliding back my way, but instead of agreeing with me, he tightened his arms around my body. "I know monsters, Sharachi, and you're not one of them, but it'll be safer for you if you turn. I'd take you back to that damn island if I could, but the Taratun council wouldn't allow it. They'd hunt and kill you before you shared our secrets with the humans on your island."

He heaved a heavy sigh, and I found myself speechless again. *He'd take me back to the island?* Despite what I wanted to believe about the monster, I could tell he meant what he said, and that left me... confused.

"I'm sorry for stabbing you again," I said with a weak smile as I gestured with my head to the bloodied dagger discarded on the floor.

His mouth quirked up at the sides, and his eyes crinkled. "Don't be. I like my females a little feisty."

I scoffed and rolled my eyes. "You like being stabbed?" I asked skeptically.

"Depends on the one who's stabbing me," he replied, and the sound of his deep chuckle warmed my insides.

I thought then of how he held me like I actually meant something to him, and my heart rate picked up again.

Do not even think *of getting involved with any more monsters,* I said to myself internally as the urge to do something stupid like kiss the horned demon started to grip me.

To distract myself, I peered at the room around us and winced at the destruction. The room was a mess with tables and chairs splintered and broken in heaps, weapons scattered around the space, goblets, platters, and jugs everywhere, and torn tapestries hanging from the walls. "Do you think Kade and Locke will be angry?"

Asher grinned, a mischievous glint shining in his eyes again. "We could tell them Darian took the Silver Sand, and his power caused havoc, so I had to bring him down. Could be funny to see how that played out."

I laughed at his suggestion but shook my head. "I think I've put Darian through enough." Lifting from the settee, I slowly walked around the room, and my smile fell as I stepped over broken wood and bent blades. Biting my lip, I said quietly, "What the fuck is going on?"

I'd been talking to myself, but Asher came up behind me. "Even though the Silver Sand didn't turn you into a monster, it could have unleashed somethin' inside you. I don't know of any monsters who can conjure and control the wind, but we'll figure it all out."

Unleashed something inside of me? As much as I wanted to turn, a sickening feeling went through me at the idea that my body was gaining some strange power. *What if I can't control it?* Before my worry could spiral, I closed off my thoughts and bent to pick up a splintered chair leg.

"Leave it," Asher said as my fingers brushed the wood. "Locke will be able to organize someone to help us discard the broken furniture and refurnish the room. We might not be part of a monster house, but his family has money, and Locke has connections."

Frowning, I left the chair leg where it was. I didn't like the idea of leaving my mess for someone else to clean up, but exhaustion was dragging at me, especially now that the effects of the Silver Sand had worn off, so I nodded and settled back onto the only piece of furniture that was still standing. Resting my head back on the settee, I closed my eyes and hardly noticed when Asher dropped down beside me.

CHAPTER 7

~ **Asher** ~

Raine fell asleep soon after settling back onto the chair, and I waited a little while before lifting her into my arms. I'd intended to take her straight to Kade's room, but as her head buried into my clothing, snuggling against my chest while she slept, I hesitated.

For a long moment, I stood there like a fool, staring at my bedroom door and wondering what she'd think if she awoke in my bed instead. It wasn't that I was hoping to get anything from her—she was asleep, and I wasn't the kind of male to take advantage of an unsuspecting female—but she'd been staying in Kade's room for the past few nights, and I had the odd desire to have her in mine as well. To have her somewhere I could be close to her and watch over her.

The need to protect her was like an itch that never left me, a constant annoying sensation under my skin, and it seemed to grow worse with every passing night. Fuck, after I saw how the Silver Sand had affected her, I'd wanted to pull her onto my lap and stroke my fingers through her hair until I'd managed to banish whatever horrible memories the drug had unearthed. But I'd had to settle with an arm around her shoulders and instead had just burdened her with my secrets. I wasn't even sure why I'd told her about my mother. Maybe because I could tell she had her own demons, and I wanted to make her feel less alone.

I knew the bond between us was responsible for my constant need to protect her, but even if we hadn't been linked, I was starting to see that the female was someone worth protecting. If Raine was a sign we could be human again, I would protect her with my life. And if she was a sign that bad things were going to come our way, then we fuckin' deserved it.

Finally moving forward, I strode to Kade's room and placed Raine carefully on his bed. Pulling up the blanket, I made sure it covered her, then I went back to the common room.

As I went to disappear into the washroom, the door to the common room opened, and Locke entered the room, followed by Kade. Their gazes swept over the destroyed space, and their entire demeanors changed, their postures hardening. Before I could even utter a greeting, Kade was before me.

"Where the fuck is she, Ash?" he shouted, snarling in my face, his spit flying onto my cheek.

I lifted my hands in the air, my palms facing outward. "Take a breath. She's fine," I said, indicating with my head toward his room. "We weren't attacked if that's what you're thinkin'. She's sleepin' it off in your room."

Kade went to storm toward his room door, but I moved to block him. "Leave her be, Kade. She's exhausted."

He narrowed his eyes at me. "Exhausted?"

I grinned, all too aware of what he was likely thinking. "Oh, I wish it was like that. But no." My brows lowered as I said, "The little human has more secrets than we thought."

Locke strolled around the room, his assessing gaze still taking in all the damage. "What secrets? And why the fuck does it look like a monster brawl happened in here?"

"And where's Dar?" Kade growled. His rounded ears became pointed, and I knew he was using his wolf hearing to detect our brother.

"Unconscious in his room," I said, answering Kade's question first.

"Unconscious?" Kade asked.

"We gave Raine a dose of Silver Sand, as I told both of you that we would, and while she didn't turn into a monster, something strange happened," I explained. I went on to tell them about her resisting Darian's song, even though he pushed himself past his normal limits and the unusual winds that had torn through the room. I also explained how Darian had been rendered unconscious.

When I finished speaking, Kade was stone-faced as he said, "And you think she created the wind?"

I shrugged. "Can't see what else would have caused it. It sure as shit wasn't Darian or me."

"I've never heard of anyone who could control the wind," Locke said, his face devoid of emotion.

Kade pinched the bridge of his nose and paced away from me. "What the fuck does this all mean?"

Locke was preternaturally still as he said, "It means the two nights are up, and she still hasn't turned into a monster. The wind is another sign that the curse is affecting her, but it's not enough. The Week of Orash is almost here, and your methods haven't worked. So now it's my turn."

"If our methods haven't worked, yours won't either," I pointed out. "You didn't see what Raine was like just now under the influence of the drug. If that didn't get her to change, I doubt anythin' else will."

"He's right," Kade agreed.

"We'll see," Locke replied, and I didn't like the cold glint in his eyes, but I kept my mouth shut. We'd all agreed to let Locke try his way after the two nights were up, and though I knew he could be a bastard when he wanted to, he was nothing like his father. He wouldn't break Raine.

CHAPTER 8

~ Raine ~

The two nights were over, and I was still human. Or at least, that's how I appeared on the outside. After the experience with the Silver Sand, I wasn't sure if "human" was accurate, but I still had rounded fingertips and fragile, soft skin, and no horns had speared through my hair. I wasn't sure whether to be happy about it or annoyed. If I was the one who'd created the vortex of wind, I was obviously no longer ordinary, but no matter what Kade, Asher, and Darian had put me through, my appearance hadn't changed.

Pulling back the blanket, I sat up, immediately recognizing the wolf shifter's soft bed and sparse room. It took me a moment to realize Asher must have carried me there, and a slight smile curved my lips at the thought of the demon. The monster was kinder than he pretended to be.

Thankfully, my bone-weary exhaustion had left me while I'd slept, and I peered at the other side of the bed, disappointed when I found it was empty. *Has Kade even returned yet?* The faint scents of sandalwood and coffee lingered in the air, but that wasn't surprising seeing as it was Kade's room. What was unusual was the way Kade's scent was mixed with the aromas of cedarwood, ash, and spice. *Locke's* scents. My brows lowered when I thought of the moody vampire with onyx eyes. *Why the hell does it smell like—?*

As if he could read my thoughts, Locke stepped from a shadowed corner of the room, blue light washing over his body, and I almost fell to the floor in my haste to jump out of the bed.

I stiffened as the monster's dark gaze roved over me, sliding up my body as if he was tracing my every curve. Lifting my chin, I forced myself not to squirm at the attention, and I internally muttered a thank you to the goddess Falia that I was wearing the same black leather outfit I'd been wearing when I took the Silver Sand. It was better than standing before Locke in only a shirt.

"What are you doing in here?" I demanded, glaring daggers at the male.

He took another step forward, and I resisted the urge to move backward, all too aware of the fact I was weaponless. Not that weapons probably would have helped against him.

"Have you forgotten our agreement, *beautiful*?" he said with a smirk, his predatory gaze never leaving me. "The two nights are up, and as far as I can see, you're still human. So now I'll be throwing everything I have at you to try to get you to change."

Ignoring the rapid beating of my heart, I folded my arms in front of my chest and stuck my hip out. "How could I forget?" I responded dryly.

His smirk grew wider as he continued to stare at me with his unnerving black eyes. I forced myself to stare back as my mind thought of all the horrible things he was going to do to me. Except...the images that came to my mind didn't look like torture, and as his scents of cedarwood and spice grew stronger around me, my body warmed in response. I resisted the urge to fan my face and swallowed, forcing myself to get a grip. *Goddess, I need fresh air.*

"I'm not afraid of you," I said, unwilling to let him know how his presence rattled me. I was lying, of course. I would have been stupid not to be afraid of him, but for the moment, his wings were nowhere to be seen, and his claws weren't out either, so that was a good sign, right?

His nostrils flared, and his gaze slid from my exposed neck to the deep *V* of my top before lifting back to my face. Then he moved so fast that my brain struggled to process what had happened. One moment he was across the room, and the next, he was in front of me, only an arm's length away. Hunger shone in his dark eyes, and it wasn't just lust-filled desire but as though the monster was actually ravenous. His tongue slid slowly along his bottom lip, and I blinked as I took in the fangs that now peeked from between his lips. *What did he say his kind drink again? Oh, right. Blood. He said they need freaking blood to survive. Fuck.*

This time I did take a step backward, hoping to get across the message that I really didn't want to be his dinner. Or did I? Even now, while he was staring at me as though I was some delectable platter of food, the bond between us hummed, telling me to get closer to him. *Confusing fucking bond.* Thankfully, I had good survival instincts and was fully prepared to gouge his eyes out if need be.

My muscles tensed as I waited for him to strike, and when he reached an arm out, I almost went to kick him in the crotch before I realized he was trying to pass me a bundle of black cloth. *A cloak?*

"Strip and put this on," he said coldly. "We leave in five minutes."

"Strip?" I frowned at the order. *Not fucking likely.* I didn't care much about being naked, but I wasn't about to just strip for him if he was going to bark at me with that attitude.

Realizing I wasn't going to take the cloak, he dropped it onto the bed beside us. "Yes," he said bluntly, then he turned away and strode across the room. Pausing before the doorway, he added, "You'll regret it if you don't." And then he disappeared into the common room.

I blew out a shaky breath as I stared at the now empty doorway. The monster was such an infuriating ass. Grabbing the cloak from the bed, I held it up, letting it unfurl and fall to the floor. The soft material was silky between my fingers, and I was surprised at how beautiful the simple garment was.

I wondered why the hell I needed to strip. *Uh, because he's going to torture you. He probably wants more of your flesh exposed so he can scar you up,* my subconscious reasoned, and I grimaced at the thought. For some reason, though, I didn't think that was the case. *Maybe he just wants a nice view?* I scoffed at the thought and let out a heavy sigh. Either way, it didn't matter. *You'll regret it if you don't,* his words echoed in my head. I might not have liked the monster, but I believed him.

Reluctantly, I peeled off my leather outfit until I was standing in only my panties. Pulling on the cloak, I tied it around myself and quickly swept my hair into a ponytail, and strode into the common room. I mentally braced myself for the destruction I was sure I'd see, but when my gaze flicked over the room, my mouth dropped open in surprise. All the broken furniture had been replaced, and everything was almost exactly the way it had been before, aside from a few more scratches on the walls and the odd missing chair or table.

None of the other monsters were around, but Locke was now sitting in his usual spot on a settee, with an empty glass vial grasped in one hand while he drank from another. He didn't look up as I entered the room.

I remembered Asher saying that Locke would organize for someone to help refurbish the space, and the need to thank the vampire rested on the tip of my tongue, but I swallowed it down. I wasn't going to thank that asshole after he'd just been creepily watching me while I slept.

It was then that I noticed he was dressed in black fighting leathers, and a long, curved sword sat in the scabbard at his side. I didn't bother wasting my time asking where we were going, nor did I ask about the others. After having destroyed the room and the strange moment I'd shared with Asher, I was kind of glad that I didn't need to face anyone else just yet.

Striding past Locke, I quickly used the water closet, drank a goblet of the pink liquid, and went to the platter of food that was on a low table. Plucking at a strange red fruit, I shoved pieces of it into my mouth. An explosion of sour and sweet danced on my tongue, and I managed a few good mouthfuls before Locke lifted from his chair and pocketed the empty glass vial he was still holding.

"Your five minutes are up. Time to go, beautiful," he said.

• • • • •• • • •• ••

Locke led us up one tunnel after another, and I almost had to jog to keep up with his long strides. For a long while, the pair of us climbed the mountain in silence, but eventually, he stopped before a narrow iron door and turned to me.

"Time to show us what monster you are, Raine," he said and pushed open the door.

His words almost sounded like a threat, and for a beat, my legs wouldn't move, but as sunlight flooded through the open doorway, landing on my face, I scurried forward, desperate for a chance to be outside of the mountain.

Crisp air greeted me as Locke led me onto a small balcony and shut the door behind us. I breathed in deeply and squinted as my eyes adjusted to the light. We were high enough that wisps of clouds floated past, and a chill wind had me clutching at my arms in an effort to keep myself warm, but the rays of light streaming from above had a smile stretching my lips. I hadn't realized it was still day.

Closing my eyes and tipping my head upward, I relished the feeling of the sunlight on my cheeks. "I didn't think monsters liked sunlight? Isn't that why you sleep during the day?" I asked Locke when I finally opened my eyes again.

"It's not pleasant for vampires, but this way, we shouldn't be disturbed," he said, and I noticed the clench of his jaw and the tightness under his eyes.

Not pleasant? What did that mean? And what did he mean about not being disturbed?

"What? Are you planning to push me off the mountain?" I joked.

He didn't immediately answer me but stepped closer. "Something like that," he said seriously, and the blood drained from my face.

"Remove the cloak," he ordered.

"Fuck you," I retorted. I'd known he was going to do something horrible, but at the thought of being thrown from the mountain, goosebumps prickled over my skin as fear went through me.

He just waited, his black eyes giving nothing away as he stared at me.

Fuck. Gritting my teeth, I kept my gaze on him as I untied the cloak and let it fall to the ground. The moment the cloth was away from me, he moved forward, so I was pressed flush against his chest, and his arms curled around my back.

What the hell? I wiggled against him, trying to push away, but he wouldn't let me.

"You're going to want to hold on tight," he purred in my ear, and I had just enough time to grab onto his shoulders before his huge leathery wings flared out from behind his back, blocking out the sun, and he flapped, launching us into the air.

My stomach lurched as my feet left the ground, and the wind stung my eyes and ears. Cold air sliced through me and my teeth began to chatter as Locke flew us higher and higher, and I cursed him for making me strip. He took us from the mountain and in the opposite direction of the sprawling city of Katakin, over a stretch of bare land until we were above a deep expanse of blue sea and high into the clouds. I realized then what he'd meant about us not being disturbed. He'd brought us out while it was still sunlight so no other monsters would see us.

"Where the hell are you taking us?" I shouted over the wind, but he didn't respond. Not that he needed to. I already had a pretty good idea.

The asshole wasn't going to push me from the mountain. He was going to drop me from the sky. Adrenaline spiked through my veins as I panicked, but there was nothing I could do. Not unless I wanted to beg the vampire to take me back to the mountain, and just the idea of begging Locke for anything had my lip curling.

He stopped above another layer of clouds, and the air became thin enough that I began to breathe in shallow gasps. The steady flap of his wings sounded in my ears, and I tried to focus on the rhythm instead of thinking about the fact the ground was miles away.

I knew I wouldn't survive the fall. I tried to console myself with the idea that he'd catch me. That he wouldn't let me die, not when he thought the bond between us meant he'd die as well, but then I wondered whether he'd found a way to break the bond and hadn't told me. *What if he no longer believes our lives are linked?* The monsters were the ones who'd said they thought that would be the outcome. For all I knew, they'd been lying the whole time. I didn't know why they would, but anything was possible.

"Don't," I rasped, hating the way I clung to him. For a brief moment, I felt his arms tense, gripping me tighter to him, but then he relaxed, his head leaning toward my ear once again.

"I warned you," he said, his deep voice calm and even. "I gave you two nights."

I squeezed my eyes shut, forcing myself not to look at the sky around me. There was no stopping him and no escape.

"Do it, then," I snarled and released my grip on him, letting the hard leather of his outfit slip from my fingers.

He hesitated a moment longer. Then he let me go.

· · · ● · ● · ● · · ·

The icy wind tore at me as I careened toward the ocean, my eyes watering and limbs flailing. Instinctively, I spread my arms and legs, making a star shape, and I stopped spinning, but I was still falling way too fast. Too fast to survive a drop into the blue-green water far below.

The wind raked cold nails through my hair and against my body, and my ears popped at the pressure of the fall. Down. Down. Down. I continued to fall to the ocean, each moment bringing me closer to death. I tried to tell myself Locke wouldn't kill me. He just wanted to scare me, but that didn't help the fear that made my chest feel as if it were caving in on itself.

Thirteen thousand feet. Ten thousand.

This was it. I kept expecting to see Locke swoop down. I kept expecting the shadow of his outstretched wings to fall over me as he dropped down from the sky, saving me from the fall. But he never came. There was only the rush of the wind in my ears and my never-ending descent toward the ocean.

Eight thousand feet. *I can't fucking die now.*

I thought of the energy that had sparked inside me when I'd taken the Silver Sand, and I tried willing it to my fingertips. If it was me that created the wind in the room, perhaps I could control the wind now. Maybe I could get it to push me to land or something?

Down I fell.

Nothing happened as I tried to conjure the energy inside me, and I growled in frustration.

From high above, the rippling waves of the ocean looked like something from a painting.

Five thousand feet.

Three thousand.

A spark of energy went through me. Light shone in the backs of my eyes, and I could feel something inside me building, stretching, and pulsing under my skin. It didn't feel the same as when I'd controlled the wind. This felt...different.

One thousand.

Five hundred.

My whole body tingled with power, but before whatever was inside me was unleashed, a sea creature burst out of the ocean below me, and water sprayed in all directions as muscled arms wrapped around my waist, slowing my descent and dragging me to the ocean.

I cried out at the impact and sucked in a breath before I was pulled under the water, but the monster didn't let us sink too deep. Warmth sparked where the creature's skin touched mine, and it took me a moment to realize it wasn't just any creature holding me but *Darian*.

His silver hair trailed around us in the water, and he winked at me as I stared at him. His huge fishtail swished in the water, propelling us back to the surface, and with his strong arms still wrapped around me in a vise grip, he lifted me back into the sunlight.

The moment my head was above the surface, my mouth burst open, and I sucked in a gasping breath and coughed. Darian released me, moving away as if trying to give me room to breathe.

"What the hell was that?" I spluttered as I began treading water. I was still annoyed that Locke had dropped me, but I couldn't help giving the siren a small smile. The last time I'd seen him, he was still unconscious, and I was happy to see him beaming at me.

"That was me making sure you didn't die," Darian responded as if he was proud of himself, and I resisted the urge to punch his arm.

"Wow, thanks for that," I said sarcastically.

His brow wrinkled in confusion. "Did you want me to let you fall to your death?"

I let out a heavy sigh. "Of course not. I just—" I trailed off and let out a frustrated sound. Darian wasn't the one I was angry at. "What do we do now?" I asked instead.

Darian moved closer to me, his silver hair glittering so bright in the sun that it was hard to look at. "Locke wants you to swim, Raine lovely," he said.

"Swim?"

"Yes, back to shore," he clarified, tipping his head in the direction of the beach and the mountain beyond that. "You can swim, can't you?"

I nodded reluctantly, resigned to what I was going to have to do. I didn't begrudge Darian for being a part of it all. I'd known Locke was going to make my life hard. But if there was the chance that getting me to swim for my life was going to bring on the change, then I was all for it.

Squinting, I peered in the direction of the mountain and then at the monster city spread beneath its shadows with its blue rivers and pointed buildings. From here, the mountain was only the size of my finger. Could I really swim that far? The water seemed to stretch for miles, an endless landscape of green and blue.

"So he wants me to drown?" Sure, I'd swum around my island, but I'd never gone far. My energy felt rejuvenated after whatever power I'd used the night before, but my limbs still ached, my body still drained from the last two nights with Kade, Darian, and Asher. I wouldn't make it back to the shore.

Darian grimaced, clearly not happy with the whole situation. "He won't let you drown. That's why I'm here. He asked me to watch you. But don't tell him I told you that."

I pieced together what Darian wasn't saying. Locke wanted me to think they would let me drown. He wanted me to be as scared as possible in the hopes it would help bring on the change, but in reality, he'd asked Darian to watch over me. I thought then of how Locke had made me strip out of my leathers. The thick material would have become waterlogged and would have been difficult to swim in. *Had he been thinking about my comfort when he gave me the order?*

The idea that, in his strange way, Locke had done something kind was too much for my already frazzled brain, so I settled with muttering a curse at the vampire. He'd still dropped me. Treading water, I peered upward to try to catch a glimpse of the monster, but he was nowhere to be seen. I had no idea if he'd just left me there with Darian or if he was hiding behind one of the enormous clouds spread across the endless blue. I wouldn't have put it past him to go back to the rooms and relax while we were out there, but either way, it didn't matter.

Bringing my attention back to the mountain in the distance, I pushed forward in the water and began to swim. I'd swim the whole damn ocean if it meant it'd get me to change into a monster.

CHAPTER 9

~ Locke ~

I flew through the cloud that had drifted past me and swooped lower until Darian and the human were again in my line of sight, even if they were just pinpricks of black against the endless blue-green of the ocean.

It hadn't surprised me Raine hadn't changed during the fall. She'd already fallen down the pit of Reask, and she hadn't turned then. But I still thought it was worth a try. I knew she'd been expecting me to torture her. She likely thought I would chain her in a dungeon and bleed her dry until she turned. Not that I'd given her any reason to think otherwise.

Darian had been surprised when I'd told him my plans for her, but he'd been happy to agree to catch her and watch her from the water. And now, seeing them together, I couldn't help the annoyance that had me clenching my jaw.

Time passed as the watery sunlight beat down on me mercilessly, the sun's rays sinking into me and sapping my energy. The sun wouldn't kill me, but it did weaken me, as it did all vampires, and I hated it. But this was the safest option for Raine.

It wouldn't be too hard to spot us out in the open, but thankfully most monsters were sleeping. I'd already told Garan we'd be out there and that his guards needn't worry about us.

I arched in the sky, coasting on another wind drift before I came around again, still watching Darian and Raine from above. The human swam slowly, but she kept up an even pace as she made her way back to the shore. She was a fighter, this one, and I had to admire that.

Stroke after stroke, she swam with Darian by her side. If she didn't change by the time she made it to the beach, I was going to have to take her into the mountain and push her until her body gave in to the curse. She couldn't stay human. If she did, she'd have to compete in the Week of Orash as a human, and it would only be a matter of time before Warrick discovered her secret. Her life and ours depended on her turning into a monster.

You would think her remaining human would be a good thing. Warrick had been searching for a cure to the curse for nearly two centuries, and if she remained human, she could be the key to unlocking how to break the fae queen's magic. But as much as I wanted to be human again, I knew my father would kill her to extract her secrets. She would become just like the outliers I brought to him. He'd carve her open as if she was nothing more than an animal if it meant he could finally solve the puzzle that tormented him. And I wouldn't let that happen.

Though I tried to suppress it, deep within me, the urge to protect her had become strong enough that just staying away from her for the last two nights had been my own personal torture. Whatever the bond was between us, the magic within me was like a parasite digging deeper with each passing moment we didn't find a way to break it. *Fuck.* I knew my brothers felt the same way. I could see it in their eyes, see it in the way they stayed by her side. Kade had already all but fucking claimed her as his mate. And even worse was the craving. Her blood called to me, threatening my control, and no amount of synthetic blood would make the need leave me. She needed to get away from me.

I couldn't decide if the little human was ruining us or healing our broken souls. When Kade's family and the other wolves had been slaughtered, he'd entered a place so dark that I couldn't drag him from it. But Raine had. She'd saved him from the depths of his despair, and for that, she'd earned some of my respect.

A large ripple on the surface of the water drew my attention, pulling me from my musings, and I dropped lower in the sky until Darian and Raine looked less like pinpricks and were the size of my fist. Neither of them noticed as I hovered above them.

I narrowed my eyes as I scoured the ocean.

There. The ripple in the water was three hundred yards away from them now. At first, I thought it must be a shark, but the shadow was too big. *A whale?* Neither of those creatures worried me. Darian could easily handle the sea creatures in his siren form, and whales were known to be harmless.

But as I stared, the ripple turned into a wave, the water rushing toward Darian and Raine with frightening speed, becoming higher and higher. Massive black spines broke free of the water's surface, tall and thin, and a monster's enormous black head sprang upward out of the ocean, its huge maw opening to reveal sharp, needlelike teeth.

Outlier.

My brows slammed down, and my gaze shot to where Darian and Raine were swimming in the ocean, seemingly unaware of the monster behind them and still far from the beach, surrounded by nothing but the sea. Panic burst in my chest as I imagined Raine and my siren brother being swallowed by the outlier. I wouldn't let them be fucking taken.

Opening my mouth, I bellowed at the monster, then I tilted my head downward, pulled my wings in, and speared toward the ocean.

The icy wind yanked painfully at my wings and tore tears from my eyes, but I didn't fucking care. The relentless sunlight stung my skin, sapping my energy, but I continued downward. Darian and Raine were down there, and I wasn't going to let the outlier have them.

Raine was mine.

· · · • · • · · ·

~ Raine ~

Air sawed in and out of my lungs, burning up my throat with each gasp, and my arms felt as heavy as lead as I forced myself to keep swimming. Stroke after stroke, I made my way toward the beach and the small shape of the mountain in the distance. It felt like hours had passed, yet the ocean stretched on, the land still so painfully far.

With my next stroke, water splashed onto my head, and a wet strand of hair dropped over my left eye. Determined not to stop, I continued forward while jerking my head in spurts as I tried to shake the strand to the side of my face. *Move, damn it*, I willed my hair. Of course, the strand refused to move, and instead, I just wasted precious energy shaking my head up and down like a crazed person.

Frustrated, I cursed and was about to stop swimming and show the hair who was boss when Darian glided up beside me, his slender fingers reaching forward to tuck the stray strand behind my ear.

"You're doing good, lovely," he said as he swam lazily beside me, his long fishtail flicking in and out of the water every so often and his silvery blue scales reflecting the sun's light like crystals. As beautiful as it was, the sight stung my eyes, and I winced, peering away from him and focusing on putting one arm in front of the other and kicking in the water.

"Thanks," I muttered quietly between breaths.

The siren was near silent as he swam beside me, and I thought of when he'd been dancing with me in the garden, his song taking me to the depths of his soul. Once again, I was reminded that the monsters were nothing like I'd expected they would be. Had he really been pushing himself beyond his limits when I was influenced by the Silver Sand? All to try to bring me back?

I tried not to think about it.

Just swim, Raine. If you don't make it to the beach, you might just die in this forsaken ocean after all. I didn't really believe that. Not with Darian beside me.

You can push through this, I told myself as I tried to ignore the way my whole body ached. But as time passed, my muscles shook from the strain, and I struggled to keep my head above the water. As my chin dipped lower, water sloshed into my open mouth, and I stopped swimming and coughed violently. Sea salt burned the back of my throat, and I inwardly cursed Locke. I knew why he was putting me through the ordeal, but I still hated him for it.

Darian came up behind me and began rubbing my back in slow circles as I continued to hack. The action surprised me, but his hands were soothing on my skin, and before long, I was calming again.

"I'm sorry for, you know, knocking you out," I said to him when I was able to speak again. I'd wanted to say it earlier but hadn't.

"That's quite all right. If the tables were turned, I'm sure you'd try to save me," he said, and his eyes sparkled at the last bit. I got the feeling he was baiting me to see what my response would be.

I arched a brow, giving him a skeptical look. "I wouldn't bet on it."

He smiled, seemingly not at all bothered by my answer. "I would."

I rolled my eyes and forced myself to begin swimming again. Not much time had passed when one of my legs cramped. *Ah, fuck, ow.* I groaned, pausing to hover in the water.

As I reached down to try to massage the muscle, the water became strangely cool, and goosebumps prickled up my arms and legs. A faint cry sounded above me, and Darian's head jerked upward.

"What in the name of the Devil Enzal?" he breathed, moving closer to me as the water began to rise around us.

Darian's gaze changed direction then, flicking to something across the ocean, and before I had the chance to even register what was going on, his strong arms wrapped around my waist and the siren began pulling me through the water at a punishing pace. Ocean spray and the wind stung my cheeks, chilling me, and I struggled to breathe in Darian's grip. His hold on me was so tight it constricted my ribcage, and for the first time, I noticed long, wicked blue claws had protruded from his fingertips.

"What's going—?" I started, but my words died off when I peered behind us. Moving fast in the water, a creature swam in our direction, its massive body slowly emerging from the water like a mountain rising from the ocean. The monster's curved back was dotted with massive, long spines that jutted into the air, and five gelatinous red eyes bulged from its enormous, spiked head. Razor-like fins protruded out the sides of its wide, scaled body, and its gaping maw opened wide to reveal a dark cavern filled with a single row of needlelike teeth that were as long as swords.

"Holy Goddess," I said as fear wormed inside me. Darian's only response was to increase his speed as he pulled me through the water.

The siren was moving so fast that the wind felt like shards of ice, but the sea monster surged after us, its massive body gliding through the water while it kept its mouth open.

As I watched in horror, the monster lifted its head higher and then closed its maw before diving into the ocean.

"Darian," I said, my voice tight. The monster wasn't close enough that its movements had the water dragging us under, but a sickening feeling overcame me as I tried to stare down into the ocean.

Abruptly, Darian changed direction, but the siren was too late. I clung to him as the outlier sprang out of the water beneath us, its open maw too wide for us to escape. It lifted us into the air, and we sunk lower in the creature's mouth as water drained from between its needle-like teeth. The rancid smell of the creature's rotting flesh made my eyes water, and I peered around frantically, wishing I had a weapon in my grasp. My bare feet slid on the outlier's slimy tongue as the water continued to lower, and I imagined myself plunging a sword into the fleshy organ. Slowly, the monster began to close its mouth, and my heart beat so loud the noise was almost deafening.

"Let go," Darian commanded, turning to me.

I blinked, but my gaze remained fixed on the monster's long, pointed teeth as its mouth continued to close. "What?"

"Just...trust me," he said, pulling my attention back to him. "Can you do that?"

"I—" I stared at his face. "I don't know."

His blue gaze was calm as he nodded and said, "Don't die, all right, lovely?" Then he pried my hands from him, shifted his grip on my body, and tossed me into the air.

A startled gasp left me as I soared toward the monster's closing lips. For a terrifying moment, I wasn't sure if I was going to make it. The gap was closing too fast, and I was moving too damn slowly. A yellow tooth sliced deep into my left leg, the deep burning sensation making it feel as though hot lava was searing my flesh, but then I was free of the monster's maw and falling back toward the ocean's surface.

The creature's gray scales were a blur in my vision as I fell past the monster's body and past a wicked fin that looked sharp enough to slice me in two had I been three inches to the right. Coming to my senses, I lifted my arms and formed a point with my hands above my head, but the force of the water was still brutal as I went headfirst into the water. A ringing started in my ears, and pressure built in my head as I sank lower into the ocean.

Darian. My heart squeezed as I thought of the siren still in the monster's mouth, but I tried to push the image of him from my mind. *The surface. I have to make it to the surface.*

Bubbles trailed upward, the air escaping my mouth, and I flapped my arms to right myself and stop my descent. Light shone on the water's surface high above me, and I pumped my arms, kicking to push myself upward. But the surface was too far, and I was too exhausted. Hours of swimming had left my body feeling like a stone. *Goddess, I take it back. Fishtail. I need a freaking fishtail.*

But my body didn't change, and I was swimming upward too slowly. Fire burned in my lungs as my body cried for air, and cold desperation sank into my bones. Darian had sacrificed himself for me, and it wasn't even going to be the sea monster that killed me.

Keep swimming. I tried to hold on to the thought, but my arms slowed, the burning in my chest becoming too much. A small spark of energy ignited inside me. It was only just there, but it was unmistakable. I tried to mentally reach for it, to will it to become stronger, but I was too weak. Too deprived of air. I wasn't going to make it.

Just as my mouth was about to burst open, clawed black fingers reached toward me and strong arms wrapped around my torso. I barely registered Locke's face before he yanked me brutally to the surface.

When my head broke above the water, my mouth burst open, and my lungs expanded painfully as I sucked in a huge, gasping breath. Air rushed into me, and I coughed at the sudden intake.

"You need to swim away from here," Locke said as he released me. His leathery wings were folded behind his back, water streaming down the thick membranes, and fury shone in his hard onyx-colored eyes.

"Where's Darian?" I wheezed. "He— The monster," I gasped.

"Whatever you do. Keep fucking swimming," he repeated, ignoring my question as he peered at something in the distance.

I followed his gaze to see the huge monster's body cutting through the water a few hundred yards away. Not far from the creature's mouth was a flash of blue and silver as Darian swam, diving under the water before springing into the air again. His powerful siren body carried him quickly now that I wasn't in his arms, and the sound of his song hung in the air.

Thank the goddess. I didn't know how he'd made it out of the creature's mouth, but I didn't care. Darian was *alive.* I blew out a breath of relief, but then I noticed how the outlier was gaining on him, its gigantic body inching closer with every second. *Fuck.*

"Doesn't his power draw creatures *to* him? Why the hell is he using it?" I said as I watched on anxiously.

"I imagine he's trying to make sure the outlier's attention remains fixed on him."

"But that's idiotic!" I said, turning back to Locke. "We have to help him."

"I will," Locke replied with a hard expression as he moved his arms and legs, treading water, but his voice sounded strange, his words sluggish. Frowning, I studied his pale gray skin, the color a shade lighter than normal.

His eyes were hooded as if he was struggling to keep them open, and his powerful shoulders were hunched slightly like his body had been sapped of all its energy. It took me a moment before I remembered what he'd said about the sunlight. About how it made vampires weak.

"Are you all right?" I asked with concern, but before he could answer, a cry sounded over the water. We both looked across the ocean as Darian pivoted, twisting his body back toward the outlier and leaping toward it, raking his claws across one of the creature's eyes before diving back into the water.

The outlier let out an awful shriek that stung my ears, then it shook its head before diving into the ocean, following after Darian.

Indecision flickered in Locke's eyes. If I hadn't known how he hated me, I would have thought he was reluctant to leave me there.

"You have to live," he said to me. "Or Kade and Asher are dead as well. The gargoyles will be here soon. I can already hear them. Until then, swim for the beach like your life depends on it because it does."

I wanted to ask what he was going to do, especially in his weakened state, but his black eyes bore into me, and I just nodded. Seemingly satisfied with my response, he said again, "Swim, Raine," and then he turned his back on me and began swimming toward the creature.

CHAPTER 10

It was my fucking fault Darian and Raine were in the water. We hadn't had any sea creatures turn into outliers before, but I should have guessed it was only a matter of time. I should have known not to risk taking them out there.

Stroke after stroke, I made my way closer to the outlier and Darian, swimming through the water and pushing my pathetic body as fast as it would go. Fuck, how I wished I could use my wings.

When I'd seen Raine fall from the outlier's mouth into the water, I'd known if I went after her it would be hard to get airborne again. But I couldn't let her drown. The urge to protect her had driven me to action as searing pain erupted in my chest, and I'd dived into the ocean determined to save her from the inky darkness of the water. When my clawed hands had grabbed her, the relief that had gone through me was almost crippling, and I'd had to fight against the urge to pull her to me and swim with her back to the beach, forsaking my siren brother.

Swim, Raine, that's what I'd just told her. My stomach hardened again as I thought about how I'd just left her, but Darian needed me, and the outlier had to be taken care of. I peered back, satisfied when I saw she was heading in the direction of the beach. Thank Halced she was strong.

Turning, I forced myself to focus my attention forward. Time seemed to pass excruciatingly slowly as I made my way through the water, and I tried not to think about how fucking impotent I felt. The ocean clung to my wings, pulling me down, and any attempt I made to lift myself and try to stretch my wings out failed miserably.

The outlier burst out of the water not far ahead of me, and I glimpsed Darian who was just managing to stay out of reach of the monster's maw. He was doing well, but I didn't know how long he'd be able to last.

The faintest flap of wings still sounded in the distance, and I thanked all the fucking seven devils that Garan and his gargoyles were on the way. They'd help slaughter the outlier.

I lifted my head again in time to see Darian disappear into the water, but instead of following him, the outlier's red gaze locked onto me. I stopped swimming, treading water as I drew my wet sword from its sheath. *Come at me, ugly.*

The ocean swelled, lifting me higher as the outlier drew closer, and as the creature neared, I dived into the water, kicking hard to gain momentum. The sea beast followed after me, its huge body submerging into the ocean, and I maneuvered in the water, swimming to the side in time to miss the creature's gaping maw.

The outlier slid past me at high speed surrounded by a cloud of bubbles, and I reached out, using my free hand to grab onto one of the massive, jagged spines protruding from its back. The force was so strong my arm was almost wrenched from my shoulder socket, but I held on, digging my claws into the creature's thick bony flesh.

The sea beast dragged me through the water, and my arm protested at the strain, but I managed to keep my purchase as the outlier changed direction and headed upward again, its head springing straight up out of the water and its mouth stretched wide as if the creature was attempting to devour the sun. I could only imagine that Darian had been the creature's true target.

The wind whipped at my soaked body as the ocean fell away beneath us, and my swiping gaze was quick enough to catch the gargoyles who now dotted the sky around us and rained arrows down on the outlier. Garan's commanding shouts and the steady flap of the gargoyles' wings were welcome sounds, but I didn't let the gargoyles' presence deter me from playing my part.

As I hung with one hand gripping the creature's spine, I lifted my sword with my other hand and drove it down, grunting at the effort as the blade slid between the monster's scales and bit deep into its pale-gray flesh.

The outlier let out a pained cry that resembled a strangled whale call and snapped its mouth shut before curving over and diving back into the water, taking me with it. I kept my lips sealed as I held on to the spine, letting the creature carry me deep into the ocean. Down it swam until the water turned frigid, and all light was sucked away, leaving only darkness around us. Something bumped consistently against my leg. The wall of a cave? There was no way to tell.

Eventually, the creature changed course, and as the water lightened, I realized it was heading upward again. Darian appeared beside the outlier, and he gave me a grim nod before raking his claws along the creature's side, his fingers sliding between its scales and staining the water black with blood.

I gripped the handle of my sword, wrenching it back out before shifting my hand to a different spot and driving it back in. My body was so ridiculously weak that my hand shook at the strain, but the blade sunk in deep, and the outlier let out another pained cry as it burst straight up out of the ocean again. Sunlight washed over me as I still clung to the beast, the water running from me in rivulets and dripping from my hair and sodden clothes.

This time, the gargoyles were more prepared. All eight of Garan's team had come, and each of them was as brave and formidable as their leader was, their hard bodies unaffected by the sunlight and made for war. Thick arrows speared into the outlier's five eyes, and a gargoyle flew in close, almost lowering himself into the creature's open maw before he dropped a sparking wooden barrel down into its gullet. The creature bucked and cried out as its eyes became a bloody mess, and my body swung from side to side as I held on.

Garan barked at his team, and the winged guardians flew away from the creature.

Drop now, Locke, Garan's hard voice sounded urgently in my mind, and I didn't waste any time. Abandoning my sword, I lifted my feet to press my boots against the outlier's body. I removed my clawed hand from the creature's spine at the same time that I kicked off, diving backward into the air. My wings flared out, and I flapped them furiously as I fell. I careened toward the ocean, my body dropping like a bag of rocks, but before I slammed into the water, the wind billowed under my wings, and I lifted into the air.

Copying the distance of the gargoyles, I flew away from the outlier, and as I reached Garan's side and turned around, the top half of the outlier exploded into a mess of blood and gore that shot out in all directions.

A small, fleshy piece of scale and skin landed on my cheek, leaving a trail of warm wetness as it slid down my face, but I hardly noticed it as it fell away. I watched as what remained of the outlier crashed back to the ocean, the weight of its body creating waves in the water.

I hadn't seen Darian near the beast when I'd jumped, but I spotted him a safe distance away, looking on as the sea beast's body bobbed in the ocean, fire continuing to burn away what remained above the surface.

Heaving out a sigh, I stayed there, hovering in the air near the gargoyles. My gaze remained fixed on the flickering flames as I thought of how our world was beginning to crumble, and I hadn't found a way to stop it. Despite Warrick's efforts from his lab in the mountain, we still knew nothing of why the curse was now affecting the animals and creatures of this world.

A dark cloud settled over me as I thought of what would happen in the nights to come.

· · · ●· ●· · ·

~ Kade ~

I made it to the beach before Asher did. As soon as the pain had started in my chest, waking me from sleep and signaling Raine's weakening life force, I knew something was wrong. Instantly, I shifted, surrendering to my wolf side. In my beast form, I had sprung from my bed, my huge paws carrying me swiftly down the winding tunnels of the mountain as my claws found purchase, gripping the stone floor.

Asher wasn't far behind me, his heavy footsteps echoing along the walls as he ran.

Something wasn't right. Locke wasn't the monster he thought he was, and I knew he wouldn't have intentionally put Raine in a situation that would result in her death. Whatever the reason for her weakened state, all I knew was that I needed to get to her.

I ran until I'd broken through one of the doors that led to the outside and only stopped when the sun shone on my fur and the crisp mountain air tickled my nose. Back when I was a boy and the curse had first given me my wolf form, my wolf side had seemed like a separate entity inside me. But now it was different. When I was the wolf, I was aware I was still me, just fueled with animalistic instincts that dominated my human side.

As I peered around at the stretch of rocky land that led to the city below us, my ears twitched as I tried to detect any trace of the human. Of *my* Mahare. As a wolf, the certainty that she belonged to me made my blood burn for her. She was *my* Raine, my female, and I wanted to claim her and howl to the world that she was mine and not to be harmed. If anyone hurt her, I would slowly tear them to pieces and make them beg for death.

The thought had saliva dripping down my fangs and my lips curling as I snarled. Dipping my nose to the ground, I sniffed, trying to pick up her scent, but neither Locke nor Raine had passed that way. Asher appeared from the mountain behind me, his axes hastily strapped to his sides, just as I finally picked up the faint traces of coconut and steel carrying on the wind. The scents came from the direction of the ocean, away from the city.

"What the fuck is that?" Asher said, and I lifted my head to see where he was looking.

Far out to sea, a huge monster with a body as wide as a small mountain sprang out of the ocean. My sharp wolf eyesight couldn't spot Raine, but my instinct told me she was there and she was in fucking trouble.

Not waiting for Asher, I launched my powerful body forward, my large paws barely touching the ground as I raced toward the ocean. The sharp pain in my chest grew stronger with every passing second, and fear made me run faster as a growl tore from my throat and shattered the air.

I thought of Locke then, all too aware of how the sun weakened vampires. Even if he was with Raine, I knew he wouldn't be strong enough to protect her. Not from an outlier that size. *Fuck.* My fear intensified then as I worried for my vampire brother, but I was quick to push the concern away. Even in his weakened state, Locke would be able to take care of himself.

The salty, pungent scent of the ocean became stronger as I made it to the beach, but Raine's scent still carried on the wind, indicating that I was headed in the right direction. As I barreled forward, the gray sand crunched under my paws, and then I was running into the water, leaping over shallow waves. When I was submerged up to my chest, I began to swim, swiping my massive paws in the water. The ocean soaked into my shaggy brown fur, weighing me down, and the salty spray stung my eyes, but none of this mattered.

My legs stroked through the water, pushing my huge body deeper until I sighted Raine ahead, swimming in the water. Relief crashed through me, but the pain in my chest reminded me she was in danger. From a short distance, it was clear she was exhausted and hardly keeping herself afloat, her head barely above the water. I could feel her life force draining from her and knew she might have serious injuries.

As I neared her, Raine's eyes widened as she stared at me. "Kade?" she rasped in surprise. Without so much as a growl, I circled behind her and sank below the water, moving beneath her. When I rose back up, I lifted Raine out of the water, and she sprawled on my back. Her shaking fingers gently grabbed the fur behind my head, and I began swimming back toward the beach, a growl of approval rumbling in my throat now that she was with me.

Garan's gargoyles passed over us, soaring toward the outlier, and I folded my ears back when the outlier's warbled cries filled the air. Internally, I thanked all seven devils they were there. With the gargoyles on the offensive, I knew they'd be able to bring down the creature. With this thought, I relaxed at the idea that Locke was still out there and thought only of Raine as I paddled back to the shore.

Asher was there to greet us when we made it to the beach, and he carefully lifted Raine from my back before placing her gently on the sand. Wasting no time, I shifted back to my human form and crouched, my gaze raking over her. A growl rumbled from me when I took in her ashen face and the long, open gash on one of her legs. Her blood leaked from the wound, sliding down her leg and staining the sand crimson.

"It's nothing," she rasped weakly and went to sit up, but her arms collapsed. Before her back landed on the sand, my hand slid under her, and I propped myself at her back.

"Darian and Locke," she said, peering up at me with worry.

"Fuckin' Enzal, is Darian out there too?" Asher commented, running a hand over his horns as he squinted out at the ocean.

I shot him a look when he peered back at us, and he cleared his throat. Squatting, he added, "Oh, ah, don't worry, Sharachi, I'm sure they're all right," and he began inspecting her wound. Blood slipped between his fingers when he tried to press the two sides of the wound together, and he gave me a grim look. "We need to get her back, Kade. This doesn't look good."

"I know," I said, nodding at him.

I waited as Asher pulled his shirt over his head and tore the fabric into strips. His deft fingers quickly used them to bandage her wound, and when it was done, I went to lift her.

Raine shook her head. "No, wait. Not yet."

A loud explosion sounded, assaulting my sensitive ears, and I followed her horrified gaze over the ocean, watching as the remains of the outlier's mutilated body crashed to the water. Above the scene, gargoyles were spread across the sky, watching on with stony faces, and I spotted Locke amongst them. A silver mass also glinted in the water, and I was relieved when I made out Darian's form.

"They're all right," Asher said reassuringly. He was staring out across the ocean as well, and he had one hand covering his eyes to help shade against the sun. "Locke and Darian better give us all the gory details later."

Raine's body sagged against me at Asher's words, and I rubbed my hands up and down her bare arms.

"Who are the gray monsters?" she asked, squinting at the sky.

"Gargoyles," Asher said with a grin, turning back to us. I lifted Raine then, and Asher kicked at the sand, burying her blood. The last thing we needed was anyone seeing the red blood and coming to conclusions that may or may not have been true.

"Garan's team of gargoyles are the main flyers who watch the city from the sky and maintain the guard towers," I elaborated, shifting her in my arms.

"Gargoyles...," she mused aloud.

Asher lifted one of his hands to rub at his chest, and then he stepped forward. "We can't wait any longer. Let me have her."

My body tensed, my arms tightening protectively around her.

"You just swam half the ocean to get her," he exaggerated and gave me a pointed look. "We'll be faster if I carry her back."

I hesitated for a moment longer, but then I gave him a curt nod and let him take Raine. One of his hands slid under her legs while the other gripped behind her back, and he turned, carrying her toward the mountain. I could have easily managed, but Asher was right when he said we'd be faster if he took her. Still, I didn't miss the way Asher's face softened when Raine let her head fall against his chest, and a slight smile teased my lips as I wondered whether he'd just used speed as an excuse to have a chance at holding her. I also didn't miss the fact that Raine didn't protest at the idea.

Asher lifted her a little higher in his arms, and he moved swiftly across the beach. I kept pace with him, keeping my senses heightened just in case there were any other surprises in store for us.

"I knew Locke planned to put me through hell, but I didn't expect that. What is that thing?" Raine asked as she tried to crane her neck and peer back at where the outlier continued to burn above the water.

My lips pulled to a thin line. "That wasn't Locke's doing."

"It's a fuckin' outlier," Asher supplied as if that was an answer he thought Raine would understand. "Biggest one we've seen yet."

She frowned. "An outlier?"

"It's a long story," I said. "Let's wait until we're back in the rooms."

Raine didn't seem impressed by my suggestion, but her mood improved when Darian appeared behind us minutes later, once again in his human form. Shortly after, Locke dropped from the sky and began walking beside him, both of them with only scratches and black blood smeared on their sodden bodies.

Raine's amber eyes brightened at their arrival, making my chest warm, despite the sharp pain that still told me her life was in danger.

Locke scowled, and his eyes hardened when he noticed the gash on Raine's leg.

Darian stepped up on Asher's other side, and his fingers trailed down Raine's cheek before he pulled his hand away. "You all right, lovely?"

She grinned at him, but the smile was forced, and the color continued to drain from her face. "I didn't die."

He smiled back at her, his eyes sparkling. "And thank the devils for that."

I hadn't known Darian to smile at any female the way he was smiling at Raine then, and I resisted the urge to point it out to him.

"We just need to get her back to the rooms and fix her up. She'll be all right," Asher said. "Glad to see you in one piece too. Should have let us know about the party."

Darian's hand clapped over Asher's shoulder and squeezed. "Next time, I'll be sure to send you an invite. We could have used the help."

"I'm betting those gargoyles were a welcome sight," he replied.

"Like seeing a blue sky after the rain," Darian agreed dramatically and smiled wider.

Slowing my steps, I fell into line with Locke, who was now striding behind us. His expression was dark, and his own weariness was plain on his face.

"You shouldn't have taken them out during the day," I said, my voice a rumbling growl as I stared straight ahead at Asher's broad back. "You know you're weaker in the sunlight."

Locke didn't peer at me. "We needed to get her to change, and taking her at night would have been riskier," he responded in a clinical voice.

I struggled to contain my anger. "It still wasn't worth it. We know the occurrence of outliers is becoming more frequent."

He was silent as if he was contemplating my words. Moments passed, and I was surprised when he finally said, "I know." His black gaze fixed on where Raine's bandaged leg bobbed in time to Asher's steps. "She'll have to compete in the Week of Orash as a human and hope no one discovers her secret."

As grim as it was, I was about to agree when Raine's muffled voice said, "There must be something else we can try." Of course, she'd been listening. There wasn't much the human missed. "We still have one night left," she added.

A growl rumbled from my chest as I prepared myself to argue. After what had happened with the outlier in the ocean, I wasn't about to let Locke put her through anything else. It had only been two nights since I'd promised to help protect her, and I'd already almost fucking failed. But when I went to open my mouth to speak, I found I didn't need to.

"No," Locke said coldly.

Raine stretched her neck, peering past Asher's body to stare at him. "What do you mean 'no'? I can still—"

"No, we're done," Locke said again, and this time, his voice was frosty as he stared her down.

Her eyes narrowed as she glared back at him, but he didn't let her protest. He stopped walking, and the moment I was far enough away, he stretched out his wings and launched himself into the air, flying to the mountain ahead of us.

CHAPTER II

~ Raine ~

When we made it back to the rooms, there was a moment when Asher's steps faltered. For a beat, he stared at the bedroom doors as if he wasn't sure where to take me, but then he was striding purposefully into Kade's room. Carefully, he lowered me, placing me on Kade's bed while being mindful not to jostle my injured leg.

I gave him an awkward smile. "Thanks." I'd wanted to protest when he'd taken me into his arms back on the beach, but with the gash in my leg and my exhaustion, I'd known I couldn't have walked. I hadn't expected the warmth that went through me when his strong arms curled around me, his scents of musk and leather making my heart race. Kade had walked beside us, and as his scents of sandalwood and coffee mixed with the leather and musk, my head had grown light.

"Anytime, Sharachi," Asher said, giving me a lopsided smile, and my body heated at the way his violet eyes peered down at me. Goddess, I had to be feverish. It was the only explanation for how the monster was making me feel. I lifted an arm, pressing the back of my hand to my forehead to check if I had a temperature, but I wasn't warm at all. If anything, I was cold. Way colder than I should have been. As if the very thought had set off a chain reaction, my body began trembling violently, and my teeth started to chatter.

Asher's smile fell, concern twisting his features as he pressed a hand to my cheek. "Fucking hell, she's freezing," he said to Darian, who had crouched beside the bed.

The siren worked quickly to unravel the rough bandage Asher had placed on my leg, and I heard him suck in a small breath of air as he inspected the wound.

I stared at the ceiling, not looking down. I already knew my leg was a mess. I didn't need to look at the ruined flesh. Adrenaline had mostly kept the pain manageable while I was in the ocean, but sometime on the walk back to the mountain, it began to feel as if my leg was on fire. I ground my teeth and focused on breathing steadily as I let the pain wash over me.

The bed dipped as Kade crawled over the mattress, taking a position behind me, and he lifted me until I was resting against his chest. The bond between us sparked, and the warmth of his body against mine had the pain lessening. Closing my eyes, I leaned into his touch, focusing on his intoxicating scents.

There was prodding at my leg, and Asher muttered a curse. He was hovering near Darian, watching as the siren inspected the wound.

My eyes fluttered open. "Is it that bad?"

"Well, it ain't fuckin' good," Asher responded bluntly as he continued to stare at the wound. Darian paused to glare at him, and a growl rumbled in Kade's chest.

Asher's expression became sheepish as he lifted his gaze to stare at Kade and me. "What? She asked," he defended, and even though I couldn't see Kade's face, I could imagine the disapproving look he was giving the demon.

"This is going to sting, Raine lovely," Darian warned, his crystal-blue eyes sympathetic as he stared at me and held up a bottle of some sort of alcohol. "And once I've cleaned the wound, I'll need to stitch it up." His long silver hair was a mess, the silver locks streaked with black blood, and I wondered whether he had his own wounds to attend to. Goddess, the siren had saved me. Had *thrown* me from the outlier's mouth, and I was still reeling from the fact that I'd be dead if it weren't for him. Or Locke, for that matter.

"Just do it," I said through clenched teeth, and Kade's comforting hold on me tightened.

My body tensed when Darian poured the alcoholic liquid over the wound, my hands curling into tight fists at my sides as the pain became almost unbearable. And then

I could feel the pinpricks and tugging on my leg as Darian stitched me back together.

Sweat beaded on my brow, and I tried to focus on my breathing. *Breathe in. Breathe out.* Darian yanked on the string a little harder as he tied the final knot, and Kade's tight hold on me kept me from jolting away.

"That's the worst over, Raine," Kade's deep voice rumbled in my ear, and my heart swelled at the way he held me, even now, while I was bleeding on his bed. At the fact that I didn't have to go through it alone.

I swallowed and nodded, knowing that if I said anything the emotion would be evident in my voice.

With the wound clean and stitched, Darian set about smearing the strange blue paste on my leg before he dressed it with a proper, clean bandage. When he was finished, he stood and smiled at me. Weariness mixed with his expression of relief. "All done. Now all you need is rest."

"Thanks," I mumbled. I didn't think I was going to be able to sleep when my leg still throbbed with pain, but when I closed my eyes and relaxed against Kade, darkness took me.

CHAPTER 12

~ **Locke** ~

Self-loathing and anger choked me as I flew away from Raine and my brothers, heading toward the mountain. If I had kept walking with them, I'd have said something I would have regretted, and I needed a moment to clear my head.

My fury stayed with me as I soared across the sky, but it had dulled by the time I landed at the base of the mountain, my feet finding purchase on the rocky ground. Rolling my neck, I made my wings disappear into my back and forced my claws to retract, then I smoothed the front of my coat and straightened.

The door ahead of me hung wide open, having been ripped from its hinges, and I didn't stop to wonder whether Kade's wolf or Asher had done the damage. I simply strolled through and began making my way along the tunnels, heading toward Warrick's lab.

It wasn't long before I was in the depths of the mountain, and I hated that the darkness helped soothe my anger even more. An image of Raine as she was sinking into the ocean came to my mind, briefly igniting my fury, but I pushed it back just as I forced away all thoughts I had of her. I couldn't be thinking about her now.

Outside the mountain, there were a few hours of sunlight left and most monsters were still in their beds, but I wasn't surprised when I found Warrick in his office. The small room adjoined his lab and didn't hold much other than a steel desk, chair, a filing cabinet, and countless sheets of paper.

Warrick sat with his back craned and his head bent down as he looked over a huge stack of papers spread out like a fan on the desk before him. The reports of the newbloods didn't appear to be in any particular order, and he scratched his chin as he peered at them as if they were all the pieces of some giant puzzle he was trying to figure out. Gosren, Warrick's goblin assistant, was nowhere to be seen, and I was thankful the sniveling monster wasn't there while I spoke to my father.

"Bear shifter should do well against the ogre," Warrick muttered, and I stiffened as I realized he was likely talking about the fights and who would be evenly matched during the Week of Orash. The Taratun council would meet the next night to discuss the initial groupings, and I knew Warrick would have a strong say during the discussion.

The urge to ask him who Raine would be pitted against sat on the tip of my tongue, but I swallowed it down. He already knew I'd taken an interest in her, and no doubt that was what had sparked his own curiosity. I didn't need to add more fuel to the fire.

"I'm sure by now you've heard about the outlier in the ocean," I said, interrupting his mutterings.

"Ah, Locke," he said, turning in his chair. His brows became smooth again, and his cruel black eyes fixed on my face. His left brow raised as he took in the bruises and cuts on my body and the monster blood splattered over me. "A messenger just left, yes. I'm glad to see you walked away mostly unharmed."

There wasn't an ounce of genuine concern in his voice, but that didn't bother me. I'd long since learned my father preferred it when he thought I was weak and broken.

"The attacks have become much more frequent recently," I said, keeping my voice even. *Since the latest round of humans were pulled here for the trials,* I wanted to add, but I didn't. The last thing I wanted was for Warrick to be scrutinizing the newbloods and Raine more than he already was. It was possible that the timing of the two was a complete coincidence. "Have you discerned any more information from studying the creatures I've brought you? Today was the largest outlier we've seen yet."

Warrick waved a hand in the air dismissively and turned back to the papers in front of him. "From what I hear, the gargoyles had no trouble bringing it down."

I wasn't surprised that he knew. The vampire had spies everywhere, and I'd long since suspected he had one of the gargoyles under his influence. But I didn't miss how he only gave credit to Garan and his team and didn't mention the role Darian and I had played. Not that it mattered. If anything, it was a good thing. When I'd spoken to Garan briefly after the outlier was defeated, I'd asked him to ensure his gargoyles didn't speak of the newblood, Raine, and the fact she'd also been out there. If Warrick had one of the gargoyles reporting to him, thankfully, it hadn't seemed that they'd mentioned her. It would have been hard explaining to Warrick why she was out there.

"We need to know why our animals and sea creatures are now being affected by the curse. If we don't contain this, Katakin could fall."

Unfazed by my comment, he began rifling through the reports, shuffling them around. "There has been no indication yet as to why the curse is changing, but I'm sure if you keep bringing me—"

I shot over to the side of his desk and slammed my fist down onto the latest report he was about to pick up. "We need answers *now*. If all our livestock starts to turn into these monsters, they'll be like a fucking army. We won't survive!"

Warrick's hands stilled, and he stared up at me with a dangerous glint in his coal-black eyes.

Slowly, I removed my fist, knowing that I'd overstepped. I wanted to fucking fight the bastard. To rid Katakin of his dark stain of a soul, and I promised myself that one day I would, but for now, he was the only council member investigating the outliers and trying to find a way to break the curse. So I stepped back, lowering my head slightly and feigning regret after my outburst.

The hardness in Warrick's eyes thawed slightly, but his eyes remained alert. "With time, I'll figure it out. For the next week, the only news the citizens of Katakin will be talking about is the Week of Orash and the newbloods who will be welcomed into their new houses. They won't be talking about a few dead monsters. We shall have to hope there aren't any more outlier attacks for a while."

"And if there are?"

A depraved smile stretched across his face, highlighting his angular cheekbones and sharp jaw. "If there are, then next time make sure you bring the outlier to me alive or at least bring me the monster's heart."

My nostrils flared as I glared at him. I resisted the urge to comment that the last outlier's heart was likely the size of a fucking bison and instead began striding back toward the door.

I'd just reached the doorway when he added, "Oh, and I look forward to watching your little shifter fight. Don't forget your mother will expect to get her hands on the newblood before she's presented."

Fangs peeked between my lips, but I didn't comment and kept my back to him as I left the room.

CHAPTER 13

~ **Raine** ~

Kade was still there when I awoke, and I blinked and rubbed my eyes before peering up at him. His head was crooked awkwardly to the side as he dozed, but he startled at my movement, his golden gaze colliding with my face.

"You didn't have to stay with me," I said as I sat up and pulled away from him.

His expression hardened as I moved away, but he didn't reach for me. "How are you feeling?"

Leaning down, I ran my fingertips over the bandage on my leg. "Better," I said, and I meant it. The pain had completely disappeared while I'd slept.

Using both hands, I unraveled the bloody bandage and carefully slid my fingertips down my leg, passing over where I remembered the long gash had been. When my fingers found only smooth, scarless skin, my lips parted in surprise. I knew the blue paste had incredible healing powers, but the gash had been so deep that I'd expected there might be a residual mark or a puckered scar. But there was nothing but dried blood to indicate that I'd even been wounded at all. *I really need to get my hands on a vial of the blue stuff before I leave this place.*

At the thought of leaving the monsters who had just saved my life, an odd pang went through me. My heart squeezed as my gaze connected with Kade's, and it took everything I had in me not to move back into his arms.

But a life with the monsters wasn't an option for me. Not unless my sister was safe and happy in Katakin. Not unless she wanted to stay.

Sliding from the bed, I grabbed a clean pair of leathers and draped them over my arm. "I ah, need to use the washroom," I said, and I forced myself from the room and away from Kade.

· · · · ● · ● · · ·

When I exited the washroom, all four monsters were in the common room. Kade and Locke were having a heated discussion near the far wall while Darian downed unhealthy amounts of wine and Asher inhaled the food on the replenished silver platter.

Who the hell is bringing us fresh food anyway? Considering Locke had helpers who had refurnished the room, I could only guess that he also had monsters bringing us food and wine.

Asher held up a chicken leg to me in salute and grinned before tearing a chunk off with his teeth. The gesture was so unexpected that I found myself shaking my head in mock disgust and grinning back at him. The demon had a way of making my absurdly crazy situation seem so insanely normal.

Ignoring Asher's bad table manners, I poured myself a goblet of pink liquid and went to sit near Darian, who was closest to the fire. From the moment I'd moved away from Kade on the bed, a coldness had seeped through me, and the warmth of the fire was a pleasant reprieve. *Or is it because I'm sitting close to Darian? Nope, definitely the fire.*

Asher watched as Darian uncrossed his legs and shifted subtly closer to me. Finishing his mouthful, the demon casually pointed to Darian with his chicken leg. "Glad to see you're up and about, Sharachi. Dar here was drinkin' himself to death with worry."

In response, Darian took another sip of his wine and arched a silver brow at him. "Says the monster who's been comfort eating as if he's about to hibernate for the winter."

I rolled my eyes at the pair of them and gulped from my goblet.

"What can I say? My appetite has grown unexpectedly," Asher replied with a toothy grin as he finished off his chicken.

Darian's blue eyes glowed as he agreed, "As has mine."

I eyed them both suspiciously. They were acting fucking weird, and I suddenly regretted my seating choice. I had enough of my own crazy to deal with. The voices in my head hadn't returned since the incident with the Silver Sand, but that didn't mean I was normal again. There was still the fact I'd probably caused the unnatural wind that had destroyed the room.

Indicating toward Locke and Kade with my head, I leaned toward Darian. "What are they talking about?"

His gaze followed mine across the room. "The outliers," he said, pursing his lips.

"Outliers?" I thought of the enormous monster we'd encountered in the ocean. "Wait, there's more than one? What are they?"

I was sitting up straight now, staring at Darian with a hopeful expression as I waited for him to give me answers.

As if they'd heard my questions, which they probably had, Kade and Locke finished their conversation and came to stand near us.

"The outliers are a different type of monster," Kade answered. "While we were all humans who were turned by the curse, the outliers were once animals. They have no remorse nor seem to have any goal other than to destroy those around them."

Animals? I frowned. "But surely you have tons of animals here? Does that mean there are hundreds of outliers?"

Again, I pictured the gigantic monster from the ocean, with its spined back and five red eyes. I couldn't imagine facing hundreds of them. "Wait. The monster in the ocean. You're telling me that it had once been an animal?"

"Yes," Kade replied with a serious expression.

Whoa. I was glad I was sitting, then, because it was a lot to wrap my head around.

"So far, only a handful of animals have turned, and we don't know why," Locke added. "The curse never affected them in the past, but in recent years, things have changed."

"But if only a few have turned, you can take care of them, right?" I asked.

Locke sighed heavily. "A few we can handle, but if all our animals start to turn, they will be like an army descending upon Katakin."

An army? I leaned back in my chair, almost wishing they hadn't told me.

"And we can't exactly kill all our animals, or we'd starve," Asher added with a relaxed shrug and a nod of his head toward the silver platter, where the remainder of a whole roast chicken sat nestled between herb-crusted vegetables.

"We're lucky we survived the last one," Darian said grimly, and I noticed the hardening of his body.

Don't die, he'd said to me before throwing me from the creature's mouth. Goddess, I'd barely survived one outlier monster. I shivered as I thought of a thousand of the creatures sweeping over Katakin city and crawling through the mountain.

I licked my lips nervously. "So what do we do?"

Locke's dark gaze locked onto me, and his voice was harsh when he said, "The Week of Orash begins tomorrow night. You need to rest."

"Rest?" I shot to my feet. "What happened to throwing everything you have at me?" If I was being honest, I could have used the rest, but now more than ever I realized I needed to turn. I was already disadvantaged as a human against the monsters, let alone against outliers. I needed to change, and taking a night off sounded an awful lot like giving up. I hadn't come this fucking far to give up.

One moment Locke was standing near Kade a few steps away, and the next, he was in my face, glaring down at me.

Darian and Asher lifted to their feet as well, but my focus was only on Locke as he said, "If I truly threw everything I had at you, you'd be so broken you'd wish for death. If it weren't for Darian and me, you'd be dead in that water. You should be grateful I'm giving you a night off."

A chill clawed its way down my spine, but I gritted my teeth as my anger rose. "Grateful? You're just worried that if I die, your miserable life will be snuffed out as well."

"If you can't see—" Locke started, but a growl vibrated from Kade, and it was loud enough that Locke didn't finish. Darian shifted, his body moving closer to mine, and even Asher's body angled more toward me.

"Back off, Locke," Kade barked, his command cutting through the air. "I won't ask again."

Locke's black gaze remained fixed on my face for a moment longer, and I thought I saw something like regret in his dark eyes, but then he turned away from me and strode toward the common room door. "Make sure she doesn't leave this room. More monsters will be in the mountain as they prepare for the beginning of the Week of Orash."

And then he was gone from the room.

I clenched and unclenched my fists and focused on calming my breathing. Locke had saved my life, but holy Mother, he was still an ass.

Kade stepped closer to me, his hand going under my chin and tilting my head up so I was looking at him. I was about to wrench my head away, but the concern in his golden gaze and the warmth of his fingers on my skin had me rooted to the spot. "Locke can be a bastard, but he's right. You need to rest."

I narrowed my eyes at him but nodded begrudgingly, my body remaining tense.

"I need to meet up with Locke, but Darian and Asher will be here with you. Stay in the rooms. Locke wasn't wrong when he said this mountain will be filled with more monsters than usual. I'll be back sometime after the sun rises." And with that, he leaned down, pressing his lips to mine. My muscles finally loosened, my anger replaced by desire that warmed my whole body.

"Where are you going?" I asked when Kade pulled back and stepped away from me, but the wolf shifter didn't answer my question. "Take care of her," he said to Darian and Kade, and then he left the room as well.

A hand rested on my back, and the bond between Darian and I hummed at the contact. "Come, Raine. You still haven't eaten anything, and you'll need your strength."

Reluctantly, I sat back down, still reeling after Locke's words and Kade's kiss. Asher grabbed a plate and piled it with food before handing it to me. It was as if the monster thought I was incapable of grabbing my own.

"How can you stand to be around him?" I asked the pair of them.

"Who, Locke?" Asher asked. "Believe it or not, he saved all of us in one way or another. He's had a complicated past. Don't take it too hard."

Darian sat beside me. "I'm sure it doesn't seem like it, but he's going easy on you. What you've been through is nothing in comparison to what Warrick put him through as a child."

"His father?" I pictured the vampire with cruel coal-black eyes. "What did his father do?"

Asher grabbed a small roasted potato and stretched out on the settee closest to us. "Let's just say blood relations are overrated," he said before popping the whole thing into his mouth.

Knowing I wasn't going to get any more than that, I began eating from my plate of food, grabbing a fork from the table and pushing a roasted carrot into my mouth. "So, are we really just going to spend the night doing nothing?" I asked incredulously.

"Doesn't have to be nothin'," Asher said, giving me a lazy smile, and I gave him a disgusted expression and flung a roasted potato at him. It probably wasn't my most mature moment, but hey, he deserved it.

Unfortunately, before the potato could hit him in the chest, his tail flicked out and the vegetable was speared onto the pointed tip. He let out a hearty chuckle as he pulled off the potato and tossed it into his mouth, then he leaned back again, folding his arms behind his head with an arrogant smile. I was glad the ass had closed his eyes so he couldn't see the flush in my cheeks.

"We'll be resting," Darian said pointedly. "I could certainly use it after what we went through."

I turned to him then, remembering how he had saved me. "Thanks," I said. "If it weren't for you, that outlier would have eaten me."

His lips molded into a smile that brightened his eyes. "It was my pleasure, Raine lovely."

· · · ● ·● ● ● · ·

The rest of the night passed slowly, with Asher, Darian, and I not doing much besides relaxing by the fire and filling ourselves with copious amounts of food and wine. I tried to prod more information out of the males, but they always gave me short answers.

As the night wore on, I became unable to sit still and ended up creating a makeshift target to practice throwing knives. Knives had always been my favorite, and I found it soothing to be able to focus on them for a while.

Planting my feet and flicking my wrist back, I released the knife in my hand. It flew through the air, landing in the center of the target I'd made out of one of the small wooden chairs.

Asher whistled loudly. "I always wondered what you humans did on that island. Now I know. The fight tomorrow night sure is goin' to be interesting."

I went over to the target and wrenched my blade from the wood. "Most islanders just wait for you monsters to pick us off. The others from my island probably haven't ever held a weapon before. Not unless you include kitchen knives."

"And why are you so different?" he asked, his violet eyes lingering on the blade in my hands.

I didn't answer. I knew he was fishing for information about me, and I wasn't about to spill my sad life story. *Uh, because some asshole monster from Katakin took my sister before her time? Because I have to find her and make sure she's all right?* No, I ignored him and continued to throw blades at my target. It was a while later when I paused and said, "This can't be all you guys do with your spare time." Because seriously if it was, they needed to find some damn hobbies.

"In our spare time, Darian and I are usually in the city, but we can't take you down there."

Oh, right. Babysitting.

"These rooms also don't have many of our belongings to let us amuse ourselves with our recreational activities. When Locke let us know the Taratun council had charged us with the duty of selectin' the newbloods and makin' them turn, we didn't have much time to gather items before we were comin' down here to the rooms Locke had fixed up for us. Naturally, I grabbed many of my weapons first."

My forehead wrinkled in confusion. "Wait, so this isn't where you normally live?"

He chuckled. "We have a few houses, but our main one is in the south of the city."

Huh. It hadn't occurred to me that they might have a home in the city, and I had the odd desire to see what their house looked like.

It felt as though an hour had passed when Darian came up beside me, watching silently as I threw another blade.

When the knife was firmly in the target, he said, "Kade might not be back for a while yet, and day has broken outside the mountain. You should get some sleep."

"How do you know it's day?" I asked, turning to him with a frown.

His lips drew down, and I wished I hadn't asked. "I can feel the magic from the sirens' song," he said.

Oh. I thought of the beautiful garden he'd taken me to and the sound of the sirens all singing in unison. It was clear it bothered him, but I didn't know what to say, so I grabbed the blade from my target and placed the knives back on the weapons shelf. Leaving Darian and Asher in the common room, I used the washroom and dressed in one of Kade's shirts.

When I was back in the common room, Asher entered the washroom after me. Ready for sleep, I stopped, hesitating in front of Kade's room. For the whole night, Darian and Asher had stayed near me in the common room, the pair of them a constant comforting presence. Over the years, I'd become accustomed to being alone, but going into Kade's empty room seemed unappealing right then.

Kade doesn't have to be your only ally. Darian's words from nights before floated through my head. The siren had proved he was more than just a monster. He'd saved me from the outlier, and something had shifted between us. I knew I could use another ally. I was also finding myself becoming way too comfortable with the wolf shifter by my side. I needed to create some distance between us.

Before I let myself consider what I was doing, I turned to Darian. He'd used the washroom before me, and water still dripped from his silver hair as he stood there with bare feet and a goblet of wine in his hands. I had to wonder at the fact that no matter how much the siren drank, he never seemed too affected. Was that a monster thing?

"I—" I swallowed, suddenly feeling like an idiot. "Did you say you had a couch I could use?"

A seductive smile lifted Darian's lips, brightening his gorgeous face, and I sucked in a breath. "For sleeping," I added quickly, almost tripping over my own words. "I just, Kade's not here yet, and I thought..." I trailed off as amusement lit Darian's eyes.

"Never mind," I said and turned back toward Kade's door. I heard Darian move behind me, and when I peered back at him, he was at his room, holding the door open for me.

"You're always welcome," he said, and despite his mischievous smile, he seemed genuine.

Seeing him standing there holding his door open made the whole situation feel like a trap, but before I could back out, his expression sobered, becoming more serious. "I meant it when I said we could be allies," he said earnestly, and I felt myself being drawn toward him.

It's just a room, nothing more. Would it really matter if I slept on his couch? "Fine," I said. I could be the siren's ally. Steeling myself, I strode over to him and into his room.

Darian's room was a similar size to Kade's, but while Kade's had a practical desk along with the wardrobe, Darian's had a luxurious couch stretched along the wall, topped with two fine embroidered cushions.

A large four-poster bed sat to the right, and a wide full-length mirror with an intricate metal frame hung on the opposite wall. I glanced at Darian's bed with its beautiful satin covers and six downy pillows. The bed was even bigger than Kade's, and I had to wonder why the hell the monster needed such a spacious place to sleep.

Because it's not just for sleeping in. Heat flared deep in my belly at the thought of what Darian did in that bed. Asher had said they liked to visit the city together, and I could only imagine what they did while they were there.

"Admit it. It's nicer than Kade's," Darian drawled from where he was standing in the doorway, his hip resting against the frame and his crystal-blue eyes watching me.

"I wouldn't say that," I responded. "Bigger isn't always better."

A wicked smile stretched across Darian's face then, and the sight of it made my heart stutter. He gestured with his head toward the bed. "You'll never know unless you try it, lovely."

I almost choked on my own laughter at his insinuation, but my lady parts didn't seem to get the joke because desire wound my body tighter. It didn't help that Darian was close enough now that I could smell his scents of sea salt and patchouli. Scents that made my core clench with need.

"Take the bed," he said as he sensed my discomfort. "I'll take the couch."

I peered at the couch with a frown. It was long but wouldn't be a comfortable fit for someone as tall as Darian to sleep on. "You saved my life. I'm not going to kick you out of your own bed."

I remembered how Darian's hands had grabbed me before he'd thrown me from the outlier's mouth. There had been a moment when I'd thought the siren had died saving me, and a gaping hole had opened in my chest. I didn't want to think about what that implied and how my feelings for the monster had grown.

Now that we were alone, I wanted to bury my hands in his silver hair and press my body against his. I wanted to touch him and remind myself he was still alive.

I knew it was the bond making me feel that way, but the feelings felt so damn real.

"What do you suggest then?" he asked curiously.

I didn't look at him as I said, "If you can keep your hands to yourself, I think this bed is big enough for both of us."

There was a beat of silence, and when I peered over at him, his eyes were sparkling in the dim blue light. "I can handle that. But if you change your mind..."

"I'll let you know," I finished awkwardly, and his smile grew wider.

Trying to ignore the rapid pounding of my heart and cursing myself for even attempting to stay in Darian's room, I pulled back the sheets on the left side of the bed and slid in. I'd become used to sleeping on the left side when I was with Kade, so Darian would have to deal. *Fuck, why did I think this was a good idea?*

· · · ● · ● · ● · · ·

I awoke to the scents of sandalwood, coffee, sea salt, and patchouli around me, and the intoxicating smells made my head spin and my mouth water. A warm body lay beside me, and I beamed up at Kade's sleeping face. *So much for staying in Darian's room to create distance between us.*

I wondered when the wolf shifter had joined me. The last thing I remembered was shifting restlessly and thinking that I'd never be able to fall asleep. *Had I really passed out right after that?*

I was further into the bed than I remembered being, and Kade had taken up his position on the left, closest to the edge of the mattress. Without thinking, I ran a hand up his bare chest, enjoying the feel of his hard muscles under my fingers. Just the thought of being apart from him had left a gnawing ache inside me, and as dangerous as it was, I was glad he was there.

I'd assumed Kade was in a deep sleep, but his muscles tensed at my touch, and his breathing hitched. I froze.

"Don't stop," he said, his voice coming out as a drowsy, scratchy rumble that had me clenching my thighs.

Moving my hand again, I traced my fingertips over his defined abs, and when I looked up at him again, his intense golden eyes were staring back at me.

"It was hard spending the night away from you, Mahare," he growled and lifted a hand to tuck a stray strand of hair behind my ear.

I swallowed, feeling way too seen beneath his assessing gaze. "Hard?" I asked with a sly smile, trying to lighten the situation.

His lips twitched with amusement. "Very fucking hard every time I thought of you," he agreed, and I snorted.

The bond between us hummed, pulling me toward him, and I didn't resist it. Leaning my head upward, I pressed my lips against his. He groaned as he kissed me back, his tongue diving into my mouth as if he'd been waiting for me to let him in, but now he was determined to show me just how badly he needed me. Reaching a large hand around, he grabbed my ass, and desire blazed through me. Shamelessly, I ground against his thick thigh, and he squeezed my ass harder.

Pulling my lips away from his, I moaned as I became desperate for more friction. I writhed harder against him and clamped my teeth onto his arm.

He stilled, his arms tightening around me. "Careful," he growled softly, his voice husky with his own desire. "Bite any harder and my wolf will think you're trying to claim me."

As his words registered, I released his arm immediately and cursed internally. *What the fuck am I doing?* I'd never been into biting before, but it had just seemed like the right thing to do. My lady parts obviously agreed too, because the wetness had grown between my thighs.

Still needing something to bite, I sucked my bottom lip into my mouth instead.

Kade's hooded gaze tracked the movement, and he braced his hands against my hips and hoisted me onto his body. My legs slid to either side of him, and my core heated at the hard press of his large erection against my center. *Of course, he's sleeping naked.* Not that I minded. I rocked my hips, sliding myself up and down his length.

His hands slid up my waist until my shirt, well *Kade's* shirt, bunched around my ribcage. Crossing my arms, I pulled it off and tossed it to the floor. Kade lifted his hands to cup my breasts and rubbed his thumbs over my hard nipples. *Oh, Goddess.* I arched my back at the pleasure.

"I can feel how fucking wet you are through your panties," Kade growled as he palmed my breasts, and the sound of his rough voice made my core spasm. Reaching down, he slid a hand between us, and I lifted enough so he could hook his fingers in my panties and shift them to the side. My anticipation heightened as the cloth scratched against my skin, and then he was dragging two long fingers down my center.

Oh fuck. I rocked my hips against his fingers.

"So fucking wet," he confirmed, and a pleased growl rumbled from him, making me ache even more.

He began alternating between stroking me and massaging my clit while his other hand played with my breasts.

Lifting his back off the bed, he sucked my nipple into his mouth at the same time as his fingers rubbed my clit relentlessly, and the pleasure became too much. I gasped as the orgasm crashed through me, and a wave of tingles swept over my body.

I was still shuddering when Kade ripped my panties from me and threw them to the floor. His hands moved to my hips, and he positioned himself beneath me. His cock prodded at my entrance, and then he was sinking inside me, stretching and filling me so deliciously that my tingles were quickly chased away by desire and pleasure that had me panting.

"Kade," I whimpered, tipping my head back as I enjoyed how full he made me feel. A growl sounded in his chest and vibrated all the way to his cock, and I clenched around him as he thrust himself in and out faster and harder.

"Well, I knew I installed that mirror for a reason," came a smooth masculine voice, and I froze, my gaze shooting to the side of the bed in shock. Kade stilled as well, his cock buried deep inside me.

I gaped at the silver-haired siren, who lay on his side with his head propped on one hand. An impish grin curved his lips, and his crystal-blue gaze slid from something behind me and came to rest on my face. Somehow, being wrapped up in Kade, I'd momentarily forgotten we were in Darian's bed. *With* Darian. *Why the hell did I think staying in Darian's bed was a good idea again? Oh right, I was supposed to be creating distance between Kade and me. Yeah, I'm an idiot.*

Twisting my head, I peered behind me to see my long red hair trailing down my bare back. A portion of my naked ass was also on display, along with Kade's bare legs. I imagined that when I moved up and down on Kade's cock, I'd be able to see him sliding into me, and the thought of seeing it turned me on more.

Swallowing, I turned back to Darian, and my brows drew down. "Pervert," I accused lightheartedly.

"Darling, this is my bed. Did you honestly think I'd be able to sleep through your delectable moans?" he responded.

"No, I just forgot you were there," I said, then bit back a moan as Kade leaned forward and began kissing my throat. Obviously, he didn't care that we had an audience.

Darian's eyes narrowed, but he gave me a seductive smile. "I find that hard to believe, but if it's so easy to ignore me, you'll have no problem continuing. I was rather enjoying the show."

My cheeks heated at the thought of Darian's gaze on me while I took my pleasure from Kade. Images of Darian's blue eyes watching me while I rode Kade to oblivion had my heart racing. It didn't help that the bond was now pulling me toward Kade *and* Darian. Nor did it help that Kade had begun circling his hips beneath me as if he was trying to remind me that his cock still wanted attention. Like I could forget when it was so deep inside me.

I raked a hand through my hair to sweep the stray strands away from my eyes and off my sweaty forehead. In a small part of my brain, common sense told me it wasn't a good idea to tease the siren, but I couldn't help wondering whether it would matter. I was already spending time with Kade. Did it matter if Darian watched? It wouldn't change the fact that I was going to find my sister and potentially leave them when the time came. And the pull I had toward

Darian was urging me to get closer to him, muddling my thoughts.

I chewed my lip. I'd never been with two guys before, but this wasn't like that, was it? He'd only be watching. *Besides, it'd be rude of you to kick him out of his own room after he almost died saving your life.* I didn't remind myself that he likely wouldn't leave even if I *did* try to force him out of his room.

In response to Darian's challenge, I began lifting myself up and down on Kade's cock again, letting him move in and out of me slowly as I held Darian's gaze.

The siren smiled as he returned my stare, but his smile fell as his attention trailed down my naked body, his gaze lingering on my breasts before dropping even lower. When he looked at my face again, his eyes were clouded with a lust that rivaled Kade's, and the urge I had to go to him made me grit my teeth. His blue eyes began to glow in the dim light, and my fingers pressed onto Kade's chest as I picked up my speed.

I kept my eyes trained on Darian as he pulled back the blanket, revealing his naked body. *Seriously, does anyone sleep with clothes on around here?* I should have been annoyed that he'd chosen to sleep naked while I'd been sleeping in the same bed as him, but I was too busy watching as he moved his hands to the massive, hard cock between his legs. Wrapping his long, slender fingers around the base of his length, he began stroking himself, and I couldn't look away.

I knew staring was rude, but damn, I'd forgotten how big it was. I was suddenly glad he was only watching because there was no way that thing would fit inside me. It was a wonder I hadn't gained a mild concussion after I had smacked my head onto it the other day.

When I finally lifted my gaze back to Darian's handsome face, his lips were twisted into a knowing smirk. *It's not that big*, I wanted to say, but we both knew it was. I had no idea what was average by monster standards, but he certainly seemed proud of himself.

Kade's teeth nipped above my collarbone, and it was then that I realized I'd stopped moving. The light touch sent another wave of desire straight to my core, and I started rocking my hips again. Kade's golden eyes glowed, and I remembered about the other times I'd been with him. He was always afraid of his wolf side taking control and trying to claim me.

He nipped my neck again, and I had an idea. "If you're going to watch, you may as well make yourself useful," I said to Darian. I'd meant to sound sassy, but my words came out almost breathless.

Darian slid his hand up and down his cock again, and I couldn't help wondering how good he would taste in my mouth. *Would he taste salty like the sea?* I stared at his massive cock. *I could take both of them, right?* I gave myself a mental shake and came to my senses. *No, wrong. Kade is already huge. You don't need Darian destroying your pussy.*

"And how can I do that, lovely?"

Darian's question drew my thoughts back to my idea.

"She wants you to make sure I don't try to claim her," Kade answered for me, clearly having understood what I was thinking. "It's been a pain trying to keep my wolf under control."

Darian's brows rose. "And how exactly do you expect me to do that?"

I continued moving on Kade's cock, and a growl vibrated from Kade's throat. "If I try to bite her, you need to force me off."

Darian became thoughtful then, but he nodded. "I think I can do that."

It was all I needed to hear. Knowing that I didn't have to worry about Kade going all wolf on me, I rode the shifter harder than I ever had, enjoying the feel of him stretching me and driving so fucking deep it made me want to scream.

Beside us, Darian sat up, lifting to his knees, and shuffled closer. He fisted his cock in time to my movements, and knowing that he was pleasuring himself while watching me drove me crazy. "Sweet Toros, you're so sexy," Darian murmured as his cock pulsed between his fingers, his face flush.

I didn't stop to think about what I was doing then. I reached out, wrapping my fingers around his cock. Darian moved his hand and sat back on his heels as I squeezed and stroked him, his face contorting with pleasure.

After a while, he moved even closer to me, and he kissed my shoulder as he pinched my nipples.

Fuck. I whimpered at the feel of both Kade and Darian touching me.

Kade gripped my waist, his hips lifting to drive himself deeper, and I couldn't take any more. I shattered, tipping over the edge for the second time. Stars burst behind my eyes, and I gasped as the world fell away beneath me.

My body shuddered, the pleasure still making my toes curl, when a feral growl had me snapping my eyes open. I noted the strain around Kade's blazing golden eyes and the sweat streaming down the side of his face.

I didn't need to ask to know what was wrong. Kade's wolf side wanted to take control. *Shit.*

Kade's face was pained, and I released Darian and scrambled backward. Because Darian was there, I'd let myself forget about the little problem we had with Kade's wolf side. I'd been bitten by Kade's wolf before, and it had hurt like a freaking bitch. Not to mention, from what Kade said, I got the feeling the whole mating thing was a big deal. Definitely not something he should be doing with a human girl who wasn't even planning to stick around.

Kade shook his head as if he was trying to stop whatever struggle was going on inside him, but his ears lengthened and became pointed. My gaze flicked to Darian. The siren was frowning, and his alert gaze was fixed on Kade.

Kade was still mostly human, but he tried to grab at me with a clawed hand as if his animalistic side was taking control. I readied myself for a fight, but before he could grasp my waist, a sweet song spiraled through the air.

I noticed the exact moment Darian's power took over the shifter. For the briefest moment, Kade shook his head as if he was trying to clear the music from his mind, but when Darian's song grew louder, the gold in the wolf shifter's eyes dimmed, and his attention moved from me to the silver-haired male who was on his knees.

Strain showed on Darian's face as if it was taking a considerable amount of power to keep Kade under his control, but his song didn't waver.

I shuffled further back on the bed as Kade prowled toward Darian. I expected the siren to knock Kade out or release him from whatever trance he was in now that his attention was away from me, but then Kade's lips crushed against Darian's. Kade devoured the siren's mouth with punishing force, his tongue tangling with Darian's, and my jaw dropped.

Holy fucking Goddess.

I couldn't believe what I was seeing. And why was watching them so hot? Darian peered over at me, his crystal-blue gaze full of mischief, and it was only then that I noticed the song had stopped. Because Kade had kissed

Darian on the lips, he hadn't been able to continue his song. Either that or he'd stopped on purpose.

In any case, I was smart enough to scoot my ass off the bed entirely when the gold flared brighter again in Kade's eyes, and he pulled his lips away from the siren's.

"Darian!" Kade roared, his face turning red. "You know the fucking rules! We don't use our magic or abilities on each other."

Darian raised his hands in mock innocence, but a smirk twisted his devilish lips, which were now swollen from Kade's kiss. "Your wolf was going to eat the girl. I agreed I'd help keep her safe from you."

Kade's gaze shot to me, panic flaring briefly until he noticed I was free of any bite marks, and then he rounded back on Darian. "No one told you to use your magic," he growled.

Darian opened his mouth to protest again, and Kade lifted his fist to slam it into the side of the siren's face. Before it connected, Darian maneuvered gracefully backward off the side of the bed, out of reach.

I moved in front of Darian before Kade could advance again. "Stop! We asked him to intervene."

"I didn't ask him to stick his fucking tongue in my mouth," Kade snarled. "Do you have any idea how many monsters he's been with? I could have caught a fucking disease."

"Funny, I seem to recall it was you who was the one sticking your tongue in *my* mouth," Darian said with a smug smile. Before Kade could push past me, I smacked Darian's chest with the back of my hand.

"Do you *want* him to pummel you?" I scolded. Of course—because like Kade's, Darian's chest was as hard as steel—it hurt like hell, but I wasn't going to tell him that. Pulling my hand away, I forced myself not to grimace.

"He could try," Darian said with a confident shrug.

Kade went to spit out another retort, but a crashing sounded in the common room, and we all fell silent. As if the sound was some kind of alarm, Kade and Darian charged from the room, not caring that they were naked.

"Fuck! Would you put those away?" I heard Asher say, and I stifled a laugh as I imagined the demon getting an eyeful of Darian's and Kade's raging erections.

Sliding on Kade's shirt that I'd discarded on the floor, I followed after the others into the common room.

"What the hell are you doing, Ash?" Kade asked, and I looked over to see Asher was collecting blades from the ground near the shelf of weapons, which was tilted toward the floor.

"Of course the fucking thing breaks on my watch," Asher grumbled.

Kade pinched the bridge of his nose. "Locke just had that new shelf installed. What did you do to it?"

"Nothin'. I went to grab my axes," Asher defended.

Darian shook his head and turned to me with a lazy smile. "Shall we get back to it, lovely?"

I turned to him and smirked before striding past him into the washroom. I could feel his eyes on me as I left him there, and I only felt a little guilty that he was going to have a serious case of blue balls.

CHAPTER 14

~ **Raine** ~

By the time I finished bathing away Kade's and Darian's scents from my skin, my stomach was a mess of knots. It was the first night of the Week of Orash, and the first time since the choosing that I'd get to see the others from my village. Not only that, but monsters from all the houses of Katakin would be attending to watch the fights, and if I were lucky, I'd learn information about Cara.

I didn't want to think about the fact that Cara herself might be there. The idea that my sister might attend sounded too easy, and I didn't want to get my hopes up. But there was definitely the chance that somebody else might know what happened to her, and just admitting that small shred of hope had my fingers shaking with nerves.

I'd just wrapped a towel around myself when there was a light rap of knuckles on the washroom door. "You'd better come out here, Raine," came Kade's voice. "She's already waiting."

She? They never told me we were expecting company. I hastily finished toweling myself and dressed in a clean leather outfit I'd left neatly folded on the bench.

When I exited the washroom, the shifter Lyr, whom I had met only nights ago, was sitting across from a now-clothed Darian. Like the last time I'd seen her, a long white braid was draped over her shoulder, but this time, pink peony flowers were weaved among her strands, and a different male was standing beside her with his arms crossed.

His body was as wide as Kade's, and his serious, no-bullshit expression made him seem like he was her personal guard. Thick, wiry muscle covered the monster's arms, and his skin was a pale gray, almost translucent. He peered at me as though I was a threat who had just walked into the room, and I had the distinct feeling that he wasn't someone I should be messing with.

Lyr peered up at my entrance, her blue eyes lighting with curiosity, and she lifted from her sitting position on a settee and moved closer to me as if she was analyzing everything about me. Standing still, I waited as she circled me and then stopped in front of me. Instinctively, one of my hands clenched by my side, but from the relaxed postures of Kade, Darian, and Asher, who watched nearby, I had the sense that I didn't need to worry.

"So this is the newblood you all won't tell me anything about," she purred. Her gaze dropped to my clenched fist, and her lush pink lips twitched upward.

"Lyr is here to help you get ready for the party," Kade said, coming closer to my side.

"Party?" I asked with a frown. "I thought you said I had to fight?"

Lyr moved back to where she'd been sitting and dropped down with feline grace, folding one leg over the other. "Is that what they told you?"

My brows pulled together in confusion. "Yes...." I dragged out the word. "*Don't* the newbloods have to fight one another?"

"Oh, they do," she replied, "but the Week of Orash is so much more than that. It's about power and persuasion. It's about ensuring your name comes up in the right conversations, cementing your place in this world."

"If you're talking about me having to schmooze the alphas in the hopes I'll be able to join my respective high house, you don't need to worry." I wanted to add that I had no intention of joining any house and that none of this would probably matter in a few nights, but I couldn't exactly say that.

"Everything you do over the next few nights will impact your future. From the way you dress to the way you speak, to the way you fight, and even to who you flirt with. Have Locke and the others not explained any of this to you?

Monsters are bastards at their best. You need to make sure you make a good impression." She stared at Kade and the others with an accusatory expression, as if she thought they'd somehow failed me by not preparing me better. *Well, she has a fucking point.*

"You don't need to worry about our lovely Raine here," said Darian as he stepped closer to my other side. "I'm sure she'll make a striking impression, and we'll be with her every step of the way."

Lyr arched a brow at him. "I hope you all know what you're doing by singling her out."

While I was glad I had Darian's vote of confidence, there was something about the way Lyr was staring at me that made me think she wasn't quite telling me the full severity of my situation. Darian and the others had hinted at the fact that the Week of Orash wasn't just about the fights, but I'd merely imagined there might be some polite chatter. If anything, I'd been counting on it. That was how I would find out my information about Cara.

But now I was picturing myself walking into a pit of vipers, which some of the monsters very well could be, and my anxiety grew as I thought of the fact that I was still a human. I was suddenly regretting my decision to stick around rather than try harder to escape for the past few nights, but I reminded myself that I likely would have gotten lost in the mountain or killed. No, participating in the Week of Orash was the most logical choice, and nothing had changed. I could smile and put on a show for the brief time I was there. Goddess, I really did hope it would be brief.

Lyr nodded toward a stack of square boxes on the table in front of her. "You can thank Locke for giving me the measurements this time. I can see the last garments I brought you don't quite...fit." Her gaze fixed on my chest for a moment, at where my breasts were barely contained in one of the leather outfits she'd given me.

Wait, how the hell did Locke get my measurements? I thought back to when I'd woken to find Locke in Kade's room. Was that why he'd really been there? Forcing myself not to think about how the vampire had likely measured me while I slept, I strode over to the boxes. Dropping down onto the chair opposite Lyr, I pulled the top box onto my lap.

Before I had lifted the lid, Lyr said, "I'm not going to do anything to her other than prepare her for the party, which I assure you will be quite a tedious process. I'm sure you all have better things to do than watch a female change clothing." I was surprised by how commanding Lyr's voice was and even more shocked when Darian and Asher disappeared from the room. Kade remained standing close by, in a similar position to the monster who stood near Lyr, and I couldn't help but smile at the thought that we now both had males guarding us.

Lyr clucked her tongue as she stared at the pair of them. "Nic, why don't you and Kade go through that matter we discussed on our way here."

"I'm not leaving you with her," the male rasped, and I was surprised by the deep gravel of his voice. The tone was even lower than Kade's.

Lyr simply stared at her companion for a long while until he finally relented. "Kade," he said, gesturing with his head for the wolf shifter to follow him. Kade's gaze slid to me, but I rolled my eyes, and he followed after the other male.

Instead of leaving the room, the males went to one of the high tables near the far wall and started discussing something in low voices. Their backs were to us, and that seemed to be enough to satisfy Lyr.

I didn't trust the shifter, but I didn't have much of a choice but to listen to what she had to say. It was true that I had no idea what to expect at the party I was supposedly going to be attending soon, and if Lyr could help me, I had to take advantage.

Now that the males were preoccupied, I pulled the lid off the box and peered inside. *A dress?* I slid my fingers along the delicate material of the folded red garment and gave the shifter a quizzical look. There was even a pair of matching red panties.

"The first night of the Week of Orash is the first chance you have to make a real impression on the alphas and leaders of the Taratun council. All the newbloods will be wearing red to signify their status as newcomers. There will be food and wine, and with this dress. I'm sure you'll have *plenty* of close company." She paused thoughtfully. "Though if Darian and the others stay by your side as they've suggested, that may not be the case."

All righty, so staying with Darian and the others will be handy to keep the other monsters at a distance, but not so great if I want to get information. I'll figure something out.

"So there's no fighting on the first night?" I asked, not sure whether I should have been relieved or freaking out. Fighting, I knew how to do. Polite dinners, not so much.

"No fighting," Lyr confirmed. "The first night will be a celebration of the newbloods and a chance for you to meet the important members of our world."

I tried to push away my annoyance. "Can't I just wear my red leather outfit?" I asked hopefully. The last dress I'd worn was the white garment I'd been in during the choosing. Dresses were impractical, and I wasn't keen to be wearing one again.

"If you went wearing that, you'd get more attention than if you just wore the dress, and I don't mean that in a good way," Lyr answered and tapped her long blue nails on the armrest beside her.

Sighing heavily, I moved the box to the side and stood to let the garment unfold. The silky red material rippled as it stretched to the ground, the color gleaming in the dim light.

"There are seven dresses in these boxes, as Locke requested," she said reassuringly. "One for each night of the Week of Orash. Even on the nights when there are fights, there will always be partying after, and you'll be expected to look divine for each appearance."

Divine? I nearly scoffed. I didn't care about looking nice. I just wanted information. But I guessed if it helped me blend in with the other newbloods, then it was worth it.

"Why don't you try it on?" Lyr suggested, indicating to the dress, and I didn't argue. It had also occurred to me that Locke had *paid* for all the beautiful dresses, and while he was an arrogant ass, he had saved my life in the ocean, so if wearing a damn dress was going to appease him, it was probably a good idea.

"I'll be right back," I said as I draped the dress over my arm and disappeared into Kade's room.

The dress fit me like a second skin, clinging to my body and molding to my curves. Along my arms, the material was like a fine netting, with embroidered lace flowers climbing up my forearms, and at my hips, there were two slits on either side, which exposed long stretches of my bare legs as I walked. I frowned, thinking about how once again, I was wearing a dress for the monsters. The only difference was that this time, they thought I was one of them.

When I didn't immediately go back into the common room, Lyr knocked lightly on the door. "I trust it fits?"

I nodded my head like an idiot, forgetting that she couldn't see me, and when I didn't respond, the door creaked open. Lyr stalked into the room, her hips swaying as she walked. I was about to tell her about personal boundaries when her gaze slid up and down my body, and she let out an appreciative sound.

"That will definitely make an impression," she said with a grin. "Locke made the right decision asking for my help again."

"And why *did* Locke ask for your help exactly?" I asked. "It can't be that hard to find a dress in an entire city."

"Perene has some influence in the city and has contacts with most of the tailors. I'm assuming Locke wanted me involved to ensure his mother wasn't aware of the garments. My tailor has no ties to the Taratun."

My eyes widened. "Wait. Locke's mother is part of the council?" Well, that was certainly news to me. "Why wouldn't he want her involved?"

So far, I knew hardly anything about the onyx-eyed monster, and I leaned forward, hoping Lyr would fill in some of the blanks.

"Yes, Perene is one of the main members overseeing the newbloods. You'd be with her and the other newbloods if it weren't for Locke and the others keeping you here. Didn't they tell you any of this?"

I shook my head.

"Well, whatever's going on here, I'm guessing Locke is just trying to protect you by getting me involved."

Protect me? I didn't hide my disbelief. "I'm sure Locke is only looking out for himself."

Lyr's lips quirked to the side, but she didn't comment. Instead, she moved over to Kade's desk and pulled out the chair. With a sweep of her hand, she motioned for me to sit down.

"I'll get my things, and then we can start on your hair," she said and disappeared from the room.

Not wanting to argue, I dropped onto the chair, and a moment later, Lyr returned with a small black case tucked under her arm. After placing the case on the desk, she opened it to reveal a selection of small bottles and various brushes of different sizes. Pulling out what I recognized as a hairbrush, she held it up.

"Have you used one of these since you came here?" she asked.

"Do fingers count?" I answered with a shrug. "I didn't exactly get to pack a bag when I was selected."

With a shake of her head, she went about detangling my knotted red waves. My eyes watered at all the pulling and tugging, but otherwise, I remained silent through the torture.

"So your island," Lyr began as she loosened another knot. "Everyone there is human?"

"There aren't any monsters if that's what you mean," I said. "Not except for during the choosing." I wasn't too surprised she'd asked the question. To the monsters of Katakin, an island with only humans probably sounded like an intriguing place.

"But..." she trailed off. "So there are only humans?" she asked again.

"Yes," I said, not sure why she was asking the same question.

"Interesting." I thought I heard a hint of sadness in her voice, but before I could ask more, she paused her torture by motioning with the brush toward the doorway. Her tone was light again when she asked, "And what about you and the four monsters you're staying with? Are you going to tell me what is going on with you and Kade and the others?"

"It's nothing," I lied.

"Oh, don't play coy. I see the way they look at you. I mean, I'm not judging. If I didn't already have my hands full, even I would be tempted by those four, but you should know they're not monsters you should mess around with. I hope you know what you're doing." Her voice came out almost as a warning.

A part of me wanted to tell her that I didn't have a fucking clue what was going on. Since arriving in Katakin, I hadn't had anyone else to talk to, and she was the first female who seemed like she might actually give a damn. But I knew better than to think that was true.

The others had told me Lyr had been the late fae queen's personal spy and a good one by the sound of it. I had no doubt she was just trying to weasel information out of me so she could somehow use it to her own advantage. Maybe she wanted to blackmail Locke and the others into owing her another favor.

Shrugging off her concern, I said, "I'm sure I'm just their latest curiosity. I'll be joining a house soon, after all. Thanks for helping me, though."

She smiled at me, but I could tell she didn't really believe me. "Don't mention it. As soon as Locke asked me about the dresses, I was happy to volunteer."

"Wait, so you're not doing this as a favor to Locke?"

She chuckled. "I organized the dresses as a favor to Locke, but something told me he wouldn't bother getting someone to help you dress for the opening party. Most of the time, Locke and the others turn up to these things looking like they either are ready for war or simply don't give a shit. Which hey, doesn't bother me, but if they're expecting to be able to keep you here without the Taratun interfering, it needs to look like you're well taken care of." Her face softened then, and she added, "Most of the monsters in the city look forward to the Week of Orash. It's not just about adding new blood to the houses. Every time, it's like a chance for new hope. *You're* new hope."

My face blanched then at what she was implying, and I squirmed in my chair. "I'm just a new shifter. I'd hardly say that makes me new hope for Katakin." I hoped she bought the lie that Locke had told me to spin—that I was a newly turned shifter—but she shook her head.

"I know why Locke asked for vials of my blood. You're still human. You have no idea what you could mean to us. To all of Katakin."

Fuck. So she knows. I had no idea if Lyr would keep the secret, but it wasn't like there was anything I could do about it. "I'm no one's hope," I replied. "I'm not even sure I'm still human."

"Well, whatever you are, don't let anyone else know," she said sternly. "Locke is right to keep you here. There are those in Katakin who won't be happy that you haven't turned. Those who would kill you if they found out your secret."

As if she hadn't just talked about me being murdered, she went back to my hair, teasing and working it until she was happy. Then she put down the hairbrush and turned her attention to the smaller brushes in the case along with various pots of different colors. Bending down in front of me, she started on my face. Her brow scrunched with concentration as she worked, and I stayed stock-still, all the while thinking about what she'd said. *You're new hope.* I didn't care about the monsters in Katakin, and certainly didn't want to be anyone's symbol of hope, but deep down

I couldn't help wondering whether it did mean something that I hadn't turned into a monster yet.

CHAPTER 15

~ **Raine** ~

When Lyr was finally done and I peered in the small mirror she held up, I hardly recognized myself. I had thought I looked tidy during the Night of the Offering when I was back on the island, but it was nothing compared to this. My hair was pinned in a loose bun behind my head, with a few soft curls left to frame my face, and black paint lined my eyes and covered my lashes. My lips were now glossed with a deep shade of red, and pink stained my cheeks, bringing color to my face.

Inside some of the boxes were different styles of heels, and Lyr had finished my outfit with a pair of red open-toed heels with lace flowers that climbed over my ankles. They weren't like the boots I'd become accustomed to, but I could walk in them and could probably even fight in them if I had to, and that was all that mattered.

I tried to tell myself that I didn't care what I looked like, and I *didn't* care, but when my mind went to four specific monsters, I couldn't help the rush that went through me when I thought that they might see me like this. Frowning, I shook my head. *None of this matters. You shouldn't care what they think.* But I couldn't squash the feelings of anticipation and exhilaration.

"Wait, don't you need to get ready too?" I asked Lyr, only just remembering what Asher had told me a few nights ago. Lyr had managed to create her own house, and I had to assume that meant she was expected at the party as well.

She waved her hand dismissively, seemingly not at all fazed that she might not have much time to prepare herself. "The Taratun council tolerates my house with my mates and me because we keep to the shadows. No one will care if I attend the celebration. But yes, I should be on my way."

I wished I could ask her more about her house and her mates, but I got the feeling divulging secrets wasn't in her nature. I helped her gather her things, and when the pair of us walked back into the common room, Locke, Kade, Asher, and Darian were all there, along with Lyr's companion Nic.

Kade's golden eyes widened as he took me in, his appreciative gaze filling with desire as he eyed my body in the dress.

"Wow, Sharachi. The leather outfits are hot, but this... Lyr, you're killin' us," Asher said with a grin and a pained expression as he admired me openly, his gaze lingering on the deep *V* of the dress.

Darian stepped forward and clasped my hand in his before spinning me in a circle. "You, darling, are exquisite."

Heat flooded my cheeks at the attention. Even Nic raised a brow at me. He still watched me with distrust, but there was a hint of surprise in his features.

Lyr gave us all a self-satisfied smile as she placed the hairbrush in my free hand. "Now you won't have to use your fingers."

I nodded at her gratefully and gave her a wry grin. "Thanks." When I turned back to the others, my gaze finally landed on the last monster in the room. Locke stood preternaturally still as he stared at me, but fury feathered his jaw.

What the hell?

"I said you could help her fit in, Lyr. I didn't tell you to make her look like..." Locke trailed off as if he was struggling to find the words, but then he finished with, "this." That last word was filled with venom, and though I told myself I shouldn't have cared what he thought, it still stung. *Definitely not going to miss this asshole when I'm gone.*

Lyr placed a hand on her hip, unimpressed with his attitude. "I think what you mean to say is 'Thank you, Lyr. You have a magical touch. Raine looks beyond gorgeous, and it's all thanks to you.'"

"She needs to blend in, not become a target," Locke said, stalking closer to Lyr, but he stopped when Nic's thick body moved to block him.

"You put a target on her the moment you brought her to your rooms," Lyr bit back. "The moment you didn't send her to the Taratun like the other newbloods. I've heard whispers, Locke. Many of the alphas already know about your special treatment of her. When they see her tonight, no one will question you if you tell them you were just infatuated with her beauty and took her to have your fun. They won't question you because they'll all be wishing they could do the same. Do you think the other newbloods aren't going to look like goddesses as well? It's the Week of freaking Orash."

Goddess, the way they were talking like I wasn't in the room irritated the hell out of me, but I could see the logic in what Lyr was saying. Pulling my hand from Darian's grasp, I turned to her before Locke could respond. "Thanks again. I really appreciate your help."

Her gaze slid from Locke to me, and she smiled. "Try not to get yourself killed, Raine." And with that, she retrieved the small makeup case she'd left resting on a table and gracefully glided from the room with Nic following behind her.

As soon as they were gone, I rounded on Locke. "Do you have to be such a dick to everyone?"

His dark eyes only hardened in response.

"You should see what he's like to the monsters he hates," Asher commented with a shit-eating grin. Locke turned his glare onto the demon, but Asher didn't seem bothered.

Blowing out a long breath, I hopped on the spot, getting used to the feel of the heels I wore. "We'd better get to the party. I'm guessing we don't need to be attracting more attention by being late."

"About attracting attention," Kade said with a grim expression. "You're not going to the party just yet."

I didn't miss his use of "you're" instead of "we're," and I didn't like where the conversation was headed. "And where am *I* going?"

They all seemed to shift as if uneasy with the situation. Locke was the one who finally answered, "To see my mother."

Perene. I thought of what Lyr had said about her, and then I thought of Locke's father, Warrick. Was Perene like that? Cold and cruel? If so, no thanks. I didn't want to see her.

"Why would we be going to see her?" I asked with a scowl. I was already riddled with nerves at the idea of going to the party, which I was sure was going to be as painful as pulling teeth.

Kade and the others didn't answer, as if they were expecting Locke to do the honors. Seemed fair seeing as it was someone from Locke's family.

"My parents are both members of the Taratun council, and my mother is in charge of overseeing the newbloods," Locke said, confirming what Lyr had told me. "As is tradition, you need to enter the party with the other newbloods and follow Perene's instructions. Once you're inside, we'll find you again."

I shouldn't have been shocked. Considering how the monsters required us to dress up in white during the Night of the Offering and stand neatly in a line for the selection, it made sense that they'd want to parade the newbloods around on the first night of the Week of Orash. Still, it annoyed me that no one had told me this until now. On the bright side, I realized it would give me a chance to talk to the other women from my village. It had only been a week since I had been lined up with them in that clearing, but it felt like much longer. Would they even be the same people, or had the fact that they'd turned into monsters made them different beings entirely?

A firm hand clasped my shoulder, and Kade leaned down to growl into my ear, "I'll be watching you from the moment you enter the ballroom. You have nothing to worry about."

Nothing to worry about? I had to stop myself from giving him an incredulous look because, you know, I was about to attend a party filled with monsters who didn't know I was still human. But all right, I had nothing to worry about. I nodded at him as if I believed him.

Darian approached me next and placed his hands on my shoulders before giving me a light kiss on the cheek. "Just keep your head up and smile, lovely. When in doubt, flattery works best. Otherwise, say nothing. You don't want to make any enemies on the first night."

I made a sarcastic mental note: *Don't make enemies.* The males were full of lots of great advice.

Asher didn't approach me like the others did, but he gave me a reassuring lopsided smile, and then Locke was leading me from the room. *Fuck. My. Life.*

· · · ● · ● · · · ·

Locke didn't speak to me as we made our way up the tunnels, which meant I spent most of the time thinking about the party and all the horrible things that could happen. Finally managing to push the negative thoughts away, I tried to focus on the positive. This was what I wanted. To have a chance to talk to some other monsters and hopefully see some of the newbloods from the previous round.

Taking a deep breath in through my mouth, I let it out through my nose and straightened my shoulders. I could do this. I'd never attended any of the celebrations back on the island, but I'd always heard the dancing and laughter. Would a monster party be like that, or would there be the screaming of tortured souls and gleeful cries instead? I guess I was about to find out.

Before we rounded the next corner, Locke stopped abruptly and pivoted toward me. I'd been so lost in my thoughts that I slammed into his hard chest. *Fuck, what is this monster made of? Rocks?* Cursing, I drew back and peered up at him. "What? Are we here?"

"Almost," he answered.

Cryptic. "All right, then...so why have we stopped?"

He stared at me, and as usual, I couldn't read his hard expression, but there was a reluctance about him. As if he hated himself for what he was about to say. "Don't let Perene rattle you, and don't believe a word that comes out of her mouth," he finally said. "She'll want to sink her fangs in deep and manipulate you in a way that fulfills her agenda."

Oh, great. So Locke's mother is a psychopath too. Now I know where he got the traits from. I realized then that he was probably warning me because he was worried I'd embarrass him. I wanted to answer with some sarcastic retort about promising to make a good impression on his mom, but the serious look in his eyes had me nodding instead.

"I'll be fine. This isn't the first time I've had to parade around in a dress for monsters," I replied.

His jaw ticked, but his eyes seemed to brighten at my confident attitude. If that was even possible when your eyes were as black as a starless night. Turning forward again, he led me around the last bend, and we approached the group of monsters up ahead. Despite their changed appearances, I recognized the other chosen women from my village immediately.

Nora's mouth dropped open with shock when she spotted me, and I had the sudden urge to rush over and ask what she'd been doing during the last few nights. We hadn't been close for years, but there was a time when we'd been inseparable, and I wanted to know if she was all right. Before I could even move closer to her let alone utter a word, a tall, thin woman in a midnight-blue dress sauntered away from the others to meet us. Her thin lips pursed as she peered at us, but her shoulders relaxed almost imperceptibly, and I had the distinct feeling she'd been waiting for me to arrive.

"You were supposed to bring her to me an hour ago," she chastised Locke, giving her son a scathing stare. "I hope you've at least prepared her for what this night will bring."

Locke remained unreadable as if he didn't give two shits about the first night of the Week of Orash, nor did he care about the fact he was handing me over to his psychopathic mother. "Perene," he said with a terse nod. "Raine here is aware of how she must participate tonight. She'll play her part."

Perene raised a disbelieving brow at her son, but then she turned an assessing gaze on me. "I hope you're right. Thank the devil she at least looks presentable." Dismissing her son with a wave of her hand, she ushered me to the back of the line of newbloods, and I stepped up behind Nora. When I looked back to peer at Locke, he was already disappearing down the tunnel away from us, as though he couldn't get rid of me fast enough. *The feeling's mutual, asshole.*

Perene hovered before me, and I hated that her attention was still on me. "The others have already rehearsed the entrance, so you'll just have to follow what they do. You will be entering one by one in a neat, well-presented line. You will come to a stop at the end, at which time another Taratun council member will introduce you all. When he is done speaking and the ceremonial toast is over, you will spend the remainder of the night meeting members from different houses and acting in a manner that befits a monster from one of the higher houses. Is that understood?"

Keeping my mouth shut, I smiled politely. The last thing I wanted to do was make an enemy before I'd even made it into the damn party.

Done with her little lecture, Perene moved to the front of the line, which was situated before a narrow iron door. As the monster moved away, Nora twisted her head toward me. The red dress that she wore was elegant, with a sweetheart neckline and streams of chiffon that flowed to the ground, but otherwise, everything about her appeared the same as the last time I'd seen her. She had no horns, claws, or tail, and her shoulder-length black hair still curved into her neck, but she seemed different somehow. It took me a moment to realize what it was. *Her eyes.* Mixed with her usual brown were flecks of golden yellow, and I couldn't stop staring.

"Raine, where have you been?" she hissed quietly. "When you didn't turn up, we all thought you were dead."

A part of me wanted to tell her about everything that had happened over the past few nights. About Kade and the others, and the strange bond I had with them. About the outliers and the trials, but instead, I said, "I'm fine. The monsters from the selection just wanted to toy with me, that's all." It wasn't just the fact that Perene and the other newbloods could hear everything I said that made me tell the lie.

Nora and I hadn't been friends for years, and I wasn't sure she was still the same person I once knew. It was possible she loved being a monster, and when she joined a house, she might have felt comfortable giving up any information I told her. What had Darian and the others said? Monsters cared about power above all else. Nora looked as though she wanted to pry and ask me more, but I said, "And what about you? Where have they been keeping you? What did—"

"Hush!" Perene snapped at us from the front of the line, and I shut my mouth. Giving Nora and me an icy glare, the older female pulled open the iron door, and instantly, all my attention focused on the chorus of chatter, laughter, and other beastly sounds that flowed out toward us from whatever room was beyond the door.

"By the Goddess Falia, it sounds like there are over a thousand monsters in there," Nora said under her breath.

I had to agree. My imagination ran wild as I tried to picture all the monsters who were making the sounds. Swallowing thickly, I flexed my clammy hands. *Just keep your head down and your ears open. You can do this, Raine.* I inwardly cursed Locke for not preparing me for this better. I understood why he'd kept me away from the other newbloods, but right now, I was wishing I had the training they'd had. The idea that I was going to be on display for a horde of monsters to gawk at made my stomach churn.

There was the sudden stamping of hooves, and a voice yelled, "Sil-ence!" All at once, the noises dimmed, and I found myself leaning forward subconsciously to make sure I didn't miss hearing anything.

"Welcome, all of you, to the Week of Orash!" the monster bellowed, his voice echoing around what had to be a large space, and his words were met with cheering and applause. When the cries quieted again, the monster continued, "It's been a decade since the last Week of Orash. That's ten years since we last tested the magic of the curse and welcomed twelve newbloods into our world.

"I am told by the Taratun council that, once again, the curse has changed all the chosen humans, but this is not a moment for us to despair. No, we should celebrate, for they are strengthened and born anew. Like the many newbloods we've had in past years, they will become valued members of Katakin! Over the following nights, we will see how the magic transformed their bodies and their minds. We will see who has the strength to rise to the top in our world. Now bring out the newbloods!"

Strengthened? Well, that's one way to look at it. The monsters cheered, roared, and cried out as the speaker finished, and I shuddered at the explosion of strange sounds. I had expected the others from my village to feel the same as I did, but as I peered at the newbloods in the line ahead of me, I could tell they didn't share my concerns. Excited smiles and wide eyes filled their flushed faces as they grinned at one another. Even Nora seemed to bounce excitedly on the spot as if she couldn't wait to walk through the doorway and see what was beyond. She twisted to shoot me a smile, and I quickly lifted my lips so she wouldn't see how I was absolutely shitting myself.

Why the hell had I thought this idea was better than escaping earlier? I was still human, and I was about to walk into a den of monsters and pretend I was one of them. I had the distinct thought that I was a like a lamb who was about to be eaten by wolves, but then I gritted my teeth. I wasn't a fucking lamb.

Perene gestured for Lana to enter the room beyond, and Lana lifted her head higher and gave Locke's mother a winning smile before stepping through the doorway. Her hips rocked from side to side as she sauntered forward, and I gaped at the dress she wore. The sheer gossamer fabric was see-through to the point that I could see the lacy red panties cupping her ass cheeks. Lana had always been confident back on the island, but now she had an air of self-importance around her. *Go figure.*

Cheers and howls erupted from the room as she walked forward until she was out of my limited line of sight, and a stream of sweat slid down my temple. *It's just walking. You can do that. Put one foot in front of the other and try not to trip*, I prepped myself.

One by one, the other newbloods stepped through the doorway before me until Nora was next. "Good luck out there," I whispered to her, and she paused to smile back at me. Excitement lit her eyes, but I could sense her hesitation. She wasn't fighting it like I was, but I could tell she hadn't accepted her new life as willingly as the others.

"You too," she replied, and then she was striding through the doorway as well.

I bit the inside of my cheek and tried to calm my racing heart. Following the timing of the others, I readied myself to step out, but before I could move, Perene crowded into my personal space. Instinctively, I recoiled, but her cold hand on my shoulder held me firmly as she leaned in close.

"I don't know how you're influencing my son, shifter, but you can't have him. It took years for Katakin to reach a stage where all monsters accepted their place, and I won't have you tempting my Locke to go against our traditions and laws more than he already has.

"The Taratun council and the order we've created is the only thing holding us all together. My son must mate with a vampire who can coax him out of the cesspool he insists on wading into. I've indulged him for these past few nights and let him have his fun with you, but make no mistake, that's all it is. By the time the Week of Orash is over, you'll belong to a house that befits you, so enjoy his attention while it lasts."

Before I had a chance to respond to her tirade, her bony hand pushed on my back, propelling me through the doorway, and I stumbled before righting myself.

CHAPTER 16

~ **Raine** ~

I made a mental note to thank Locke for the pleasantries of his mother, but as the stares of hundreds of monsters landed on me, I straightened, pulling my shoulders back, and began walking to where the other newbloods were standing in a line at the center of a raised dais.

The cheers of monsters stung my ears as I walked, and the sounds of their unnatural cries and cruel laughter sent a shiver down my spine. I could feel their curious gazes locked on me, judging me with every step I took, but I didn't stare back. Not yet. Sweat slid between my breasts, and I ignored the instinct that screamed at me to run, instead focusing on making sure my heels didn't slip on the glossy floor. After what felt like an eternity, I stopped to stand a short distance away from Nora, and only then did I finally peer out at the room.

Ho-ly Goddess. My breath caught in my throat, and my eyes widened as I took in the massive ballroom spread before me. Hundreds of monsters filled the space, standing in groups on a polished floor of fine white marble. Some of them appeared almost human, and I guessed these were mostly the shifters, incubi, and succubi, but the rest had blatant monstrous traits. There were monsters with rams' horns and furry tails, ogres and trolls with muscled bodies the size of small mountains, and wraiths with skin the color of ash. A group of males stood proudly, their antlers so large they were like the branches of trees sprouting from their heads, and their long faces and pale white eyes had fear trickling down the back of my neck.

Everywhere I looked I was met with hungry gazes, and I fought against the urge to run. Nights ago, Kade had told me about all the monsters in Katakin and what their strengths and weaknesses were. I found it useful now to know exactly what kinds of monsters stood before me, but the knowledge of how absolutely fucked I was made me want to hightail it out of there. I was always ready to fight if I had to, but I was smart enough to know when I'd lose. This was definitely one of those times.

Despite my fear, I couldn't help but also gape at the beauty of the monsters and the space. Everyone wore garments that were easily as stunning as my own, made from rich silks, furs, and other fabrics. The females wore gowns that sparkled in the dim light, their necks glittering with large jewels and diamonds, and the males wore suits or shiny fighting leathers that fitted tight to their bodies.

Along the left side of the room, pale moonlight streamed through tall arched windows, shining on the three diamond chandeliers hanging from the domed ceiling and making the space glimmer with silvery light. Sweeping blue velvet curtains had been pulled to the side of the windows, and the walls gleamed golden, white, and blue from the fire torches lining the room and the opulent paintwork that detailed intricate curved patterns.

The monsters stood around high tables decorated with vases of beautiful black flowers, and there were satyrs strolling around with silver platters topped with goblets or small bites of food. On the opposite side of the room to the windows were thick pillars and large archways that led to a space beyond, but I couldn't see what was in that area.

All right, that's enough gawking, I scolded myself. Forgetting about the dazzling space, I focused my attention on the double doors at the other end of the room, the only other exit I could see aside from the small door I'd just walked through. Burly Minotaur guards with the bodies of men and the heads of bulls stood on either side of the doors, and I had to wonder whether it was their job to make sure none of the newbloods escaped. Then again, when I peered at the others from my village, it didn't look like any of them actually *wanted* to leave. Lana preened at the attention of the monsters, smiling and jutting out her hip as if she was a queen and they were her subjects, and the rest of the newbloods had smiles that were just as big.

"Citizens of Katakin," bellowed a centaur who was standing beside Lana. It was the same voice I'd heard when I'd been waiting beyond the door. The top half of the monster's body appeared human with silky black hair that trailed behind his head, a handsome face with a chiseled jaw, and a bare, muscular chest, but his bottom half was that of a powerful black stallion with four muscular legs and thick tufted hooves. *Whoa.* If Kade hadn't already told me about all the monsters in Katakin, I would have struggled to believe that so many different beings existed.

"I present to you the newbloods from this round!" the centaur continued, and a deafening cheer came from the monsters in the ballroom. The sound of their warbled cries and roars vibrated in my head, and I clenched my jaw as I resisted the urge to cover my ears. After a while, the centaur stamped his front hooves to quiet them again. "As is tradition, tonight we enjoy the beginning of the Week of Orash, but come tomorrow night, the newbloods will battle one another, fighting with their weapons and bodies to showcase their new skills, strength, and dominance. By the week's end, all monsters will have a house, and some may even have a mate. Let us toast and begin the celebration!"

At that, the applause became even more frenzied, and bile climbed up my throat. A silver goblet of fizzy pink liquid was thrust into my hands by a ghostly female monster, and I eyed the pink liquid before turning my head to peer at the other newbloods. Nora and the others didn't hesitate to take long gulps from their goblets, and Lana licked her lips dramatically when she was finished.

I turned my attention back to the goblet in my hands. Did it also have the Acaralia in it? I wondered then whether the newbloods were even aware of what the pink water was, but then I noticed Perene glaring at me from the side of the dais. Reluctantly, I lifted the goblet to my lips. The scent of sweet alcohol burned my nose, and there was no way I was drinking the stuff. Tipping the cup up, I pretended to swallow before moving it away from my mouth again.

And then the newbloods and I were being ushered down a short flight of steps and onto the ballroom floor. Immediately, we were each swarmed with monsters and separated from one another. I stole a look at Nora who was surrounded by a group of human-looking monsters, but she didn't peer my way as she grinned and began chatting animatedly with those around her.

"Well, aren't you a delectable creature," hissed a voice with way too much interest, and I turned to the brutish-looking male who had come to stand directly in front of me. The monster towered over me, and his slitted green gaze roved appreciatively over my body in a way that made my skin crawl. He was attractive in a harsh sort of way, with short black curls framing his face and a square jaw covered with stubble, but his close proximity had me on edge.

"I'm Losak, alpha of the House of Silat," he hissed, puffing out his chest. "High house of all the shifters save for the wolves. And this here is Quinn, my second." He gestured toward the male beside him, who had neatly combed brown hair and glowing pink eyes.

"Welcome to the city, newblood," Losak said, and this time when he hissed, a forked tongue flicked out of his mouth and slid along his lower lip.

I forced a polite smile to my face. "Thanks. Katakin is certainly an interesting place." He likely expected me to tell him my name, but he hadn't actually asked, so I wasn't going to just give it to him.

Losak smiled broadly as if he knew I hated every second I was standing there talking to him, and he loved every moment that he made me uncomfortable. Quinn didn't do much other than leer at me as if he thought I was his dinner. *Is everyone in this damn place a psychopath?*

Lana's flirtatious laughter floated over to me, and I slid my gaze in her direction. She was sitting perched on the end of the dais with one leg crossed over the other and was surrounded by a mass of monsters. The vampires, ghouls, and centaurs stood captivated, as though they thought she was the most fascinating female to cross their paths. One of the monsters closest to her said something, and she laughed louder as if it was the funniest thing she'd ever heard.

"You aren't drinking," said Losak, bringing my attention back to him. "Do you not wish to celebrate?"

I thought about telling him, "Uh, fuck no," but by some mercy, Darian appeared on my right side and Asher on my left. Kade stood behind me.

"Ah, Losak, I see you've met our lovely Raine here," Darian said as he wrapped an arm around my waist and pulled me close, practically claiming me in front of the shifter alpha. Losak glared at the siren with his slitted gaze, but I leaned into Darian, quite happy for the shifter to think I was off limits. There was something about Losak that had warning bells chiming in my gut.

"We were just getting acquainted," Losak responded with a tight-lipped smile. "No need to intrude. *Raine* was doing just fine here without you," he added, and I didn't miss the way he emphasized my name. *Great.*

Asher stepped up beside Darian with a casual grin on his face. "Ah, don't be like that. We're all here to have fun, aren't we? Why don't you go speak to one of the other newbloods? We'll take it from here."

Irritation crossed Losak's face and a vein pulsed at his temple, but his lips curved into a wicked smile. "I was surprised when I heard you've been keeping the shifter newblood as your little pet. Though, now that I've seen her with my own eyes, I quite understand the fascination. Still, I'm sure you must be tiring of her. Why don't you let someone else have the chance to enjoy her for a while? After all, she might be joining my house."

Enjoy me? I scowled, and even though I knew it'd likely be a death sentence, the urge to jab Losak in the throat had my fingers twitching.

A warning growl rumbled from Kade's chest, and Losak's gaze flitted to him.

Asher's smirk grew wider. "You know the rules, Losak. Until the Week of Orash ends and Raine joins a house, she's free to be with whoever she wishes. Luckily for us, she seems content to stick around."

I'm not sure I would have used the word 'content,' but I appreciated what Asher was trying to do.

Losak's gaze fell back on me then, and his eyes locked with mine. It wasn't exactly an unkind look, but it still made me uncomfortable. "If I were you, shifter, I'd be taking advantage of my situation. Don't waste your time with these rejects when you can sample the monsters from different houses. If you want to know what it's like with a real alpha, come visit me."

Darian's arm tightened around my waist, and Kade's growling grew louder, but Losak and Quinn backed away, disappearing into the throng of bodies around us.

A few surrounding monsters stared at me, and I could tell that some of them wanted to approach, but their gazes were wary as they took in Kade, Darian, and Asher. I was surprised to find their attention mostly focused on Asher, as if they thought he was the most dangerous threat. While the monster was the largest of the four, he was also the one with the most carefree attitude, so it shocked me that they'd be most afraid of him.

Now that Losak was gone, I leaned away from Darian, and he hesitated before pulling his arm from my waist. I knew I should have been annoyed that Kade and the others had come to my side straightaway—I wasn't going to get any information out of the other monsters with these three scaring everyone off—but I couldn't help but feel grateful. I was completely out of my depth in a ballroom of monsters, and it was nice to know I wasn't alone.

"You all right, Sharachi?" Asher asked.

I bobbed my head in response. "Never been better," I said with an exaggerated smile, and Asher snorted.

"Be wary of that one, lovely. Losak is known to be unpredictable," Darian cautioned as he peered off into the crowd.

"How the fuck did he know about Raine staying with us?" Kade growled, looking as though he wanted to wolf out and hunt Losak down.

I was about to tell him to calm down, but it was then that I noticed how they were all dressed, and my mouth almost fell open. Each of them was wearing a finely tailored black suit that fitted tightly against their perfectly sculpted bodies and tall, muscly frames. They were all clean, their hair neatly arranged, and if it was possible, their scents seemed stronger somehow, as if they were permeating the air and swelling around me, drawing me to them. While most of the monsters around us were gawking at me, I didn't miss how many of the females and even some of the males stared at Kade and the others appreciatively. The thought annoyed me, but I couldn't blame them. Darian and the others looked like gods, and I was just the little human in their midst. Their toy, or so the other monsters clearly thought.

Kade's gaze roved the area as if he was searching for anyone else who might be a threat, and a moment later, his attention fixed on a figure across the room. *Zacal.* The alpha of the House of Worzel and a handful of his wolves were chatting with Nora near a stone archway. Though he appeared deep in conversation, every so often, Zacal's poisonous gaze slid our way.

"What are they talking about?" I asked, tilting my head back toward Kade.

Kade's posture was rigid as he glared at the male wolf alpha. "Nothing you need to worry about."

I narrowed my eyes, not believing what he'd said. I thought of how Kade and I had recently fought with Zacal, and the image of Kade's wolf growling in Zacal's face came to my mind. Zacal was likely still salty about it, and I could only imagine the lies he was telling about that night.

I went to ask Kade about one of the other wolves standing with Zacal when my gaze locked onto someone else across the room. I hadn't even realized I'd been searching for him until Locke's black gaze held mine with an intensity that made me feel exposed. Leaning against one of the back walls, Locke stood with a goblet in his hands, his posture relaxed as if he hadn't a care in the world.

As I watched, Perene led Lana over to him, and I ground my teeth before looking away. I didn't need to see that. What had Perene said? *My son must mate with a vampire who can coax him out of the cesspool he insists on wading into.* It was now obvious who Perene had in mind to become Locke's mate and supposed savior. The thought of them together made me sick, but I reminded myself that I didn't give a damn about the asshole.

Motioning toward my drink, I asked Asher, "What's in this?"

The demon leaned closer to me, and his scents of musk and leather became stronger, making my mouth water. *Fuck. What is wrong with me?*

"It's safe," Asher explained. "It contains Acaralia, but instead of mixin' it with water, they've combined it with alcohol."

Right. So it's still birth control.

I remembered something Losak had said then and asked, "Wait, what did Losak mean about me taking advantage of my situation?"

Darian was the one to answer me this time. "We've told you that you have to be of the same type of monster to join specific houses, but you also have to be the same type of monster to mate with another. So shifters mate with shifters, centaurs mate with centaurs, and so on. But there are no rules against bedding different monsters as long as it's purely recreational. However, when you join a house, while you're still allowed to bed monsters from other houses, it gets trickier. Some houses have running conflicts with other houses, and if you bed someone from an enemy house, your alpha may disapprove and punish you. The Week of Orash is one of the few times when you can bed whoever you wish without repercussions. You don't have to think about the impact it may have on you or your house. So, let's just say, over the next few nights, there will be a lot of...connecting."

"He means fuckin'," Asher clarified for me with a grin. "There will be a lot of fucking."

I rolled my eyes at his shit-eating grin but became unsettled when I thought of Losak's words: *If you want to know what it's like with a real alpha, come visit me.* I mean, I'd suspected it was some sort of proposition, but I hadn't thought he was literally inviting me into his bed. Having sex with the alphas of the higher houses wasn't exactly on my to-do list. I was going to have to be careful not to give any of the damn monsters the wrong idea.

Now that I knew the fizzy pink liquid in my hands wasn't poison, I downed the whole goblet. If I was going to survive the night, I could use a little bit of liquid courage.

Darian gave my empty goblet to a satyr passing by us with a tray of drinks, then he linked his arm with mine and began leading us through the crowd of people. "Well now, let's move along. There really are some people you should meet."

CHAPTER 17

~ **Raine** ~

It was easier to appreciate the magnificent ballroom now that I was surrounded by Darian and the others. Everywhere I looked, the space screamed opulence, and if it weren't for the fact that Darian had shown me his garden, I wouldn't have believed something so beautiful could exist in the mountain. On the right side of the room, opposite the windows, we passed one of the tall archways that led to a sitting area. The space was dimly lit by blue torches, and white chaise lounges were grouped in pairs and shrouded by white gauze that streamed down from above.

"What is this place?" I asked Darian as he led me past another archway and across the room beneath one of the sparkling chandeliers.

The siren leaned closer to me, his breath tickling the side of my face. "This is the main ballroom of the royal castle. The ancient structure was built on the side of the mountain, with its lower levels carved from the rock itself. When the monarchy fell and King Adrien was overthrown, the Taratun council found ways to repurpose the spaces. Tunnels were made deep into the mountain in the years following, along with the majority of the caverns and rooms, but the original foundation of the castle remains."

A castle? It certainly explained the grandeur. As we passed a high table, I reached out to touch one of the black bell-shaped flowers, but Kade swiftly knocked my hand away. "They're poisonous," he warned. "Stay away from them."

I stopped to gape at the wolf shifter. "*Why* would there be poisonous flowers at a party? What if someone accidentally touches them?"

Asher shrugged as if the fact the monsters used dangerous flowers to decorate the room was the most natural thing. "Monsters have a sick sense of humor. If anyone touches the petals, they might get a bad headache and hallucinate."

"For anyone who isn't immortal, it would kill them," Darian said with a grim expression, leading me away from the table and vase of flowers.

Oh great. So they're death flowers. I wanted to chastise Darian and the others for not telling me that incredibly important information straight away, but I knew it'd be too risky. The other newbloods wouldn't be as wary considering the flowers wouldn't kill them, and I had no idea who might be listening to our conversation.

Darian continued to lead us through the mass of monsters until we reached a female with milky white eyes, skin the color of smoke, and an ivory velvet gown that reached down to her pointed white heels. The shades of gray on her mottled skin seemed to move as I stared as if her skin was a living being on its own. *Creepy.* The female was surrounded by a handful of other monsters who had a similar ghostly appearance, and I quickly scanned their faces.

A slender female had her head turned away from us, and her mousy brown hair was arranged into a braided bun above her head. The shape of the female's body and the color of her hair was so familiar that my heart began to race as hope exploded inside me. *Cara?*

Before I could say anything, the female turned my way, revealing a heart-shaped face dotted with freckles and pale gray eyes. I blinked as I continued to stare, but then my chest caved inward as disappointment went through me. It wasn't her.

Oblivious to my internal frustration, Darian stepped forward and dipped his head toward the female in the ivory dress. "Mabel, you look spectacular as always," he complimented her with a flirtatious smile.

The female with the heart-shaped face was looking at me now as if she knew I'd been gawking at her, and I carefully avoided her gaze, moving my attention to the pale-skinned female called Mabel.

Mabel lifted her pointed nose into the air as her assessing gaze swept over us. "Darian, I was wondering when you'd come to say hello. I see you've brought your delightful new friend to meet me," she said, her unnerving white gaze fixed on me.

"It's Raine," I said with a tight smile, getting way too tired of being called the "pet," "newblood," or "friend."

She raised her brows. "Raine," she repeated. "As Darian has alluded, I'm Mabel, alpha of the House of Faren, high house of shadows." She paused then and gestured to the room with a bony hand. "I trust you are enjoying the festivities. The other newbloods have informed me that Katakin is vastly different from what you were previously accustomed to. Much more..." She circled her hand in the air as if she was trying to find the appropriate word. "...civilized," she finished.

I nearly snorted in her face. I wanted to point out that back on the island we were more civilized than monsters who stole and tortured humans to get them to turn into them, but as I peered around at the milling figures in extravagant garments and the opulent ballroom surrounding me, my words died in my throat. Instead,

I said carefully, "This room certainly is spectacular. I've never seen anything so grand."

"I imagine not." Mabel nodded as if satisfied with my answer and turned to a handsome wraith beside her, who handed her a goblet of wine. Taking a sip, she pulled the goblet from her thin lips and changed the subject. "I hear you are enjoying your time with Locke and his friends. I must admit, I was surprised when rumors of your little welcoming arrangement reached my ears."

Welcoming arrangement? It didn't take me long to understand her meaning and make sense of the amused glint in her eye. *So everyone does think they're keeping me as their own personal sex toy.* Without thinking, I opened my mouth to tell her that it had been more like a weird little prison than a sex pad, but Darian spoke first.

"Our darling Raine has been most satisfied. In fact, she's in no hurry to leave," he said with a smug smile, and he trailed his fingers up my bare arm that was still linked with his. Tilting his head to the side, he gave me a subtle look.

At his comment, I remembered we needed the monsters to believe Darian and the others were only keeping me close because they were playing with me. I forced a smile onto my face. "Yes, I'm *very* happy with how I've been treated so far."

Though Mabel's smile stretched wider, there was no warmth in her gaze. "Perhaps they should be reprimanded for keeping you all to themselves. I hear you have become a powerful shifter. I'm always intrigued by what new abilities the curse bestows on newcomers, and I'm looking forward to seeing you fight. I'm sure we will become firm friends."

From the way she said the word *friends*, I was betting we didn't share the same views on what the word meant, but I smiled and politely said, "I'd like nothing more." All right, so now it sounded like I was kissing ass, but pissing off the alpha of the House of Faren didn't seem like the best idea. Goddess, I knew it was expected that all the newbloods become acquainted with the alphas, especially those from the high houses like Mabel, but I wondered how long I had to talk to her to fulfill my obligation.

As I racked my brain for a seemingly appropriate question to ask the alpha that any normal newblood would ask, my attention went to the heart-shaped female with the pale-gray eyes. She was practically drooling as she stared at Asher and had been for almost the entire time Mabel talked. Asher was acting oblivious, though the small quirk of his lips showed that he noticed, and I couldn't take it. I glared at the female, making it clear that it was annoying me because it damn well was. I wasn't sure *why* it was, but it fucking was. All the guys got looks often, but this female pressed her thighs together as if she was about ready to rip her dress off and bend over for Asher.

Mabel followed my glare, and the moment the alpha turned toward the wraith, the female's face morphed, her expression turning from appreciation to downright disgust as she stared at Asher. I mean, her lip curled, her nose wrinkled, and I could practically hear her sniff as she made a show of dismissing him.

If I hadn't seen it with my own eyes, I wouldn't have believed it. *Un-fucking-believable.* Now I was irritated because she was acting as if Asher had some kind of disease. I had thought it was strange the way Mabel's gaze never went to Asher as if she refused to acknowledge him, but seeing how the heart-shaped female had changed, I was sure something was going on. When we finally finished speaking with Mabel a few excruciating minutes later, and Darian began leading us back through the crowd, I couldn't stop thinking about it.

Now that I was paying attention, I realized that most of the alphas didn't acknowledge Asher. Many of the monsters from the lower houses appreciated him as much as they appreciated Kade and Darian, taking in their muscled bodies, but nearly all of the monsters from the higher houses ignored Asher as if they were content to pretend he didn't exist. If the demon noticed, he didn't seem to care and had a perpetual grin glued to his face.

I moved closer to Asher, becoming more bothered by the situation with every passing moment. "Why are they looking at you like that?" I hissed.

Asher winked at a pretty siren female, and she frowned and turned her back to him. "Like what?" he asked.

"Like *that*," I said, motioning to the female who was ignoring him.

"Oh, her. She's from the House of Saceris."

"And *why* is she treating you that way?"

He gave a casual shrug, seemingly not disturbed by it. "Remember when I told you my mother went crazy?"

"Yeah."

"Well, she didn't just try her cure on me. A few monsters in the House of Thorem woke up as she tried to hack their tails off or sawed at their horns. They all healed, but the reputation of the house suffered when others heard that our alpha was strugglin' to control one of his own. Some of the monsters, especially those from the higher houses, choose to ignore me now. I don't think they believe I'm crazy like her, but it's more as if they don't want to be associated with the son of the monster who went insane and tried to destroy her house."

I stopped walking, disbelief rooting me to the spot. "But that's absurd. Your mother was unwell. You can't be blamed for that."

Asher gave me a lopsided smile. "Don't worry about it. By the end of the night, even the females from the high houses will be crawlin' all over me. They're just worried about their reputations, but if their alphas leave, things will change. They like to pretend they're too good for me, but they can't stay away."

My brows slammed down as I struggled to understand how he had so willingly accepted the situation. "Wait, so they ostracize you because of what happened with your mom, but when their alphas go away, then they want you? That's messed up. I thought anything goes during the Week of Orash?"

"Yeah, I guess my situation is a special one," Asher said with a shrug. He didn't seem bothered by it all, but I found myself growing angry. Angry at the monsters for treating him that way and angry that he accepted it. Fuck that. Back on the island, I was treated as a bit of a freak because I spent my days training rather than learning to sew and weave like the other girls. But for the most part, the villagers had accepted me.

I stared at Darian and Kade, but while they looked sympathetic, it was clear they'd also accepted the situation. "None of us have a house," Darian said calmly. "To an extent, we've all been shunned."

As he said it, a scantily dressed goblin on our right glared at Asher as she passed.

"Who's that?" I asked Kade.

"Belongs to the House of Axeran," he replied. "One of the high houses."

I glowered at the female and had to stop myself from going over and slapping the haughty look from her face. Determined to do *something* with myself, I gave Asher's hand a tug. Taking the hint, he leaned down.

"You deserve better, Ash," I said, then I slid my arm behind his neck and pressed my lips against his.

I'd meant it to be a quick kiss. I'd wanted to show him that I didn't care what the alphas of the high houses thought, and neither should he, but the moment his lips touched mine, tingles rushed through me, and my body warmed as I found myself desperate to be closer to him. Surprise touched his features, but then he was kissing me back, his tongue dominating my mouth.

All thoughts of the alphas and haughty females disappeared from my mind as his large hands wrapped around me, pulling me closer to him, and I melted against his body. The rational part of my brain knew the bond was at fault, but right then, I didn't care. My arms moved from behind his neck and slid down his broad chest as I savored the feel of him under my fingers. Goddess, he was huge, his muscles straining against the formal shirt he wore. The male was built like a house but had the face of a god, and his hands on me were like fire. I was surprised the females from the higher houses managed to keep themselves from ogling when their alphas were around because the male was sex on legs. The scents of musk and leather enveloped me, and I rubbed against him, desperate for more friction.

His large hands slid up my sides, and he leaned down to groan against my ear. "Fuck Raine, unless you want me bendin' you over right here, you might wanna stop rubbing against me like that."

I shivered and my core clenched at his words, but I was finally aware of my surroundings enough that I noticed Darian and Kade were watching us intently. They looked as though they wanted to join us, and the thought of it had my body growing warmer. For the briefest insane moment, I thought about asking the three of them to go back to the rooms, but then I came to my senses. Slowly, I pried myself from Asher and blearily took in the stares of the monsters around us. The scantily dressed goblin was watching from not too far away. Her jaw hung open, and even though her eyes heated with lust, I had no doubt she was about to tell her alpha about what she'd just witnessed. I gave her a saccharine smile and turned to Asher.

His violet eyes glowed, and his shit-eating grin was back in place. Without worrying about who was looking, he adjusted his pants. "Knew you liked me, Sharachi. There's no denyin' it now."

"What? I don't—" I began, but I *did* like him. I could still feel his hands on my body as he held me against him, and it took all my effort not to walk back into his arms.

"You, my dear, are perfect," Darian said, smiling at me as if he was proud of what I'd just done. Linking his arm in mine again, he began leading me back through the crowd.

• • • • • • • • • •

For the rest of the night, Darian and Kade introduced me to the alphas of different houses while Asher stayed by my side. We met centaurs, trolls, banshees, ogres, and a number of other monsters whose names I couldn't remember.

Aside from Mabel, the wraith alpha of the House of Faren, high house of shadows, Darian only introduced me to one other alpha from the higher houses. Kenric was a massive orc and alpha of the House of Axeran, the high house of giants, and I was surprised to find the orc to be a cheerful monster with an aptitude for lame jokes.

As the night wore on, I asked Darian why he and the others weren't introducing me to any of the alphas from the other high houses, and he explained that Losak, whom I'd already met, was a basilisk shifter and alpha of the House of Silat, the high house of shifters. Zacal, I already knew from when Kade and I had fought against him and his wolves. He was the alpha of the House of Worzel, high house of the wolves.

Then there was Drustan, an arrogant vampire from the House of Nesarin, who was the alpha of the high house of vampires. Cordelia was a siren and the alpha of the House of Saceris, high house of the water monsters, and Darian was especially hoping to avoid her. Lastly, Borren was a hotheaded demon and the alpha of the House of Thorem, the high house of demons. Asher had shut down when we'd passed by the alpha, and I didn't need him to explain why. I hadn't forgotten what he'd said about the alpha of the House of Thorem putting his mother out of her misery. The thought made me shudder, and I was happy to stay away from the alpha.

While they introduced me to the alphas, I made an effort to keep an eye out for Cara, but my heart ached when I didn't find her. I hadn't realized how much I'd gotten my hopes up until my stomach plummeted as the night grew late.

I'd been introduced to a few of the newbloods from the last round, but while I vaguely recognized some of their faces, I hadn't found out any information about Cara. By the end of the night, the twelve newbloods from the last round had been accounted for, and not one of them was my sister. It made no sense. I'd also wanted to try to speak to Nora again, but anytime I looked her way, she was swamped with monsters. Annoyance and frustration went through me, but I kept pasting a smile on my face. *This is only the first night. Take a breath, Raine.*

At some point, a band on the dais had begun playing upbeat music and monsters moved to the middle of the ballroom, dancing to the rhythm.

Darian led us away from the last alpha we'd been speaking to and took my hand in his. "Shall we?" he asked, gesturing his head to the monsters who were moving their bodies in time to the music.

I groaned and shook my head. After the night I'd just had, dancing was the last thing on my mind. "Actually, can we go?" I hadn't gotten the information I'd wanted, but I'd try again the next night. Right then, I wanted to rest my feet.

"We've introduced Raine to enough monsters. No one will notice if we leave now," Kade said, and I shot him a grateful look. "We should take her back to our rooms so she can rest for the first fight tomorrow night."

"Well, thank fuck that's done," Asher grumbled, and he turned to Darian. "I'll never understand how you can stand talkin' to all those pretentious bastards."

"If we don't play the game, we'll be destroyed by it," Darian replied with a humorless smile. "But yes, I think that's enough for tonight. Let us all retire."

"Retire?" Asher asked. "We haven't been able to relax in weeks. How about we finally have some fuckin' fun?"

Fun? At first, I didn't realize what he meant, but then hurt went through me. I knew I shouldn't have been surprised. Darian and Asher talked about how they shared females, and from the way they talked, it sounded like they did it often. But still, I couldn't help clenching my jaw at the idea that they wanted to be with someone else.

Many alphas had left the party by now, and the remaining monsters were bleary-eyed and deliriously happy as they felt the effects of the alcohol and Silver Sand in their systems. Around us, females had begun to brush past Asher, Darian, and Kade, their flirtatious touches and lingering gazes making it clear what they wanted. I had the disturbing desire to break some of their fingers for touching the guys, but I kept my hands to myself.

A few females from the House of Axeran who'd been ignoring Asher earlier were now ogling at him as if he was the most delicious thing they'd seen all night. The sight of them made me sick.

Darian's blue gaze slid to me, and I could see the hesitation in his eyes. Before he could say a word, I blurted, "All right, Kade, let's get out of here." Then I turned and started toward the double doors at the other end of the room, ignoring the pang in my gut when I didn't hear Asher and Darian following after us.

· · · · ·· · · · ·

~ Asher ~

It had been weeks since Darian and I had gone out drinkin' and brought females back to our beds. Weeks since I'd been able to forget about the fuckin' world and have some damn fun. I didn't care that the females around me were only interested in one thing. Just like I didn't care that some of them were only givin' me attention now that their alphas had left the party. Sex was sex.

But as an attractive banshee with midnight hair ran her fingers up my chest, I found myself wishing her hair was the color of fire instead. As she appreciated my muscles with her spindly pale fingers, I kept remembering the way Raine had kissed me in front of everyone with lust in her gorgeous amber eyes.

You deserve better. Her words haunted me. Not because I believed them but because I knew she meant it. Raine had listened to my tale about my mother and how the higher alphas shunned me, and she was disgusted. But not by me. She'd pulled me closer, planting her beautiful pink lips on mine, and fuck the devil if I wasn't going to reciprocate.

Coconut and steel had invaded my senses, and her beautiful body called to me in a way that demanded I respond. Just her lips on mine had my cock growing hard and my chest aching as the need to claim the female nearly overwhelmed me. But I had to let her go. What could a fucked-up demon like me offer her? For the remainder of the night, I'd struggled to keep my hands off her, and now I needed a release.

The banshee turned around and ground her ass against me in time to the music, and my brows lowered. I should have been enjoying this. I should have been rock-hard and ready to pound her against the wall like I usually was when I was out to enjoy myself, but now that Raine had left, my cock was limper than a fuckin' uncooked sausage.

It wasn't just what Raine had said or how my nickname had rolled off her tongue that had me questioning things. It was the memory of her against me, of her body molded to mine, and the insatiable need I had to protect her at every fucking moment. I knew it was the bond that compelled me to protect her, but I wasn't so sure that it was the bond that made me want her so badly. The female had the beauty of the Devil Sharachi, but it was her heart and spirit that had captured my attention. And I wanted her back in my damn arms where I was now sure she was supposed to be.

I peered over at where a female demon and siren were dancing on either side of Darian and pawing at him as though he was the fucking Devil Halced himself. His blue eyes were dim, and I could tell he was as interested in them as I was in the banshee still shaking her ass against my limp dick.

My siren brother was still at the party because of me. I'd seen the way he'd stared after Raine and Kade, even more obviously than I had. He was letting these females rub themselves all over him for my fucking sake, and while I loved him more for it, it made me sick inside.

What was I doing? Placing a hand on the banshee's shoulder, I gently moved her away from me and stepped back. She swiveled and tried to shuffle closer again, but when I shook my head at her, she huffed in annoyance. Tipping her nose up at me as if she just remembered I was beneath her, she disappeared into the throng of dancing monsters and soon found a wolf shifter to grind against.

I stepped over to where Darian had a bored expression on his face. "Ready to get out of here, brother?"

His eyes brightened at my question, and his lips twisted to the side. "I thought you'd never ask. What changed your mind?"

Scratching the back of my head, I mumbled, "Somethin' Raine said is bothering me."

Darian's lips curled upward, but he didn't bother asking me what it was. "Another time, ladies," he said, stepping away from the siren and demon who gave him sad, pouty faces before they began dancing with each other as though they were trying to allure him back to them.

He didn't even spare them another glance as I led the way out of the ballroom.

CHAPTER 18

~ **Raine** ~

The sounds of voices woke me from sleep, and I groaned as I pulled myself from the bed. Kade wasn't in the room, and I rubbed my eyes to wake myself up. Yawning, I walked into the common room wearing nothing but one of Kade's big shirts.

Asher, Kade, and Locke were already up and dressed, though Asher was missing his shirt. Sweat gleamed on his hard abs and soaked his shaggy brown hair, but I didn't let myself appreciate the sight. I hadn't forgotten how he and Darian had stayed at the party to have a good time, and my chest still felt hollow at the thought.

"How long have you been up?" I asked no one in particular as I avoided their gazes and grabbed myself a cup of pink Acaralia water.

Asher flexed his muscles and grinned. "Hours. Darian and I had to work off some energy."

Hours? Anger coursed through me, and I wasn't even sure why. "Hm," I said.

Intent on ignoring him, I peered at where Locke was again staring at the map I'd seen him with nights earlier. *I really am going to have to get my hands on that.* I wondered what the vampire had been doing the night before. He hadn't joined us when Darian and the others had introduced me to the alphas, and the last time I'd seen him was when Perene had been leading Lana over to him. I tried not to think about what the thought of Locke and Lana together did to my insides.

A fresh platter of food was laid out on one of the tables, and I piled up a plate and found a spot on an unoccupied settee. When I'd finished the food, Darian exited the washroom, and I took my turn washing my face and changing into one of my red leather outfits. Somehow during the night, my clothes had all been laundered and left neatly for me in the washroom, and I could only assume Locke was behind it.

Taking my time, I braided my hair into a single braid that would keep the hair out of my eyes. When I went back to the common room, all four monsters were waiting for me, and even Locke had tucked away his map.

"What?" I asked with a frown.

"It's the first fight tonight," said Locke as his serious dark gaze fixed on my face. "You'll be up against demons, an ogre, a succubus, sirens, a banshee, a bear shifter, and a vampire. The only rule during the fights is that the newbloods must not kill their opponents. But you're still human. Or at least, you appear to be. A newblood could kill you without even trying to."

"I get it," I retorted dryly. "I'll try not to die."

I didn't miss how he'd said 'appear to be' like he wasn't sure if I was human or not. No one had mentioned the fact I'd turned the rocky ceiling to sand during Asher's first test, and neither had anyone talked about the fact it was likely me who had conjured the unnatural wind while I was under the influence of the Silver Sand. In any case, I hadn't been able to do anything magical since, so I had to still be human. Right?

"You can't use magic tonight, Sharachi," Asher said as if he'd been reading my thoughts, and he stepped closer to me. "Everyone thinks you're a shifter, and shifters don't have that kind of power."

"I don't think that'll be a problem. I doubt I could do it again even if I wanted to," I replied. In truth, I *had* been wondering if it was possible because if I found a way to control it that would be badass, but I hadn't felt anything that resembled the energy I'd felt both times I'd used the magic before.

Moving into my space, Kade lifted my arm and started strapping leather armor to my arms and shoulders. "No one can see the color of your blood, Raine. All it would take is a flash of red and our world would turn to chaos."

"Yes, I would rather appreciate it if I didn't have to entrance an entire amphitheater of monsters to protect you," Darian added.

Asher bumped the siren's shoulder. "Don't tell me you wouldn't love the attention."

"Would *you* want the alphas all clamoring for you?" Darian retorted with a raised brow. "I'd like to keep my lips away from the likes of Zacal and Drustan."

Asher snorted then, clearly enjoying the visual he was getting, and I couldn't help grinning as well.

"And I'd like to not have to rip all their heads off," Kade growled as he finished strapping leather to my other arm.

"Oh, don't act like you'd hog all the fun. I'd help you out," Asher added with a grin.

I swallowed against the lump forming in my throat. I knew they didn't want me to die because of our bond, but the fact they were talking about protecting me as if it was completely natural was making me feel all sorts of strange. *Am I really getting emotional at the idea that they'd willingly murder monsters for me?*

Yes. The answer was a definite yes, because not only did I feel tears prickling in my eyes, but warmth heated low in my belly at the thought. I knew it wasn't because they were talking about killing others for me. Not really. It was the ease with which this was all happening. The way they were acting as if I was *theirs.*

The scents of cedarwood, ash, and spice grew stronger then, and my attention went to Locke as he stepped closer to me, his onyx gaze boring into me. I braced myself for whatever threat he was about to spew at me, but instead, he said, "When you fight, remember those females are no longer your friends. They're newbloods now, and they all have the instincts of monsters. They will desire power above all else, and taking you down shows everyone that they are stronger than you. Trust no one, not even if they're on your team."

Huh. Advice. I did not see that coming. Wait. "Team?"

He nodded as if it was common knowledge. "For the first fight, the newbloods are usually split into two groups. The team that wins will continue to fight the following night. You need to be on the losing team."

My brow wrinkled. "The losing team?"

"You can't ask her to do that. It'll ruin her chances of being offered a position with a higher house," Asher protested on my behalf.

"The more she fights, the more likely it is that someone will find out she's human. She'll lose if she wants to survive," Locke responded, not bothering to look at Asher but continuing to stare straight at me. As if he thought staring me down could convey how serious he was.

Well, he was wrong because that stare just made me want to piss him off. Luckily for him, I was smart enough to see the reasoning behind what he was saying. I *did* want to survive, and I couldn't have cared less about losing the interest of any of the alphas from the high houses.

"He's right," Kade added. "Raine, you should stay at the back and feign a hit to the head before falling to the ground. No one would question you if you didn't get back up."

Feign a hit? I hated the idea of looking weak, but I could do it. "All right. Pretend to get knocked out. I can do that," I said with an unhappy nod.

Asher stepped forward with a leather weapons belt and strapped it around my waist. When it was secure, I made my way over to the weapons shelf and slid two knives into the leather, then I grabbed a sword and slid it into the scabbard at my side.

Goddess, it was good to be armed again. Feeling like I could take on the world, or at least like I could take on a few newbloods, I turned back to the others and smiled. "All right. I'm ready to get my ass kicked."

· · · ● · ● · · ·

I waited behind an iron grate in the bowels of a gigantic amphitheater, along with five other newbloods and two hulking Minotaur guards. It seemed Locke was right about us being split into teams, and I assessed the females who were with me. Lana and Nora were there, along with Bri, who had turned into a demon. The two other newbloods weren't women I'd spoken to when we were back on the island, but one had ocean-blue eyes similar to Darian's, so I guessed she was a siren, and the other appeared human, so I wasn't sure what she was. All of them wore fighting leathers similar to my own and had weaponry strapped to their sides.

A thunderous roar came from the crowd above us, and I leaned against the cold, stone walls of the space we were in and tried to calm my racing heartbeat.

"You ready?" Nora asked as she propped herself against the wall beside me.

I thought about admitting I was shitting myself, but that didn't seem like something a power-hungry newblood would say, so I settled with, "You bet."

She grinned at me, anticipation and excitement brightening her eyes. "This is going to be fun."

A part of me wanted to agree. I enjoyed pushing my body and wielding weapons, but this wasn't like training on the island. I was pitted against monsters, and I didn't have the abilities they had. Another roar came from somewhere above us, and the walls shook, making streams of sand fall from the stone ceiling above our heads. The blood pounded in my ears, and I clenched my fists.

Slowly, the iron grate began to lift, and the Minotaurs stepped forward. "Time to move," one of them barked as they began ushering us into the tunnel beyond the grate.

Determined not to let his meaty hands touch me, I strode out behind Lana and Nora, making my way along the tunnel until we exited out onto a wide stretch of sandy ground. I only made it a few steps before I froze, the sheer size of the amphitheater around us making my heart squeeze.

Situated at the top of the mountain, the amphitheater was constructed of massive slabs of grey stone that reached into the sky far above our heads. Thousands of monsters watched from the rows of seating encircling the fighting arena, their gleeful chatter audible over the icy air that penetrated my leathers and chilled me to the bone. Stars spread across the sky, the tiny dots seemingly insignificant against the mass of stone towering over me, and I swallowed as my throat became painfully dry. *Fuck.*

Chewing the inside of my cheek, I forced myself to move again, spreading out as the others on my team had done and adding to the end of our line. Splashes of black stained the sand beneath our feet, and my stomach roiled when I realized it was blood. Monster blood. *Well, that explains the frenzied cheering coming from the arena while we'd been waiting down in the tunnels.* I didn't let myself think more about it and lifted my gaze. On the opposite side of the amphitheater, the newbloods from the other team emerged from their own hidden tunnel and trekked across the sand, taking up similar positions to us.

Trying to focus my mind, I eyed the members of their team. A hundred yards away stood Gina, a pretty brunette who I knew had been turned into a banshee. A short distance from her stood Sasha, the daughter of one of the bakers back on our island. While Sasha had always been tall, now that she'd been turned into an ogre, she stood over seven feet high.

I didn't know the names of the remaining newbloods, but I could tell two of them were demons because of their horns and tails. I could only guess the other two were sirens as Kade had told me three of the newbloods had become sirens, and there were still two unaccounted for.

At the thought of Kade and the others, I turned my attention to the stands, scanning the faces of the monsters. Losak, alpha of the House of Silat, was sitting with a few other members of his house in the front row, and when my gaze fell on him, he gave me a wolfish smile. I quickly averted my eyes, and it didn't take long before I spotted Locke, Kade, Asher, and Darian, sitting in the front row further to my left. Darian gave me a reassuring smile, and Asher winked at me, but Kade and Locke looked as stone-faced as I felt.

The loud stamping of hooves drew my attention away from them, and I peered at where the centaur from the night before was standing on a balcony high up on the right side of the amphitheater. The area he was in had been sectioned away from the other seating, the stone walls making it more private. Behind him, Perene, Warrick, and a few monsters I didn't recognize were sitting on elegant cushions and drinking from silver goblets, and I could only guess these were more members of the Taratun council.

As the crowd joined in, stamping their feet, the chatter of voices quieted. The jarring sound of boots, claws, and hooves against stone became so loud it made my head pound, but abruptly the noise ceased, and a tense silence filled the air. The centaur smiled broadly and gestured dramatically with his hands. "And now, for the event we've all been waiting for," he bellowed, "Let the first fight of the newbloods begin!"

At that, monsters cheered and howled, but I refused to tremble at the sound. *Focus on the fight, Raine. You just need to stay back and pretend to be knocked unconscious.* In theory, it sounded easy, but with over a thousand monsters watching my every move, I knew I'd have to make it look convincing.

Lana and the newblood from my side who appeared human, shot forward at the same moment that Sasha, the ogre, and the two demons from the opposite team came toward us. The five of them clashed in the center of the arena, and chaos erupted. Fangs sunk into flesh, giant limbs swiped through the air, and bodies were flung to the ground.

I shuffled my feet on the sand and grabbed my knives from my belt as Lana's teeth sank into one of the demons.

The demon thrashed for a few moments before the severe blood loss rendered her unconscious, and her body fell limp. Lana smiled wickedly as she let the newblood drop to the ground. Black blood dripped down her chin, and she made a show of running a manicured finger along her bottom lip and sucking the blood from it. Monsters in the stands shot to their feet, their applause growing wild as if the sight of the blood drew them into a frenzy.

Not far from Lana, the human-looking newblood from my team managed to place her flat hand on Sasha's chest. For the briefest moment, the ogre's eyes glassed over, the monster's green gaze filling with lust, but the newblood from my team had moved too slowly. Before she'd touched the ogre, the ogre had already started to bring her arm down, and despite the haze of lust, the monster's arm kept coming down until the ogre's fist smashed into the side of the newblood's head. The newblood from my team fell to the ground, her eyes rolling into the back of her head and black blood trickling down her temple. She didn't get back up.

Oh fuck. I was starting to doubt whether I could successfully fake being rendered unconscious without actually sustaining brain damage or worse. *If I get hit by that thing, it'll kill me,* I thought grimly.

"I hope that whatever you shift into, it's something badass," Nora said to me from a few paces away. "I told Samara her succubus power wouldn't always save her."

Succubus? I figured she had to be talking about the newblood who'd just been taken out by the ogre. I opened my mouth to reply, but the two newbloods with blue eyes from the opposite team began to sing, and I turned my attention back to the fight. *Sirens—I was right.*

In response, the siren from my team started up her own song, and I guessed she was trying to redirect their magic, but it wasn't long before their power overwhelmed her, and she was striding toward them with a desperate love-sick gaze on her face. Nora and I tried to grab her arms to hold her back, but her silky skin slid from our grasps. The moment she was within striking distance, Sasha's large green fist smashed into her, and her body crumpled to the ground.

I winced, but there was nothing I could do to help her. Gina, the banshee from the other team, started wailing in a pitch that was so high even the sirens on her team looked like they were in pain, and I quickly clapped my hands over my ears to try to block the sound. Beside me, Nora's clothes ripped from her as she shifted and grew, brown fur sprouting from her skin as she transformed into a massive bear that equaled the size of the ogre. Standing on her hind legs, she opened her maw wide, and her roar shattered through the banshee's wail.

Nora dropped back onto all fours and sprang forward, her bear form sprinting toward the banshee. As she ran and moved closer to the noise, black blood leaked out of her furry ears, but she didn't stop until the banshee's body was limp under one of her fat paws.

I removed my hands from my ears only to realize I'd made a mistake. The two sirens started up their song again, and I felt the moment their combined power gripped my mind. My knives fell from my hands, thudding to the sand at my feet as I smiled and strode toward them.

"Fight it, Raine. Their power is nothing to you!" Darian's shout cut through the fog in my mind, and I blinked, my footsteps slowing until I had stopped walking altogether. I had no idea whether it was against the rules for him to call out to me like that, but the interruption was all I needed. The effects of their power washed over me, and I shook my head as my mind cleared. *Their power is nothing to you.* I repeated the thought in my head and began striding forward again. At first, the sirens must have thought I was still under their spell, as their smiles were wide and confident, but as soon as I picked up my pace and drew the sword from my belt, the smiles fell from their perfect lips.

Moving in close, I advanced on the one on the left, spinning and delivering a roundhouse kick to her head that had her out cold. When the other siren tried to come at me from behind, I pivoted, swiping her legs out from under her and lifting my sword to her throat. She glared at me but didn't move as I kept the blade to her neck.

It wasn't until the thunderous applause stung my ears that I realized the fight was over. The centaur who had spoken earlier was standing at the end of the balcony, and once again, he stamped his hooves on the stone floor. Again, the monsters in the stands copied until the sound reached deafening levels. Just when I was sure my eardrums would burst, the stamping abruptly stopped, and an eerie silence fell over the amphitheater.

My chest rose and fell in measured breaths as my gaze fell on the remaining members of my team. Lana was standing near another unconscious demon, her chest covered in black blood, and her fangs still elongated as she smiled at the crowd. Near her, Bri stood with a sword in her hand, and from her stance, I guessed she'd also been fighting the demon. A few yards away from them, Nora's bear towered over the fallen ogre with triumph.

"Well, wasn't that exciting?" bellowed the centaur, and in response, the applause around us grew loud once again. When the noise quieted enough for the centaur to speak, he continued, "The first fight is over, and it looks as though we have a winning team! Tomorrow night, the winners from this round will face off against one another in one-on-one combat. But now, let us celebrate tonight's victors!"

CHAPTER 19

~ **Raine** ~

My hands gripped my knives loosely as I eyed Samara across the arena. The celebration the night before had been much like the party on the first night of the Week of Orash. Monsters had flocked to me to congratulate me for being on the winning team, and I'd played my part and acted as arrogant and proud as the other newbloods. Thankfully, no one asked me how I'd been able to overcome the sirens' power.

Tonight, for my one-on-one fight, I'd been pitted against the succubus who had been on my team. *Samara*. Again, my arms and shoulders were strapped with leather, but in contrast, Samara wore a gauzy red dress that ended at her knees. A huge slit ran up the center of the dress, and whenever she moved, her long legs were on full display.

I knew she was sour about the fact she'd been taken out by Sasha, the ogre, the night before, and I suspected her dress was intended as a statement. That she was powerful and didn't need any extra protection to fight against me. Samara didn't have any weapons strapped to her, but she still had her succubus power, and I knew better than to underestimate her.

After the previous fight, Locke had scolded me for getting too involved in the fight but pretending to be knocked unconscious wouldn't have helped me. I still would have been on the winning team. In any case, the vampire again instructed me to lose my next fight. If I lost against Samara, I wouldn't have to compete for the remainder of the Week of Orash, so I could see the logic in that. The tricky part was I had to do it without letting Samara draw blood. Considering the succubus didn't have any claws or weapons, I was liking my odds, but it was still risky.

The centaur, whose name I'd since learned was Henral, announced our fight, and the monsters in the stands watched Samara and me intently, the crowd seeming to hold a collective breath as everyone waited to see who would make the first move.

Samara finally ventured forward, darting across the sand toward me, and I kept my gaze trained on her. She was fast, her movements graceful, and it wasn't long before she was within striking distance. My fingers twitched on the hilts of my daggers, adrenaline spiking through me as the urge to either move away or attack had me gritting my teeth, but I stayed where I was. *All right, Raine. You just need to block her a few times, then pretend to get hit and fall to the sand. Sounds simple enough.* Except I also needed to make sure she didn't touch me. According to Kade, the power of a succubus was similar to a siren's, except instead of bewitching their victims through music, a succubus's power was transferred through their touch.

In a blur, Samara's left hand lashed out, and I kicked it away instinctively. As if she'd expected the action, Samara spun around, and her long fingers clamped around the exposed flesh of my right hand.

The moment our skin collided, my body relaxed, and all thoughts of defense and self-preservation floated from my mind as her power seized me. Samara's lips twisted into a victorious smile, and I barely noticed the look of malice in her eyes. All I saw was how perfect she was. From her curved hips to her full lips stained with red, I wanted her more than I wanted anything. As she shook her head, her long black hair flicking behind her shoulder, desire made my body heat and my head grow light.

"It seems the shifter newblood is now under the influence of our new succubus! This fight will be over before it's even begun," a voice floated to me from somewhere far away, but I didn't care about what they were saying, nor did I care about the faint sounds of booing and cheering coming from somewhere around me.

The daggers slipped from my grasp, and I went to step closer to Samara in a daze, hoping to press my body against hers and feel her soft skin against mine. Before I'd even moved forward, one of her hands landed on my shoulder, stopping me.

"To your knees," she commanded, and I obeyed, dropping down until my knees hit the sand. My lips parted at the impact, and as Samara bent her knee, exposing a long stretch of bare leg, I moved forward, running my tongue up her calf, up the side of her knee, and further up her thigh. Even though it was my body that was moving, it was as though I had no control over my movements.

"Mmm, so good," she said, tipping her head back and letting out a wicked chuckle. Warmth radiated through me at her praise, and I continued to kiss and lick her leg, savoring the taste of her.

Peering down, she smiled at me and brushed aside more of her dress, revealing tan skin even further up her thigh.

My tongue slid higher, and desire made my core spasm. I'd give her anything she wanted. She was my queen and—

Thunder rumbled somewhere in the distance, but I dismissed the sound, my tongue inching higher up Samara's thigh.

Anything she needed, I would—

The rumbling grew louder, and this time the sound vibrated in my skull. The sound was so familiar and so full of fury that I blinked once. Twice. Slowly, I realized it wasn't thunder, it was growling, and the sound called to me like a familiar song.

Kade. That one thought freed my mind from whatever prison it had been in, but it wasn't enough to break Samara's power. My body kept moving, my tongue continuing to taste the newblood as if I was a puppet and Samara was the one pulling my strings. Slowly, sensation began to return to parts of my body, but it wasn't happening fast enough.

I could see Samara's cruel smile for what it was now. She wasn't just trying to win this fight. She was trying to humiliate me. *But why?* My gaze flicked to the stands, and it didn't take me long to figure it out. Along the front row, Zacal sat among his wolves. He was leaning forward, his chin propped on his hands, and his yellow eyes watching me with an intensity that made my blood cold.

His gaze went to someone across the amphitheater, and though I couldn't turn my head to see who he was looking at, I could take a guess. *Kade.* This whole thing wasn't just a fight between newbloods. Zacal had somehow made a deal with Samara, and this was a message to Kade that we shouldn't have fought against him.

Well, fuck that. Like hell was I going to lose now. I had regained control of my toes, lips, and jaw, but my tongue was so damn close to reaching Samara's pussy. *Had she planned to make me eat her out in front of everyone?* If we were back on the island, I never would have thought something so absurd, but we were in Katakin now, and Samara was no longer human.

With what felt like a monumental effort, I managed to pull my tongue back into my mouth, but my nose still slid higher up her thigh. Kade's growl grew louder in my ears, continuing to ground me. Shit, I was so damn close...

Feeling returned to parts of my neck and jaw, and it was enough. Reaching forward, I opened my mouth and clamped down hard at the top of Samara's inner thigh.

Warmth filled my mouth accompanied by the coppery taste of blood, and Samara's shriek pierced the air. She recoiled from me, jumping backward as if I was a crazed animal. The moment we were no longer touching, her power released me entirely, and I rolled my shoulders and shook out my limbs, once again in full control of my body.

Lifting to my feet, I spat her blood onto the ground and wiped my lips with the back of my hand.

She bent over, glaring at me as she clutched at her wounded thigh. "You fucking bitch! You bit me!" she yelled.

"Maybe next time you should try finding a willing participant," I said coldly.

Her cheeks turned beet red, and she straightened, ignoring the trail of black that dripped down her leg.

Whoa. Did my teeth really do that?

"You're going to pay for this," she seethed. In a rage, she reached forward, trying to grab at me again, but I was ready for her and easily dodged her outstretched hand. Springing upward, I landed a fist on her stomach, followed by another on her nose. She staggered backward, grabbing at her face, but I spun and delivered a side kick to her head, and she fell to the ground.

Around me, monsters in the amphitheater cheered and howled, but I ignored them. My chest heaved as I stared at Samara's crumpled body, her red dress tattered and smeared with black. Now that she was unconscious, she almost looked human again, but just as guilt started to seep into me, I remembered Zacal's intense gaze and Samara's wicked smirk.

In the front row, the wolf alpha glowered at me now, his top lip bared and fangs protruding from his gums. I knew I should have been worried. From the look on Zacal's face, it was clear I was now on his shit list. But then again, I probably already had been.

Not far from him, Losak was standing as he applauded me, his slitted eyes fixed on me with way too much interest. I tried not to return eye contact and turned my head to Kade and the others.

All four of them were standing and staring at me. Kade was gripping the railing in front of him as if he was about to jump into the arena and sprint to me, but he nodded and remained where he was. Darian smiled at me as he clapped slowly, and Asher had the widest shit-eating grin stretching across his face.

Locke stared at me as if he wasn't quite sure whether he should be applauding me or punishing me, but slowly he lifted his hands and brought them together in two slow claps. That was it. *Two.* Maybe he wasn't the hard-ass he always pretended to be. Or maybe he was, and he just enjoyed the bloodshed. Either way, I grinned at him.

CHAPTER 20

~ Raine ~

"Is going to the party tonight the best idea? Zacal didn't seem too happy that I took Samara down," I said as I walked with Kade, Asher, and Darian through the tunnels toward the after-party. A scarlet red dress pulled tight against my body, the silky material wrapping around my neck, crossing over my breasts, and molding into a skirt that ended above my knees.

"Zacal won't attack durin' the party. He'll be too afraid of losing," answered Asher.

Kade grunted his agreement. The wolf shifter hadn't stopped frowning since they'd met up with me after the fight.

Darian straightened the collar of his shirt as he walked. "Unfortunately, all newbloods must attend the after-parties during the Week of Orash. If we don't make an appearance, Perene and the council will make our lives difficult."

"And how long are we expected to be there?" I asked. In truth, as much as I hated attending the parties, even if I'd had a choice, I still would have gone. It was where I was hoping to find information about Cara.

"Until you've let enough monsters hear themselves speak to you, and you've reinvigorated their feelings of self-importance," Darian drawled.

"Or until you've let enough of them fuck you against the wall," Asher added with a stupid grin, and I scowled at him in disgust. Darian and Kade glared at him as well.

"What?" Asher replied with an innocent shrug. "I'm just sayin'. The Taratun don't care about who the newbloods talk to. They care that the newbloods are participating in the party and actin' as the main entertainment. Keeping the alphas of Katakin happy, as it were."

"Anyone lays a hand on Raine, and they won't have a hand anymore," Kade snarled.

"Or a head," Darian added, raising a finger into the air.

Fucking? My curiosity peaked at the thought of all the monsters in the party suddenly deciding to get their freak on. I mean, did that include the centaurs? *How...* I didn't ask.

"*I'll* decide who's allowed to touch me, thank you," I chipped in, ignoring Kade's hard stare. "And I didn't see any monsters going wild the last two nights, so I think we're safe."

"Safe," Darian mused, rubbing his chin. "Now, I don't think I've ever heard that word used to describe one of these parties."

"The mood changes throughout the night, Sharachi," Asher explained with a hint of mirth. "Monsters take their fun seriously, and as the night wears on, you'll see more of it."

Oh. Ohhh. My mind then went to two nights earlier when Darian and Asher had stayed back at the party while Kade and I had returned to our rooms. This whole time, I'd imagined they'd picked a single female, but now I was picturing them being part of a full-on orgy, and that just pissed me off more.

"So I imagine you and Darian had a great time the other night," I said to Asher while trying to keep my face blank.

"To the contrary, we left not long after you and Kade. I was finding it to be rather a bore," Darian replied.

A bore? My gaze slid to Asher then, and his violet eyes peered back at me intently. His face was suddenly serious, and I swallowed thickly.

"A lot has changed since you turned up, sweetheart," he said, and I wasn't sure if it was his new nickname or his penetrating gaze, but warmth flowed through me.

• • • • • • • • • •

When we entered the ballroom, the party was in full swing. Alphas crowded around the newbloods, and monsters laughed and danced.

There had been three one-on-one fights that night. I'd bested Samara, the succubus. Lana had defeated a siren named Indira, and Nora's bear had taken down Bri, who was a demon. Even more monsters encircled Lana and Nora than the night before, and numerous gazes watched me as my heels clicked along the marble floor. I'd only made it a few steps before a monster who appeared to be made from stone was shoving a goblet into my hand. He clapped me on the back, sending pain shooting up my spine while slurring, "Congratulations, newblood!"

Asher shouldered him away from me, but soon there was a whole swarm of monsters blocking my path. It was as if taking a chunk out of Samara's leg had made me even more desirable. *Monsters seriously have strange requirements when it comes to picking their friends.*

After a few short conversations, Darian and the others managed to lead me to a less crowded space further into the room. I was able to breathe evenly for a few brief moments before I was approached by a demon with twisted horns poking from his short black hair and watery green eyes.

The demon smiled at me, but it wasn't a nice smile. "The shifter who can resist a succubus's power. You'll have to let me know your secret."

Around me, Kade, Darian, and Asher stiffened.

"Back off, Jarin. You have no reason to speak to her," Asher said, pressing closer to my side.

"I'm also *dying* to know what kind of shifter you are," the male added, ignoring Asher's warning. There was something about the way he said it that had the hair raising on the back of my neck.

Pretending to be unaffected by his questions, I smiled. "For your sake, let's just say no one can force me to do anything I don't want to, and if I told you what I was, well, that would ruin the surprise now, wouldn't it?"

The male's green eyes narrowed, and he folded his arms across his chest as he scrutinized me. "Forward *and* feisty. I can see why so many of the alphas are talking about you."

Talking about me? I could tell he was baiting me into asking him for more information. Instead, I said, "It seems you already know much about me, and yet, I know nothing about you."

At that, Jarin pulled back his shoulders and puffed out his chest, and I had to stop myself from rolling my eyes. "I'm Jarin, alpha of the House of Bateran. Being a shifter, there's no chance of you joining my house, but that doesn't mean we can't have some fun before the week is over."

"Raine won't be going anywhere with you," Kade growled, positioning himself slightly in front of me. Kade was easily a head taller than Jarin and twice as thick, and

I had to give Jarin points for not stepping back from such an imposing figure.

"Why don't you waste the time of some other unsuspectin' female, Jarin," Asher said harshly. "We all know what happens when you're left alone with newbloods," he added with a grin that didn't quite meet his eyes.

Asher must have hit a sore spot as Jarin's nostrils flared with anger at the comment. Glaring at Kade and Asher, he turned to leave, but before he went, he said, "I'll see you around, shifter." And then he was moving away from us, disappearing into the sea of bodies.

"What happens when Jarin is left alone with newbloods?" I asked, rounding on Asher the moment Jarin was gone.

Darian, who was still standing behind me, was the one to answer. "Jarin was one of the monsters who selected the last round of humans. He tried to rape one of the girls before they'd turned, but the act must have frightened her enough that it brought on the change. The girl named Piper transformed into a gorgon with a head full of snakes."

My brows rose in surprise. "Snakes?"

"Yep. One look and Jarin had been turned into stone," Asher added with a wry grin. "Unfortunately, the effect didn't last."

"Huh. Sounds like he got what he deserved." I wanted to hope that Jarin had learned his lesson, but something told me he hadn't. Still, I was glad Piper had gotten some revenge.

My expression became thoughtful then as I contemplated the very important information I'd just learned. Jarin was one of the monsters who'd selected the humans during the last round. *He has to know where Cara is.* While I'd spoken to all the newbloods from the last round during the first night of the Week of Orash, I hadn't been able to outright ask them about Cara. Not with so many other monsters around us. The last thing I needed was someone figuring out why I was there.

I'd been wracking my brain trying to think of a way I could speak with some of them privately, but Jarin... If he was there for the selection, he knew more than those newbloods would. He could give me answers. I was sure of it.

· · · ● · ● ● · ·

When we finally made it back to the common room, I kicked off my heels and trudged straight to Darian's room, purposely letting my feet drag on the floor. For the remainder of the night, I'd been distracted as I forced a smile to my face and chatted with the monsters who approached me. Every so often, I would scan the crowd, searching for Jarin, and when I glimpsed his green eyes and twisted horns, relief would rush through me. I just had to hope he would still be there when I returned without the company of Kade, Darian, and Asher. Locke hadn't joined us at the party, so I didn't think he would be an issue.

"Goddess, I'm tired," I groaned and stretched out my arms before opening my mouth in a wide yawn. I wasn't exactly lying because I *was* exhausted. From fighting Samara's succubus power and a night once again pandering to alphas' egos, I could have curled up on the floor and slept right there. Still, I wanted to make it really clear that the only thing I was planning to do in the near future was sleep. Dawn wasn't far away, and before long, the party would end as the remaining monsters in the ballroom would crawl back to their beds. I needed Kade and the others to copy me and fall asleep as quickly as possible.

Darian was quick to follow me, but I face-planted on his bed and pretended to fall asleep immediately without even changing my dress. It wasn't my finest moment, but I hoped it was believable enough. I mean, the monster was a siren with incredible hearing so there was the risk he could hear my heartbeat and would know I was faking it, but I kept my face relaxed and my breathing steady and hoped for the best.

There was a beat of silence as Darian stood watching me, but then he chuckled under his breath, and the next thing I felt was his slender fingers draping a blanket over my body. I had to stop myself from biting my lip as I imagined his long fingers removing my dress instead, but I managed to keep still, and before long, his steps receded until I assumed he was back in the common room.

A short time passed before he returned and lowered himself onto his bed, far on the side opposite from me. Keeping silent, I waited until his breathing slowed and I was sure he was asleep, then I slowly slid from the mattress.

Peeking into the common room, I checked it was empty before dashing across the space and snatching up my heels. Making my way to the weapons shelf, I strapped two daggers to my thighs, then I crept from the room and closed the door behind me.

· · · ● · ● ● · ● · ·

My first thought was that I was free. That I could disappear into the mountain and maybe escape into the city. But I had no idea where I would go, and Jarin was a real lead. A real chance for me to find my sister. If I escaped into the city, I had no idea where I would start to look for her. *And the fact you don't want to leave Kade and the others has nothing to do with it either, right?* I ignored the voice in my head.

By now, I had memorized the twists and turns I had to take in the tunnels to get to the ballroom, and it wasn't long before I was standing in front of familiar double doors. Shrieks of laughter, groans, and pounding music floated to me out in the tunnel, and I mentally prepared myself for whatever grisly scene I was about to enter. What had Asher said? *The mood changes as the night wears on.*

I let out a deep breath through my nose. *All right, this is no big deal. I'm just a human going into a room full of randy, intoxicated monsters who are looking to have some fun.*

I knew going to the party without Darian and the others wasn't the smartest idea. Even though I'd bested Samara only hours earlier, I still hadn't shown any true strength.

Just get in there, get the information you need, and get your ass out. Steeling myself, I took another deep breath and entered the room.

I had tried to prepare myself for what I'd see, but I was still shocked when I stepped into the ballroom. *Holy Mother Falia.* Asher was right about the atmosphere changing as the night wore on. On the dais, the four-monster band still played music, the rapid thudding of the drums and strumming of wooden musical instruments making my bones vibrate. But monsters were no longer just dancing and chatting with one another. Moans, grunts, and groans filled the air as monsters sought their pleasure not just from the wine and music but from one another as well. Gray smoke curled in the air, obscuring some of the monsters, but others were on full display, not caring that they were in plain sight of everyone else.

A female demon giggled as she walked past me, holding the hand of a male centaur. The centaur was handsome, with long brown hair that waved over his muscular shoulders and brown eyes that sparkled with mischief. His head turned to me, and his movements slowed as he gave me a roguish smile, his heated gaze sliding down my body as if he was imagining everything I had to hide under my dress. *Whoa.* My cheeks warmed, and I was grateful when the demon tugged playfully on his hand and he turned from me, continuing the follow her across the room.

Swallowing, I gave myself a mental shake and made my way through the room. Picking my path carefully, I avoided any wandering hands or unnaturally long tongues and peered around as I searched for Jarin. *Great plan, Raine. And what happens if you find Jarin but he's busy with uh...activities? Fuck.* I didn't have an answer.

Ducking beneath an archway, I scanned the private area on the right side of the ballroom where the white chaise lounges were grouped. Thankfully, the sheer material draped over the couches seemed to be purely decorative, as it didn't stop me from seeing who relaxed on the seats. If Jarin was in there, I'd spot him. The unfortunate part was that it also meant I could see all the other monsters.

My gaze landed on where a Minotaur was lounging naked, his bronze skin tinted blue from the light of the torches spread around the space. Two vampires were drinking from him, one with her fangs buried in his neck and the other with her teeth clamped onto his wrist. At first, I thought they were killing him, but then I noticed the stupid smile on his face. His eyes rolled into the back of his head before closing, and he moaned as the vampires continued to suck and lick at him.

Well, fuck. If I hadn't already realized going back to the party alone was a bad idea, I did right then. Swallowing hard, I moved faster, passing by the Minotaur and his friends. *I need to find Jarin quickly and get the hell out of here.*

I wondered then whether I should have told Kade, Asher, and Darian the truth about my sister and about me wanting to find Jarin. Did it really matter if they knew? *They could try to stop you*, common sense whispered to me. No, I had to do this alone.

Winding my way through the dwindling crowd, I avoided eye contact with any monster who looked my way. Something told me that not all monsters would gracefully accept refusal.

Yeah, like the rapist you're trying to find. I'd almost forgotten what Asher had said about Jarin and the newblood, but I was comforted by the feel of the daggers on my thighs. Jarin might have been a demon with instant healing abilities, but that didn't mean it wouldn't hurt if I stabbed him repeatedly.

Moments passed, and I had almost given up hope of finding him when I saw him with another demon near the far wall of the ballroom. The face of the other demon seemed to be in a perpetual scowl as they talked, and I wondered what they were discussing.

Moving behind a stone pillar, I waited until the other male had left before stepping into the open again. *All right, Raine, act sexy.* Curving my lips into what I hoped was a seductive smile, I swayed my hips as I strode over to Jarin.

The demon spotted me immediately, and surprise flared briefly on his face before he smoothed his expression and grinned at me. His green eyes watched me hungrily as I sauntered toward him, his gaze traveling up and down my body and lingering on the swell of my breasts. Nausea gripped me, and I resisted the urge to grab my daggers.

Stopping in front of him, I leaned to one side, resting a hand on my hip.

"Where are your guardians, little newblood?" he asked, though his gaze still lingered on my breasts rather than my face. "I was starting to think you never went anywhere without them."

"Guardians?" I replied with mock laughter. "Let's just say I have my own plans for how I spend my time."

Jarin raised a brow and finally lifted his attention to my face. "Do you now?"

I stepped close to him and brazenly slid my fingers down the muscles of his lean chest. He was thin in comparison to Asher, Darian, and Kade, but there was still strength there. For a moment, I doubted myself and whether I'd be able to get him to talk, but I pushed the doubts away. "I've been told that during the Week of Orash, anything goes. I'm hoping you might be able to give me the excitement I'm after."

He licked his dry lips. "And what kind of excitement would that be?"

I leaned in closer, ignoring my repulsion of the monster and brushing my lips across the shell of his ear. "Take me somewhere a little more private and I'll show you."

He chuckled darkly. "Now why would I do that? Having an audience is half the fun."

I cursed inwardly. I'd been worried he would say that. Biting my lip, I feigned innocence and said, "I guess I was just hoping to have you all to myself."

His eyes narrowed, and for a moment I thought he'd seen through my act, but then he smiled widely. Turning, he led me to a quieter space behind one of the archways. The moment I followed him into the shadowed area, he slammed my back against the stone of the archway. It wasn't enough to make me cry out, but I winced as pain worked its way down my spine.

"You'd better hope you're enough to satisfy me, shifter," he said gruffly in my ear, and his wet lips collided with my neck.

Bile rose in my throat as one of his hands groped at my breasts while his other hand slid down my rib cage, but I swallowed it down.

"I hear you had the pleasure of choosing the humans from the last round," I said casually as I tried to hide my disgust. *It's just groping. I can handle groping.*

"Mm-hmm," Jarin mumbled as he made an appreciative sound. One of his hands squeezed my hip, and I couldn't stop myself from squirming against his grip. Seeming not to notice, he gripped me tighter, not caring that his fingers were digging in painfully.

I cleared my throat. "It must have been fun watching them turn when you brought them here. How many turned on the first night?"

Instead of answering me, he palmed my breast while the hand that had been squeezing my hip trailed lower, his fingers starting to slide beneath my dress.

Oh, fuck this. Before he could discover the daggers on my thighs, I grabbed onto his shoulders with both my hands and drove my knee hard into his groin. Surprised, he grunted and reeled back, staggering away from me as his hands dropped to clutch at his pants.

He lifted his head and fury shone in his watery green eyes, but I didn't give him the chance to attack. In a swift movement, I'd drawn my daggers, and I shot forward until he was the one with his back pressed against a wall. Lifting my blades, I poised them under his neck, one crossed over the other. The knives were small and too short to be able to sever his head in a single clean swipe, but I would have been able to cut halfway through if I wanted, and the blood loss would have made it hard for him to retaliate.

"What is this?" he seethed, his body shaking with anger.

"Not so fun when you're the one being handled, is it, asshole?"

Jarin glared daggers at me, and I was sure he was imagining killing me in a thousand different ways. Too bad for him I wasn't going to let that happen.

"Ten years ago, you were one of the monsters who selected the humans for the trials," I snarled. "There was a pretty girl with mousy brown hair and wide brown eyes. She was only sixteen, younger than the women who are normally selected. You're going to tell me where the fuck she is."

As I spoke, Jarin's expression changed his fury morphing into something akin to fear as recognition lit his eyes.

"Where is she?" I growled in his face when he didn't answer. "And what the hell did you do to her?"

Jarin's dry lips turned into a sneer, and he opened his mouth to speak, but before any words came out, his gaze darted to where a figure stood watching us from not too far away.

Jarin's lips snapped shut, and I frowned as I made out Warrick's tall frame. The vampire stared calmly at us, his cruel black eyes filled with curiosity and amusement, but he didn't come any closer.

Fuck. I knew I should have quickly released Jarin in the hopes that Warrick hadn't overheard anything, but I was so close. Too damn close to just walk away. Turning back to Jarin, I pressed my blades harder against his neck until a trickle of blood ran down his skin. "What were you going to say?"

Genuine terror shone in Jarin's eyes now, and I wasn't foolish enough to think it was because he was afraid of me. His gaze kept frantically darting in Warrick's direction as if the older vampire's presence had him on edge. Inwardly, I cursed in frustration. I'd been so damn close to getting answers about where my sister was. My hands trembled as I held my blades tightly to Jarin's throat, anger coursing through me.

Warrick strolled toward us then, his steps slow and unhurried. "Raine, is it?" he said when he was only a few yards away. "I must congratulate you on your most impressive victory against the succubus tonight."

The cold rasp of Warrick's voice had a chill rushing down my spine, but I didn't change my position. When I didn't speak, he continued, "Whatever Jarin here has done, I assure you he's not all bad. Leave him be, and I'll ensure he never bothers you again."

Jarin's face paled at Warrick's words, and I became keenly aware of the threat behind me. Moving slowly, I pulled the blades from Jarin's throat, then I pivoted as I stepped back, making sure that both monsters were in my line of sight.

Sheathing my blades, I gave Warrick an easy smile. "Jarin seems to think all females exist only to serve his needs. I was merely trying to educate him on the matter, but I appreciate your offer. I'm sure a respected monster like yourself has a greater chance at getting the message across." All right, so I wasn't the best at flattery, but at least I wasn't lying about Jarin being a disgusting male specimen. I just hoped Warrick believed Jarin's wandering hands were the only reason I'd had my blades to the demon's throat.

Warrick tilted his head, watching me carefully as he gave me a slow nod, but the vampire didn't say anything else.

Well, that's creepy. "Uh, I'll be leaving now, then," I said awkwardly and backed away from the pair of them.

Warrick continued to stare at me intensely, his black eyes watching me until I had walked away and was again bathed in the blue light of the ballroom. I skirted around monsters and high tables until smoke drifted past, and I was sure the vampire could no longer see me. Letting out a shaky breath, I thought about making my way back to the rooms but decided it would look too suspicious if I left immediately. So instead, I found an empty chaise lounge that was far from where Jarin and Warrick had been, and I dropped onto the soft furniture.

Now that I was alone, I became more aware of the wild pounding of my heart and sweat coating my palms. I thought of the fear that had crept into Jarin's eyes the moment he'd spotted Warrick. *Why is he so afraid of the vampire?*

I wondered then whether Warrick had heard the questions I'd been asking Jarin. If he had... Realization crashed down on me, and my heart began racing faster. *Did Jarin refuse to speak because he was worried Warrick would hear him? Does Warrick know what happened to my sister?* I was only guessing, but my stomach roiled at the thought that Warrick might have had his hands on Cara. Dark thoughts entered my mind, but I pushed them away. If I thought like that, I'd never find her.

There are thousands of monsters in the city, possibly hundreds of thousands, and they can't all attend the Week of Orash. Even if Warrick does know something about her location, it doesn't mean she's dead, I consoled myself.

Goddess, I needed something. Something that would help me survive the nightmare I was in. A satyr approached me with a tray of goblets balanced on one hand, and I lifted as I gratefully took two of them. Fizzy pink liquid almost sloshed over the sides of the goblets as I sat back down, and I downed the contents of one goblet and then the other.

Placing the empty goblets on a side table, I stood as I contemplated hunting the satyr down for a third, but a hand grabbed my arm and swung me around. Instinctively, I bent and grabbed a goblet with the intention of throwing it at my attacker's face, but Locke's smooth voice had my body relaxing, despite the words that came from his mouth.

"What are you doing here?" Locke asked harshly. His onyx eyes burned with anger as he peered around us like he was ready to maim any monster within my vicinity.

The bond between us hummed at the contact of his fingers on my arm, but I ignored it as I held up the empty goblet and forced myself to grin. "Asher said this place becomes quite the party as the night wears on. I wanted to see it for myself."

Suspicion shone in Locke's gaze, and I felt the need to really sell the lie.

Not too far away, two monsters with silky blue skin were enjoying each other's company, and I gestured to them with my head. The male's muscles flexed as he rutted into the female from behind, and I curved my lips into an appreciative smile. "I thought I could have as much fun as I want until I join a house?"

Locke's gaze raked over the monsters, and his expression hardened as he released my arm. "It's not safe for you here. Monsters are unpredictable, especially when they've been drinking or taking Silver Sand. I'm taking you back to the rooms. *Now*."

"Well, you're no fun," I said, acting disappointed, but relief went through me as he led me from the ballroom. In truth, I wanted nothing more than to be away from the eyes of monsters. I hadn't spotted Warrick or Jarin again, but I couldn't shake the feeling that I was being watched.

Locke walked me briskly down the tunnels that wound toward the rooms we stayed in, and we were halfway back when the two goblets of wine I'd consumed started making my head buzz. A giddy smile had climbed its way onto my face when Locke stopped abruptly and pushed me against the wall of the tunnel. The air rushed from my lungs as I let out an "oof." *Seriously, what is it with monsters and walls?* I was going to have some bruises peppering my spine when the night was over.

"You don't ever go to the parties by yourself," Locke ground out. "Do you think this is some sort of a game?" Fury twisted his serious features, but I was finding it hard to keep a straight face. I wasn't sure if I should have been annoyed at myself for being stupid enough to down two goblets of wine when I was so vulnerable or if I should have been glad because it made tolerating Locke's intensity way more bearable. *I'm going to go with "glad" right now.*

It crossed my mind that it wasn't long ago that Jarin had pressed my back to a wall, but this was nothing like it had been with Jarin. There was something about Locke that made me feel safe when I was with him. The bond between us made me want to pull him closer, and my hands felt useless at my sides. Still, I managed to glare at the vampire.

"Get your hands off me, Locke. If I want to have fun while I'm still not tied to one of your damn houses, I will." I couldn't tell Locke about my plans to find Cara. Now that I suspected his father knew about her whereabouts, it was just another reason for me not to trust him. For all I knew, he was part of whatever had happened.

I had expected Locke to threaten me and give me some lecture about how until he found a way to break the bond between us, I had to lie low, but instead, a cold hand slid up between my thighs, and I sucked in a sharp breath. A slight smile lifted Locke's lips as he brushed his fingers over my daggers, then he ran his fingers along my panties, pressing the fabric against my sensitive spot.

"I thought Kade, Asher, And Darian were giving you all the 'fun' you needed," he said against my ear. His cool breath tickled my skin, sending a pleasant shiver through me, and the faintest hint of longing sounded in his voice.

Pretending I didn't know what he was talking about, I said, "As much as I love to train, it's not quite—" I didn't finish. My words caught in my throat as Locke pulled my panties to the side and slid two fingers up and down my center. He stroked through the wetness between my thighs as if he was savoring the feel of me, and my lips parted in surprise as need uncoiled in my belly.

I swallowed hard and shifted my back against the wall as his fingers circled my clit, teasing me slowly as if he had all the time in the world. Gritting my teeth, I stopped myself from begging him to give me more.

He smirked down at me. "If you need something, human, you ask us. No one else." His face grew serious then, his brows lowering as he got right in my face. "Do you understand?"

Opening my mouth, I went to protest because, you know, fuck orders, but he trailed his fingers lower, sliding the tip of one of them into me, and I nodded instead. "Yes," I breathed.

"What was that?" he asked as he continued to tease my entrance.

"Yes," I said, louder this time. "I'll ask you guys if I need something."

He teased me for a moment longer, his black eyes fixed on my face as if he didn't quite believe me, but then he said, "Good." Pushing his finger into me, he slid it in as far as he could before pulling it back out. My breath hitched at the sudden sensation of him moving it in and out of me, and my back arched against the wall, my hands stretching out and my fingers pressing against the cool rock.

Locke braced himself against the wall with a hand above my head, and his nose dipped to the curve of my neck, his cold lips brushing against my skin. He moved his slick finger faster inside me, and I bit my lip to keep from moaning. *Oh fuck.* I wanted more. So much more, and I cursed the stupid bond that was between us. It had to be the reason I wanted him so badly.

He pulled his head back, lust shining in his eyes as he took in my face. In a sudden burst of movement, his wings speared from his back, flaring in the dim blue light before curving around us, almost as if he was trying to shield me from the outside world.

My chest tightened at the thought, but I made myself focus on the pleasure building in me. On the way his fingers made me feel like nothing else mattered.

Wait. Wings? I vaguely registered what the appearance of Locke's wings meant. Usually, whenever his wings were out, his claws were too.

Panic shot through me at the idea that Locke's finger was now clawed as he fucked it into me, and I imagined myself getting mangled down below, but as he continued to finger me, it was all pleasure. As if he could sense my fear, he slowed his movements like he was trying to show me that he wouldn't hurt me. I knew I should have been disgusted at the thought of his claws. I *wanted* to feel disgusted, but even if his finger was clawed, he made me feel alive. His touch drove away thoughts of Jarin and Warrick, and somehow, even though he was the one pushing me against the wall, I felt more powerful than when I'd had my blades pressed to Jarin's neck.

Sensing that I'd calmed, Locke slid a second finger into me, and he pumped them faster inside me. The pleasure became so intense that I let go of the wall, and I buried my hands in his dark hair, enjoying the feel of his silky strands between my fingers.

He groaned at my touch and flicked at my clit with his thumb, and I gasped as a wave of pleasure rushed over me, making my head spin. Stars dotted the backs of my eyes, and I gripped him as my body shuddered. Locke's breathing was harsh, but when my body relaxed, he dropped his wings, folding them behind his back, and pulled away from me.

Cold settled into me as he moved away, my hands falling back to my sides. *Oh fuck.* I blinked as I stared at his tousled hair, still shocked at what he'd just done.

His lips quirked to the side as he stared back at me, and he lifted his hand that was still glistening with my release. Bringing his fingers to his lips, he licked them clean like I was the most delicious thing he'd eaten in ages, and as I took in his wicked claws, I swallowed. Rationally, I knew he could have made his claws appear after he'd fingered me just to mess with me, but I didn't care. As I watched him lick his lips, desire began building in me again.

"Don't go searching for fun outside our rooms again, Raine," he said, and then he turned toward the tunnel again and began walking.

His words echoed in my head, and I couldn't help but wonder what he was implying. That I could have fun with anyone in the rooms? Did that also include him?

Pushing off from the wall, I straightened before smoothing down the front of my dress. Then I trailed after Locke.

· · · ● · ● · · · ·

~ Locke ~

It was hard for me to walk with a rock-hard cock between my legs rubbing painfully against my leather pants. I thought about asking if Raine would give me a hand, but I knew I shouldn't. She'd seemed to enjoy my company enough, but I hadn't meant to pleasure her. I'd intentionally been keeping my distance, watching from afar while my brothers stayed by her side during the parties. With every night she stayed in our rooms, I felt my desire for her grow, and that was dangerous. I had more enemies than my brothers had, and the scent of her blood called to me, making me want to drown in her. I didn't need my father setting any more of his attention on her either.

While Kade, Asher, and Darian had dark pasts, they weren't like me. They hadn't been twisted like I had been when I was a child. I knew they saw me as the strongest of us, but at times, it felt far from the truth. I was unhinged and fueled by anger. No, I'd keep away from her. I'd find a way to break our bond, and then she'd be free of me. I didn't acknowledge how that made me feel.

The incredible taste of her lingered on my tongue, and I could still feel her phantom hands buried deep in my hair. When Raine had told me she was at the party to have fun with other monsters, I'd suspected she was lying, but the idea of it still drove me mad. I had become overwhelmed with the irrational need to erase the thoughts of any other fucking monsters from her mind.

It didn't bother me that she spent time with Kade and Darian, and I wouldn't have cared if she'd been with Asher. But the thought of her with an outsider had fury burning through me, even though I knew it was what I wanted. She needed to join a house and find a place in Katakin away from us, but we were still bonded. I told myself the bond was the only reason I cared who she was with and when the connection between us was broken, I'd have no trouble sending her on her way, but deep inside, I knew there was more to it than that.

Fuck, I hated to imagine what would have happened if I hadn't still been at the party. When Kade and the others had left, I'd stayed behind. I'd spotted one of the monsters who'd witnessed the last outlier attack, and I'd taken the opportunity to speak with them. When I had first noticed Raine's scents of coconut and steel a while later, I'd thought I was going crazy. That my borderline obsession with her was messing with my mind. But then I'd detected her again, getting hints of those same delicious scents that made my mouth water and my pants tighten. I'd gone searching, half expecting I'd come up empty-handed, but then she was there before me.

At first, fear went through me as I wondered whether she'd been hurt. Whether some monster had dragged her there to have his way. The most depraved tortures went through my mind as I thought of what I'd do to any monster who touched her against her will, but a quick assessment of her body calmed me.

Fucking Halced, what is happening with this female? I'd never had those feelings when I'd been with any other monster.

I thought again of how wet she'd been for me, and my gaze slid to where she walked at my side. I wanted nothing more than to pick up where we'd left off. To press her against the wall and fuck her until she stopped biting her beautiful pink lips and gave in, crying out my name as the pleasure drove her mad. But instead, I rolled my shoulders and kept striding forward, using what willpower I had to concentrate on keeping my hands to my fucking self.

CHAPTER 21

~ Raine ~

The next night, I was glad to learn I didn't have to fight. All the newbloods who had lost the first group fight were given the chance to battle against one another in a kind of redemption fight. The winner would redeem themselves and gain a spot with the finalists the following night.

I sat in the stands with Asher and Kade on one side and Darian and Locke on the other. Locke hadn't spoken to me since our time in the tunnel, and that suited me just fine. It was easier to imagine he'd simply had a lapse in judgment than contemplate whether there was any other reason for his actions.

I wiggled on the stone seat and focused my attention on the sandy arena below us. The fight had just begun, and all six of the newbloods were quick to go on the offensive, attacking the others as if they were determined to repair any damage to their reputations.

The two sirens stayed close to one another as they fought, but before they were able to sing a single note, the ogre had them down with two harsh blows to their heads. On the other end of the fighting sands, the banshee and two demons were battling it out in hand-to-hand combat. The banshee delivered quick punches to the demons, then she opened her mouth and wailed.

Immediately, I covered my ears, as did the other monsters in the stands, but the ogre and one of the demons went down hard. Black blood oozed from their ears as they writhed on the ground in pain before falling still. If I hadn't known death was against the rules, I would have worried they'd been killed. Within a matter of minutes, only the banshee and a single demon remained standing.

I was surprised to find that the demon was Bri, the girl from my village with chestnut-colored hair and green eyes that shone like emeralds. Small green horns peeked from her hair, and her forked green tail hovered in the air behind her.

Bri had always been a placid, quiet person, and as far as I was aware, she had never fought before arriving in Katakin. Now she kept her ears covered with her hands, and she launched herself at the banshee. The narrow tip of her boot collided with the banshee's throat, making the female cut off her wail and splutter instead, and Bri's triumphant smile was terrifying. The banshee clutched at her neck, and

Bri followed up with a back kick to the banshee's chest that left the banshee sprawling to the ground, gasping for air.

The crowd went wild at the violence, their bloodthirsty howls and cries making my skin crawl. Across from us, Borren, the demon alpha of the House of Thorem, was eyeing Bri with more interest and appreciation than I'd seen him show toward her during the previous nights. From the way Bri's sharp gaze found his, I was guessing it was exactly the attention she was hoping for. I wondered whether Borren would be interested in offering her a place at his house, and even if he'd want Bri as his mate. Kade had explained that monsters chose the strongest mates they could find, and I had no idea if Bri had shown she was powerful enough for the demon alpha.

Henral, the centaur who always spoke at these events, announced Bri's victory to the crowd, and once again, my eardrums protested at the deafening cheers that followed.

Bri's grin stretched wider as she beamed at the applause, and I was happy for her. I might not have been willing to accept a place for myself in Katakin yet, but I was glad she had.

"That didn't take long," Asher mused from my left side. He was leaning back with his hands folded behind his head and his booted feet on the railing in front of him.

"Sirens and banshees always make the mistake of thinking their voice is their strongest weapon," Darian said thoughtfully, as though the three newbloods were his pupils and he was disappointed in them.

"But isn't it?" I asked, turning to him with a frown. "I mean, the banshee almost won just by wailing."

"It is the most powerful weapon they wield, but I believe all monsters are only as strong as their entire body, no matter the power they have. For sirens, the gift of song works better when combined with other assets like combat skills and fast reflexes. It's too risky to rely on one's powers alone because if that's their only strength, as soon as it's gone, they have nothing. As we have seen tonight and also the other night when you won against Samara."

Right, Samara. The succubus who tried to get me to eat her out.

As if he was having a similar thought, Kade's face hardened. He hadn't said much about Zacal or Samara since that fight, but I could tell it was still bothering him.

Sighing, I forced my attention back to the arena. Bri had been escorted from the sands, and monsters were beginning to retrieve the unconscious newbloods. Now that the fight was over, monsters in the stands began to rise and shuffle down the rows of seating as they filtered from the area.

"We should get going," Kade said as the wraith who had been sitting on his left side disappeared, his ghostly body vanishing into thin air. Kade stood, and Asher followed. I moved behind them, and we began picking our way to the aisle.

Seriously handy, I thought as I passed the empty seat where the wraith had just been. *Maybe I should rethink my monster preferences. Being a wraith looks like it would have a lot of advantages.*

Darian and Locke walked behind me, and the siren must have noticed my hesitation. Moving closer, he leaned down and whispered in my ear, "Trust me, it's not as fun as it sounds, lovely. You'll want to be solid when I touch you, not slipping through my fingers like smoke." One of his hands gripped my waist, and I shuddered at the contact.

Before me, Asher's steps stopped, and he twisted his head back to grin at us. "Can't say being a wraith would be my pick, but we'd make it work."

I stared at him incredulously. *Goddess, why are we even discussing this? It's like I can't even have a private thought anymore.* "It's not like I get to pick anything," I retorted, but Darian shuffled closer to me, and the hardness in his pants prodded against my back, distracting me. My throat dried out, and I swallowed as desire ignited within me.

I fought against the bond that sparked between us and went to step forward. Only, I'd forgotten Asher was standing still, and as I moved, his perfectly shaped ass pressed against my front.

"I thought we were getting out of here?" I said through gritted teeth, pretending as if being sandwiched between two sexy-as-sin monsters wasn't making me feel lightheaded.

Asher turned his head to give me a crooked grin, but he started moving again, and I focused on trying to keep my breathing steady as we left the stands.

"You all right there, Sharachi?" Asher asked with a knowing smirk as we stepped out into the tunnel that led down into the mountain.

I narrowed my eyes at him in annoyance. "Just peachy," I said with a smile. My gaze trailed from him to a smug-looking Darian, and I added, "It's a good thing we're attending the after-party. I need wine if I'm going to deal with you two."

· · · · · ● · ● · · ·

The night was growing late, and the upbeat tempo of the band's music filled my ears. After only stopping at our rooms briefly to change, we'd made our way to the ballroom to fulfill our obligation to make an appearance at the party. Because I hadn't participated in the fight that night, there were fewer monsters who were vying for my attention, but that suited me just fine. I was quite happy for them to flock to Bri and offer their congratulations. Besides, Bri didn't look like she minded.

Lifting my goblet, I downed the remainder of my wine, enjoying the way the fizzy alcohol warmed my chest. "So, what poison is on display tonight?" I asked, indicating to the nearby vase, which held a stunning bouquet of scarlet roses.

"That would be paralysis for an hour and nightmares for a week," Asher answered casually from beside me.

I gaped at him. "Paralysis? And let me guess, death for any human who touched it?"

"Actually, it would be agonizing pain for a night while the human was paralyzed and plagued by nightmares, and then it would be death," Darian added in a matter-of-fact voice as he held up a slender finger.

Oh, great. Is that all?

"Stay away from them," Kade growled as if he thought I'd be dumb enough to touch them. His confidence in me was inspiring.

"Yes, because I'm about to just willingly go near the death flowers," I retorted dryly.

"It wouldn't be the first time you'd done somethin' stupid," Asher said with a shrug.

"You do seem to have little regard for your own well-being," Darian added.

Hey! I opened my mouth to argue but shut it soon after when I thought of all I'd done since arriving in Katakin. I *had* stabbed Asher and tried to kill Kade while he slept. Not to mention the fact I made sure I'd gotten chosen for the selection in the first place by insulting Locke. They had a point. Still, I didn't like them banding together against me.

"Funny, I remember you were all the ones putting me in less-than-desirable situations," I said.

"Yeah, but you wouldn't have died," Asher pointed out. "You just thought you would."

Unbelievable. I refused to argue with him any longer and turned my attention back to the flowers. There were dozens of vases with the roses around the room, all of them propped on high tables and short stone pillars. Even though I guessed the monsters all knew they were poisonous, none of them seemed to care about getting close to them so long as they weren't touching the delicate decorations. *Ballsy.*

I remembered what Asher had said about them being there because monsters had a sick sense of humor. "How often do monsters accidentally touch them?"

Darian pulled his own goblet away from his lips. "I dare say, almost never."

"Except when they're given a helpin' hand," Asher said with a mischievous grin, and he started moving to a group of monsters not too far away.

A male troll stood talking to three female goblins, and it was clear from his flirtatious grin that he was trying to get more out of them than just friendly conversation. I couldn't hear what he was saying, but the females shifted uncomfortably and looked as though they were trying to move away from him. Seeming not to get the hint, or perhaps he didn't care, the troll kept stepping toward them, encroaching into their personal space. The huge monster swayed on his feet, liquid sloshing from the cup in his left hand. Some of his drink landed on the chest of the goblin in the middle, and she stared down in horror at her soiled dress. The troll was so focused on the goblin closest to him that he didn't notice the other female's distress, and neither did he sense Asher approaching. At least, not until the gazes of the females darted toward Asher, but by then, it was too late.

"He wouldn't," I whispered, clapping a hand over my mouth as I stared on in amusement.

"He would," Kade answered seriously.

As if to confirm Kade's point, Asher grinned back at us and then pretended to slip. His shoulder slammed into the troll's, and the other male couldn't stop himself. The goblins cried out in shock as the troll stumbled to the side and his head became buried in the bouquet of roses.

The troll shouted and quickly lifted himself, but before his massive fist could swipe at Asher, his body locked up and his hands fell limp at his sides, his goblet clattering to the floor. The troll's legs buckled, and he toppled away from the table, his body falling heavily to the ground.

The goblins blinked as they stared at the paralyzed troll, and Asher gave them that lopsided smile of his. "Ladies," he said, and he strode back to us with the stupidest grin on his face.

I stifled my laughter as the goblins, who had regained their composure, prodded at the troll with their heeled feet. When they were sure he wouldn't move, they all poured the remainder of their drinks onto him before disappearing into the crowd.

"Was that really necessary?" Darian asked Asher with a reprimanding tone when the demon had joined us again.

"I was just givin' Raine a demonstration," Asher replied innocently, taking his spot beside us.

I grinned at Asher, somehow certain that he'd just used me as an excuse to help the goblins out. Asher cared more than he would admit. The monsters of Katakin definitely didn't deserve him.

"Is anyone going to carry him away?" I asked thoughtfully as I eyed the troll, who was still prone on the floor. Monsters were passing by him as if he was nothing but another piece of furniture.

Asher shrugged. "That guy would weigh a ton, and I get the feelin' he doesn't have many friends. Either someone from his house will collect him soon, or he'll move when the paralysis wears off."

"And won't he be mad at you when he can move again?" I asked.

He nodded. "Yep."

"And you're not worried?"

"Nope."

Huh. I wasn't sure if Asher's lack of concern was because he thought he could easily best the troll or because there was a reason he knew the troll wouldn't be able to attack him, but I didn't prod any further.

By now, the three goblets of wine I'd consumed had made my head blissfully light, and the pounding of the music was making my body move involuntarily. Aside from when I'd danced with Darian, I hadn't danced since before Cara had been taken. I *didn't* dance, but Darian had shown me how expressive it could be. It was like fighting, just without any weapons involved. My fingers twitched as I wished I was practicing knife throwing or moving around an obstacle course, though I knew I'd probably be abysmal at those activities in my current state. In any case, right then I couldn't do either of those, so dancing it was.

Understanding what I was doing, Darian, Kade, and Asher followed me to a more open space closer to the band, where countless other monsters were moving their bodies to the music. Smoke curled around the dancers, and the scent of ash and the sweet smell of roses hung in the air. I stared back at the three males, who were eyeing me curiously.

If I'd been in a rational state of mind, I would have known it was a bad idea to tease them, but right then I didn't care. I hadn't seen Warrick or Jarin all night, and I couldn't help but feel like it was a bad sign. As the hours passed, I grew more on edge, and I didn't need any of the alphas thinking I was acting suspiciously. So, I had downed the wine. I had no plans for later that night, and dancing with the monsters wasn't going to change anything. Closing my eyes, I moved my body to the beat and let the music flow through me, the deep notes sinking into my bones.

At first, I danced on my own, swaying my hips from side to side and reaching my arms into the air as if I was trying to touch invisible stars above me, but then three hard bodies crowded around me, moving in time to the thudding beat as they flowed with me.

I breathed in Kade's scents of sandalwood and coffee, Darian's sea salt and patchouli, and Asher's musk and leather, and my body loosened even more. Deep in my heart, I couldn't help feeling I was right where I needed to be, but there was an odd, niggling thought in my mind. As though *someone* was missing.

Opening my eyes, I peered out through the gap between Darian's and Kade's broad chests to where Locke stood leaning against a far wall, his dark gaze watching us intently. I had the sudden urge to beckon him over to us, but I didn't. He knew where I was. Dismissing the vampire, I focused on the sound of the music.

By the time the next song started, with the alcohol in my system and the heady scents of Kade, Darian, and Asher around me, I forgot all about why it was a good idea for me to keep my distance from the monsters. The urge to get close to them made my body tingle, and I stopped fighting it.

Spinning around, I planted my lips on Kade's and melted against him. My tongue slid into his mouth, and he responded, his own tongue tangling with mine. His large hands curled into the small of my back, pressing me harder against him as our bodies moved to the rhythm of the music.

When I finally pulled back, another set of hands found their way onto my body, and Darian's mouth was on my neck. I twisted my head in his direction, savoring the feel of his lips on my skin.

Asher closed in on my other side, trapping me between him and Darian, and I slid my hands up Asher's hard chest. He grabbed my hips as I swayed my ass, and it wasn't long until I was pressed against him, and he was crushing his lips against mine.

The songs passed in a blur of us teasing one another and me enjoying the way they stared only at me. When the last song was coming to an end, Darian's lips brushed against my ear. "As much as I hate to say it, it's almost dawn, lovely. We should return to our rooms."

I responded by leaning back against him and sliding my hands behind me until I was rubbing at the hardness in his pants. "So soon?" I said, innocently blinking up at him.

His teeth clamped onto my earlobe, and he grabbed me between my legs and pulled me harder against him. I bit my lip to stop from moaning.

"Unless you want us taking you right here in front of everyone, we might want to head back," Kade growled from next to Darian. Smoke curled around his face, and his golden eyes glowed as he spoke. From his expression, I knew he was serious and need clenched low in my belly. Was I really willing to sleep with them? I'd only intended to dance and let off some steam, but I couldn't deny that I wanted more. So much more. "We'd better get going, then," I said with a smile.

Kade's response was to let out a growl that had wetness sliding down my thighs, and he lifted his chin to the others. "Let's go."

I stumbled as we moved toward the doors. I wasn't sure if the strong pink wine I'd consumed was to blame or if it was because of the bond and the fact I'd been around Darian and the others for so long, but Asher lifted me into his arms, and I buried my head into his chest, breathing him in as he carried me the rest of the way.

CHAPTER 22

~ Raine ~

When we were back in the common room, Asher propped me on my feet. My head still buzzed, but the sensible voice in my head had me second-guessing the situation I found myself in. I mean, what the hell was a female supposed to do with three dicks at once? It wasn't exactly a question I'd ever thought I'd be asking myself.

"You sure you wanna do this, Sharachi?" Asher asked, and I turned my head to him. In the time I'd been standing there, he'd already peeled off his shirt and he stood there half-naked, his pants low enough that his magnificent *V* was on full display. I knew I should have said 'no.' I shouldn't have wanted the monsters, but I did.

I craved all of them, and I was starting to realize I didn't care if it was the bond or not. I was beginning to feel as though I belonged with these monsters, and one night with all three of them wouldn't kill me. Or so I hoped.

I must have been drooling as I stared at Asher because when I didn't immediately respond, Darian said, "I'm guessing that's a 'yes'." He'd appeared on my other side holding a goblet of wine.

"Ash, do you mind? Your bed's the biggest," Kade asked from behind me.

The playful grin that Asher gave us had my stomach doing flips. "It's about bloody time," he said and strode toward his room.

I laughed and followed him. Asher's bedroom was similar to Kade's and Darian's, except his bed was indeed the largest. The four-poster frame had patterns carved into the mahogany wood, and the mattress looked as though it was wide enough to fit at least six monsters. Above the bed, two massive axes were crossed over each other and suspended from the wall. The silver steel gleamed wickedly in the dim blue light coming from the torches around the room, and the intricate swirls on the weapons had me eyeing them in appreciation.

Asher moved to my side. "Forged them right before we learned we were in charge of the selection for this round of newbloods. Figured they'd brighten up the room."

Grinning at me, his stomach crunched as he jumped onto the bed, and he stretched himself out, propping an elbow under his head to keep it upright.

Darian moved gracefully onto the bed next to Asher, his goblet now nowhere to be seen, and the pair of them looked like sexy gods who had just fallen from above. *No, not gods,* I reminded myself. *Monsters.* But staring at them, I was really starting to wonder at the difference.

Turning my head to the side, I asked Kade, "Can you get my straps?"

He stepped up behind me, and his hands moved to untie the silk ribbons behind my back. When they were loose enough, the dress slid from me and pooled onto the ground. I dropped my panties next and slid my heels from my feet before stepping ass naked over my dress and crawling onto the bed, taking up the empty space between Darian and Asher. I didn't give myself time to second-guess what I was doing. I wanted this, and so did they.

Turning toward Darian, I leaned into him, my blood pounding at my throat. Lifting a hand, I ran my fingers along his smooth jaw, and he moved forward, pressing his lips to mine. The kiss was slow and unhurried, as if Darian planned to make the moment last as long as possible, and I reveled in the taste of his sweetness with hints of the sea on his tongue. My chest warmed as the bond between us urged me to get closer to him, and my hand slid along his muscled arm.

Asher shuffled closer behind me, and then his warm lips were kissing my shoulder as he wrapped an arm around me, his large hand splaying over my belly. A rustling sounded as clothes fell to the floor, and then there was movement near my feet. A moment later, Kade's warm tongue was sliding up my bare legs, and I shivered in anticipation.

Breaking from Darian's kiss, I turned to Asher, my lips finding his instead. His tongue dominated mine in the most delicious way, and I let him push my back against the bed, my head sinking into the pillow. He reached a hand up and massaged one of my breasts, his thumb rubbing over my hardened nipple.

Darian undressed to the side of the bed as Kade's tongue licked higher. When Kade reached the apex of my thighs, his hands moved my legs apart. He kept kissing and licking my inner thighs as his hand reached forward, and he slid a finger along my center. My mouth parted in a gasp at the sudden sensation, and Asher moved his lips from my mouth to the breast he'd been working on.

Kade's fingers circled my clit, and then he slid them into me, his tongue licking at my clit instead. *Oh fuck.* I bit my lip as pleasure wound through me. Darian climbed back onto the bed and kissed the curve of my neck as his hand worked on my other breast. My eyes closed, and I moaned at the feeling of being touched in so many places at once.

Kade kissed and licked me, his fingers fucking into me until I was a panting mess and close to exploding, but before I could crash over, he pulled back. My eyes flew open, and I was about to protest when he lifted my legs. I kept them straight as he rested them against his shoulders, my feet reaching past his ears, and he grabbed under me, lifting me until his hard cock was prodding at my entrance.

Holy goddess.

Asher moved away to undress his bottom half, and Darian gave both my breasts attention as Kade's cock slid inside me. I let out a cry of pleasure, and an answering growl rumbled in Kade's chest.

"You like him filling you, don't you, lovely?" Darian lifted his head to purr in my ear, and I sucked in a sharp breath at his dirty words.

Kade's eyes blazed gold as he continued to move his cock in and out of me, and I grabbed onto the sheets, crushing the fabric in my fists.

Fangs peeked from Kade's mouth, and he shook his head and snarled, making a sound that was more animal than usual. The fangs shrank down to rounded teeth again, and Kade barked at Darian, "Dar, don't use your fucking power this time."

"I make no promises," Darian responded with a sly smile, and I chuckled at the pair of them.

My laughter was cut off as Kade began fucking me harder, the muscles of his shoulders and biceps bunching as he drove his huge length deeper inside me, moving in and out of me at a relentless pace again and again as he drove me to oblivion.

Darian sat back on his knees and flicked at my clit, and I gasped. Reaching out, I wrapped my left hand around his massive cock and began stroking him. He moaned at my touch, and I grinned at the sound.

Asher moved back on the bed and sidled up to me again. With Darian's fingers on my clit, Kade's cock pounding inside me, and Asher's teeth clamping over my nipple, I crashed over, the climax rushing through me as I arched my back and let out a panting cry. Tingles spread over me, goosebumps prickling my skin, and Kade pumped into me a few more times before he growled and found his own release, spilling inside me. I shuddered with the aftershocks of my orgasm, my chest rising and falling rapidly.

Gently, Kade pulled out of me and moved my legs from his shoulders before lowering me to the bed. Leaning over me, he pressed a soft kiss to my lips and pulled back again. His eyes were glowing golden, but he remained in his human form.

"Didn't want to find yourself kissing Darian again?" I asked with a grin between heaving breaths.

His brows lowered, his face becoming serious. "No" was his only response, and Asher, Darian, and I all cackled.

Kade moved back, and Darian, who had stopped playing with me when Kade set me down, ran his finger up and down my center. I didn't think I'd want more after the orgasm I'd just had, but desire built in me again. When Asher sucked on my earlobe, his teeth lightly grazing my skin, and his hands found their way to my breasts, I was already squirming with need again.

"Get on your hands and knees for us, lovely," Darian ordered, and my gaze lowered to take in Asher's cock. It was almost as long as Darian's but thicker with more of a curve, and metal piercings ran down its length. *Whoa.* I swallowed in intimidation at the sight of it, but I moved as Darian asked until I was on my hands and knees, my ass bared to the cool air.

Asher moved behind me, his hard cock pressing against my ass cheeks while Darian moved closer to my head. I raised a brow at Darian as he positioned himself so his cock was close to my head.

"Yeah, I see what you think's going to happen, but I'm not sure if you know, but your cock is monstrous. If I try to go all the way down on that thing, I'm going to choke to death," I pointed out.

Darian's abs tensed as he laughed. When his laughter died down, he said, "Just do whatever you feel comfortable with. But I suggest you refrain from using your eye."

I made a face, remembering how his cock had smacked my eye when we were in the garden. Before I could come up with a retort, Asher reached under me, sliding his fingers along my wetness, and his touch had my words dissolving in my throat. The constant need I had to always be with them flared again as his fingers worked on me, and then he was sliding the tip of his cock into me. His hands gripped my hips as he teased me, never letting his cock slip in past the head.

Letting out a huff, I pushed my hips back, but his hands held me tightly, not letting him sink in any further.

Asher chuckled. "Not yet, sweetheart."

Frustrated, I stretched my neck out. Darian had been stroking his cock in front of me, and I took him in my mouth, glad to be doing something to get my mind off Asher's relentless teasing.

"Seven devils," Darian cursed under his breath as I worked on him. Reaching down, he pulled my hair into a ponytail behind my head and tugged. The slight sting of pain on my scalp had a moan escaping from me, and I took more of him into my mouth until his cock hit the back of my throat, and my eyes began to water.

"Fuck, Raine," Asher rasped, and as if he was rewarding me, he pushed his cock into me. I was so slick from Kade's release that there was only a slight sting due to his thickness, and then it was all pleasure. His piercings hit places inside me that made my eyes roll to the back of my head, and I squirmed at the onslaught of sensation.

As Asher fucked me from behind, Darian dominated my mouth, and the pair of them moved in tandem, the tug of Darian's hands on my hair bringing me closer to another release.

Kade pressed soft kisses to my back and peered at my face. "You all right there, Mahare?"

I was so consumed with pleasure that I barely registered his words. I mumbled a yes that came out as more of a mewl, and Kade smiled, "That's our Raine."

My chest warmed. *Our Raine.* Determined not to think about how those two words made my heart ache, I flicked my tongue over Darian's cock until the siren was groaning and spilling into my mouth. Swallowing, I let him pull away, and Asher reached out for me. With Kade's help, he lifted me until I was upright with Asher resting on his knees behind me. My legs shook, but his hands cupped under my ass as he lifted me up and down on his length, making me gasp as he buried deep inside me.

Asher leaned forward to kiss my neck, and I reached back, trying to touch him. Instead of my fingers digging into his shaggy hair, my hands brushed along his horns. His whole body froze as he tensed at the touch, and I realized what I'd done. *Shit.* I thought of what Asher had revealed to me about his past and his mother. I wasn't exactly sure what his mother had done to him, but I suspected his horns might be another sensitive issue.

"Sorry," I said, hastily pulling my hands back. I went to move away, thinking he'd want me off him, but he held me in an iron grip.

"You good, Ash?" Darian said from close by.

A few beats passed as Asher's breathing calmed, but then he said to me, "You're not going anywhere, sweetheart. Just... not the horns."

My throat tightened at the way his voice cracked, but I nodded. Slowly, he relaxed and began moving me again. It didn't take long before pleasure made me clench around him, and sweat was beading on my brow.

Darian reached down to circle my clit with his fingers while Asher moved deep inside me, and soon I was crashing again, pleasure whipping through me as Asher roared his own release. When our shudders subsided, Asher's head tipped down, and he nuzzled my neck, his breath hot on my skin. Darian helped me move further back on the bed and pulled me against his chest while Kade helped clean me.

Lifting my hand, Darian kissed it before peppering soft kisses up my arm, over my collarbone, and up my neck. Unable to help myself, I laughed at the almost ticklish sensation, but he cut off my laugh with a kiss to my lips that took my breath away. When he pulled back, he said, "You, my dear, are even more of a treasure than I thought you would be."

A treasure? The sincere expression on his flawless face left me speechless.

I stared at his glowing blue eyes until Kade dropped down on my other side and turned me toward him. Leaning down, Kade pressed a soft kiss to my slick forehead. "We're going to have to find a way to break the rules, Mahare. Because there's no way you're leaving us to join a house."

I swallowed down the lump building in my throat. "And what if that's what I want?"

"*Do* you want to join a house?" Asher asked from where he'd stretched across the end of the bed. He'd pulled on his pants, but his chest was still bare, and I didn't miss the fact that he'd moved close enough to allow my feet to touch his abdomen.

"No, of course not," I said automatically, and the three monsters around me relaxed at my response.

I knew then that I should have said yes. Because even though I wasn't planning to join a house, if Cara wanted to return to our island, I would escape with her in a heartbeat. If I made them think I was planning to join a house, it would have made the transition easier, even though I was becoming painfully aware of how much a part of me didn't want to ever leave them.

"Well, I guess we'd better get Locke on board, then," Asher said with a grin, and he reached down and began massaging my feet.

I groaned and closed my eyes as he applied pressure in all the right places. Goddess, the sex had been amazing, but Asher's hands on my feet were downright magical.

No one talked about the Taratun council and how the idea of me staying with them was impossible. They didn't even have a house, and I was a newblood. If anything, the parties during the Week of Orash had shown me how I was expected to join a house and integrate into their society. I didn't think they'd be happy if I decided to join Kade and the others.

But Asher simply kept massaging my feet, and I gave in to the lull of sleep with Kade and Darian pressed by my sides.

CHAPTER 23

~ **Locke** ~

I watched from a shadowy corner as Raine danced to the thudding tempo that filled the ballroom. The result of multiple glasses of wine had made her cheeks red and her eyes glassy, and she danced as if she was determined to forget about the world. I didn't blame her. Kade, Darian, and Asher surrounded her, and I found myself wanting to join them.

My need for the little human had only grown since I'd tasted her in the tunnel, and being away from her was all but driving me mad. But I didn't move from my spot. Raine was an enigma. A distraction. And I couldn't let myself be drawn into that. More than that, I couldn't let her be drawn to me. Being with me would bring her nothing but pain. I hadn't found a way to break the bond between us, but I would, and then she'd be free to join a house. I didn't let myself wonder whether she wanted me to break it. She couldn't stay tied to us.

The night bled by, and eventually, Raine and my brothers left the party. Rather than follow them, I left the ballroom and headed higher up the mountain. Finding the exit I was after, I made my way onto a small balcony, and then I was in the air with the cool wind sliding past my wings.

It wasn't long after that I landed on a cobblestoned street in the heart of the city. I avoided the blue light of the lanterns, sticking to the shadows and making my way to the back of a dark stone building. It didn't take me long to pry open the lock, and then I was inside the massive, domed structure, my feet barely disturbing the dust coating the blue and white checkered floor of the ancient library.

Watery moonlight shone through the domed glass ceiling above my head, and I peered around at the stained wood shelves that covered the curved walls of the building and the hundreds of ancient leather-bound tomes. The woody and musty scents of the books lingered in the air, and my chest expanded as I breathed in deeply. When I exhaled, my body relaxed, and my muscles loosened for the first time that night.

It took me only a few moments to pile some books into my arms, and then I was making my way over to one of the fabric couches that sat tucked away from the great glass windows that dotted the front of the building. Placing the books on the small table next to the couch, I lit the lantern I'd left there.

I knew visiting the library for the third time in a single week was too risky, but I had to keep searching. There'd been a time when the double doors at the front of the building were always unlocked, and the space was a hive of activity rather than as quiet as Katakin's ancient graveyard. The fae queen, Izla, had frequently visited the library and often added to the shelves, bringing tomes of brightly colored fae fairy tales to add to the collection of texts, but when her curse had first spread throughout the kingdom, the city had erupted into chaos.

When the citizens discovered the queen was behind the curse, the library was just one of many places that was attacked and targeted because of her known involvement there. Thankfully, a group of monsters had banded together, saving the structure and the books within, but many of the stones on the left side of the building were still blackened, and the scorch marks forever told the tale of the incident.

Only young at the time, I couldn't recall every detail of what had happened over the months following the curse, but I remembered the Taratun barricading the doors of the library and forbidding anyone from entering it. The shelves contained mostly fictional works, and it was announced that believing in miracles was the reason we'd allowed the fae witch into our kingdom and were cursed for our hospitality. Therefore, from then on, we were only to live in the present and real world of Katakin.

Shoving thoughts of the past from my mind, I settled onto the chair and pulled one of the books in front of me. *The Broken Kingdom* by Sharou Zanae. Considering the number of works by Sharou, I guessed they were a prolific writer back in the fae kingdom of Zalei, Queen Izla's home world.

Rifling through the yellowed pages, I searched the fae fairy tale for any talk of magical bonds. I didn't bother looking for anything that hinted at curses. I'd searched these books countless times in the past and found nothing that explained how to end the curse—or rather, any talk of curses at all—but it was possible I'd missed information that indicated about bonds. I hoped to come across something that could help but found nothing but the same charming, if delusional, tale.

"Pretty sure you've read that one before," purred a voice, and I stilled, my hand pausing on the next book I'd been about to grab from the pile as Lyr materialized from the darkness. She stood near the closest row of shelves, leaning back with one leg folded over the other as if she'd been there for a while.

I frowned, annoyed that I hadn't noticed her. The female had a gift for blending with the shadows, but if I hadn't been so engrossed with the book, I would have picked up her heartbeat. It was a reminder I needed to stay vigilant.

"It's one of my favorites," I drawled. It wasn't a lie. I enjoyed the story, which spoke of a dream kingdom beyond the stars. When the people of the kingdom forgot how to dream, a monster burrowed out of the earth and tormented the city. A young boy was the one to figure out the monster was a nightmare, and they had only to dream again for the monster to disappear. When I was younger, I'd often imagined Katakin was the dream kingdom and that I'd be the one to bring us from the darkness of the curse, but I was beyond such hopes now. Especially because it had become painfully clear that I was the fucking monster, and no one was waking up from this nightmare.

"You shouldn't be here," she said. "The Taratun could have you killed or imprisoned. No one wants to remember the old ways, and looking through fae fairy tales might make you appear as a fae sympathizer."

Even though I believed Lyr would be the last person to out me to the council, I lifted to my feet and glared at the tiger shifter. "You know as well as I do that I'm no sympathizer. Why are you here, Lyr? Shouldn't you be at the party, spying on the alphas and newbloods?"

Lyr was once Queen Izla's personal spy, but though her job had ceased when the queen disappeared, she still listened to the whispers of those in Katakin and kept abreast of any rumors that floated through the high houses.

"Raine still hasn't changed," Lyr said with a matter-of-fact voice. "And I want to know what you're planning to do about it. I was passing by when I noticed you entering the back of the building. From the looks of it, you're hoping to find an explanation in these fairy tales?"

Fuck. I knew if Lyr had seen me enter the building, others could have too. I tilted my head, listening for any signs we had other company, but the library remained quiet. When I turned my attention back to Lyr, she was still staring at me expectantly. I didn't bother trying to lie. The female was as smart as she was cunning, and I didn't doubt she'd been paying special attention to Raine.

"She hasn't," I admitted, "and now that we've announced she has shifter blood, no monster will want her to join their house without seeing what she shifts into."

Lyr seemed thoughtful, but then she said, "I could offer for her to join my house."

"What?" I kept my face neutral to hide my shock. In two hundred years, Lyr had never taken an interest in the newbloods and offered them a place with her and her mates. But we were running out of options, and the urge to refuse her offer didn't leave my tongue. If it came to it, letting Raine join her house might be the best we could do.

She shrugged and rubbed her chin. "We'd have to figure out what to do when Raine does change, but it could be a solution for now."

"Why would you do that?" I asked suspiciously.

Her ice-blue eyes peered back at me, giving nothing away. "I told you, the peace in Katakin is as fragile as ever, and announcing that Raine is human would cause anarchy."

"And you've always kept to the Taratur's rules," I said dryly.

Lyr's lips quirked up at the sides. "Just know that for now, I'm also interested in keeping Raine alive. You don't tell me all your secrets now, do you?"

I resisted the urge to grab her by the neck and squeeze the information out of her. Whatever Lyr's motivations were for wanting to help Raine, I knew she wasn't just offering out of the goodness of her heart. Lyr always had a plan.

I glanced at the pile of fairy tales on the table. We were running out of options, and I had been wondering what the fuck we would do if we made it to the joining ceremony, and Raine still hadn't changed. This was the only option that seemed somewhat plausible. "I'm hoping it won't come to it, but if it does, Raine might have to accept your offer," I relented.

"I'll make sure I'm there if the time comes." Lyr purred, and then she was gone, her body having melted back into the darkness. I scowled at where the shifter had been standing. Lyr had always been true to her word, and I had no reason to doubt her now, but I still hated that she knew about Raine. Knowing I couldn't do anything about it, I sat back down and grabbed another book from the pile.

・・・・・・・・・・・

It was over an hour later when I sensed another heartbeat, and Kade entered the library. My brother smelled of sex and Raine, and those scents had my cock growing hard again. I cursed under my breath.

"I didn't think you'd come," I said, swallowing down my jealousy when he approached. Like Darian and Asher, Kade and I had shared females in the past, mostly to make sure we kept each other in check, and explicit images of Kade and I sharing Raine had me grinding my teeth in frustration.

"I always show up," Kade responded as he stopped before me.

My lips twitched at that. I could only imagine how hard it must have been for him to leave Raine with Darian and Asher rather than keep enjoying her.

"Find anything?" he asked.

I shook my head. "Maybe this is a fucking fool's errand."

"It's better than doing nothing. What are we going to do if Raine doesn't change soon? We're lucky no one's said much about her not shifting so far. Even if she wins the fights, if she doesn't shift soon, the alphas will think she's weak."

Sighing heavily, I leaned back in my chair. "Lyr was here. She offered to let Raine join her house if none of the other monsters will have her."

"Raine's not joining anyone's house," Kade growled. "She's staying with us."

"We have nothing to offer her," I said bitterly.

"We'll make it work, even if it means running from the Taratun."

There's nowhere for us to run, I thought, but I didn't say it. Kade's glowing golden eyes showed just how close he was to shifting, and there was no point in us arguing. Not when I wanted the same thing he did, as reluctant as I was to admit it.

I tipped my head toward the shelves where I'd pulled my books from. "Are we going to talk all night, or are you here to help?"

Kade grunted, but he moved over to the shelf and pulled out his own stack of books. "We're making this work, Locke," he growled as he dropped down next to me. I didn't answer.

CHAPTER 24

"Great work out there," I said, bumping Raine with my shoulder as we walked down the tunnel back to our rooms. "Knew you'd win against that demon."

She blew out a long breath. "Piece of cake." Sweat covered her brow, but otherwise, she appeared untouched.

"Don't pretend you weren't shitting yourself like the rest of us," Kade said from behind me.

Raine turned to stare at me with a raised brow, but I kept my face sincere. "Never doubted you, Sharachi."

She smiled, and I could tell she didn't believe me, but what was I going to say? *You're a great fighter, but it was a bit hairy there for a while. I was sure you were goin' to get yourself sliced and reveal you're still a human. Then I planned to leap over the railing and fight any monsters who tried to get to you. But hey, it turned out great because you kicked ass.* No, she didn't need to hear that. But it had been close. *Too* close.

There had been two one-on-one fights that night. The vampire against the bear shifter, and Raine against the demon who'd won the redemption fight the night before.

The fight between the vampire and bear shifter had been close, but the vampire had used her claws to slice a gash into the shifter's flank before leaping onto the beast's back and sinking her fangs into the bear's neck. Raine's fight had taken longer, but it had ended with Raine's sword poised at the demon's chest and without any of her blood being spilled.

Thank fucking Halced the red-haired female could fight like a devil. As usual, the crowd applauded her victory, but I hadn't been deaf to the whispers of the monsters seated in the stands. Raine had been in three fights and still hadn't shifted, and some were starting to suspect that she shifted into something weak and was too embarrassed to change. Worse, some were starting to question if she was a shifter at all. If she didn't shift during the final fight the next night against the vampire, an alpha might take it upon themselves to fight her and try to draw her creature out. And that would be a fucking disaster because then I'd have to get my axes out.

From the way Losak, alpha of the House of Silat, had watched her during the last fight, I was willing to bet he'd be the first in line. With Losak being the leader of the high house of shifters, if Raine had been a shifter and wanted to join a house, accepting an offer from him would have been the best option for her. Wolves were the most common shifters and had been able to form the House of Worzel, but the only other high house for shifters was the House of Silat, which housed all manner of other shifters from Losak the basilisk to Alec the giant eagle shifter.

But I wasn't letting Losak, the scaled bastard, anywhere near her. Not when I knew she didn't want to join a house. And not now that I realized how she fucking belonged with us. It wasn't just the sex, though that had been incredible. When I was with her the night before, I'd felt it in my very soul. This female was meant to be with us and only us.

You deserve so much better. Her words from nights ago repeated in my head more often than I cared to admit. She hadn't judged me when I'd told her my story, and she hadn't judged me when I'd frozen up when her hand had brushed my horn.

Oh, it had felt good. *So* mind-numbingly good to have her touching me there, but I'd been ruined to the point that sometimes I confused pleasure with pain and warmth with fear. But Raine hadn't shied away. In the past, I'd always been careful not to let any females touch my horns or tail, and if they did, the night would be over for me. But not with Raine. With her, I'd almost considered asking for more. But I couldn't. Still, she hadn't turned from me when I'd become cold.

My gaze slid to where Raine walked beside me. Her brows had lowered, her face molded into the same serious expression she'd worn from the moment she'd awoken in my bed with Darian and me beside her.

Snaking my arm around her back, I rested my hand on her hip and pulled her closer to me. "Ah, don't tell me you regret last night," I said casually. Darian, who was walking on her other side, didn't turn to look at her, but his blue eyes were sharp as he stared straight ahead, and I knew he was paying attention. Locke was striding behind us with Kade, and the vampire hadn't commented about us all being with Raine, though he'd no doubt figured it out.

Raine's body relaxed at my touch, and I grinned.

"Would it hurt your ego if I said I did?" she teased.

"A little," I admitted, squeezing her hip.

Her lips twisted to the side, but then her smile fell as if she remembered something she'd been trying to forget. "I don't regret it, but I don't see how this would ever work."

"We're good at findin' ways to bend the rules, Sharachi. Don't sweat it," I said.

From the look in her eyes, I guessed she wasn't just talking about the Taratun and the fact she was supposed to join a house, but I didn't question her about it. I was too busy thinking about if it was possible to break the rules in this situation. Newbloods were spectacles and the shining examples of how monsters always found their places in Katakin. The Taratun wouldn't accept a newblood defying those rules. Especially not just so the newblood could join my brothers and me.

But I wasn't going to let Raine walk away from us if she didn't want to. And while we were bonded with whatever strange magic was between us, we couldn't let her out of our sight. *We'll find a way.* I'd have to chat with my brothers later.

CHAPTER 25

~ Raine ~

As much as I wanted to pretend that being with Kade, Asher, and Darian hadn't meant anything, I knew it had. Every time I'd been with Kade, I'd been able to convince myself that it didn't really change anything, but not now. Waking with Darian and Asher beside me and Kade's scent clinging to my skin had my heart feeling so full that tears welled in my eyes. That was right. Fucking *tears*.

I'd managed to blink them away, but that wasn't the point. In a short time, these monsters were making me feel things that weren't just pleasurable, they were downright dangerous, and I needed to get out before the thought of leaving them made me want to scream. I already knew it would be difficult, but I wasn't in so deep yet that I wouldn't do it.

I was quiet as we made our way to the after-party that night, wearing another of the red dresses Locke had ordered for me. With a sweetheart neckline and beaded lace-up corset, the dress made it hard for me to breathe, but aside from the impracticality of the thing, it was stunning. A skirt of red velvet draped to the floor, a single slit in the middle showing off a generous amount of my legs as I walked. Thankfully, despite the slit, the dagger I'd strapped to my thigh was hidden from view.

I'd enjoyed letting loose the night before, but now that I was sober again, I reminded myself what I had to do. Sleeping with Kade and the others wasn't helping. "Will Warrick be at the party?" I asked Asher.

Asher nearly stumbled at my question, and he lifted a hand to his chest, clearing his throat. "Who knows? He's usually in his lab and seems reluctant to leave the place."

Kade peered at me from my other side. "Why do you ask?"

Asher wrapped his hands around his ax handles that traveled up near his waist. "Don't worry, sweetheart. We won't let him anywhere near you."

Slowing my steps, I turned to him. "Wait. He has a lab in the mountain?"

"It's deep beneath the mountain, actually," Darian clarified from where he walked beside Asher. "But like Ash said, you needn't worry about him."

Knowing they must have thought I was still scared from when Warrick had entered the rooms nights ago, I made a show of relaxing my shoulders. *Better that they think I'm asking because I'm still freaked out.* "I'm glad. He gives me the creeps," I said.

Asher chuckled and wrapped a thick arm around my shoulders. "He gives everyone that feeling. That monster is about as twisted as they come."

I thought about Locke then. The vampire would have been the best monster to ask about whether Warrick planned to attend the party. Then again, I got the feeling he didn't care much for his father. "Why isn't Locke with us?" I asked.

Kade let out a sigh. "He'll be at the party."

I didn't say much else as we walked to the ballroom. I was too busy remembering how pale Jarin's face had become after Warrick had spotted us together the other night. If Jarin made an appearance again, I was determined to finally get some answers from him.

When we entered the ballroom, some of the alphas came up to congratulate me, and I talked politely with them as I scanned the crowd for any sign of Jarin. As time blurred past, I began to wonder whether Warrick had done something to permanently silence the demon. I couldn't help but feel that Jarin had been about to divulge some secret the other night that Warrick wasn't happy about. If Warrick was as cruel as they said, who was to say he hadn't done something to Jarin? I cursed under my breath, hoping I was wrong.

I was still scanning the crowd when feminine laughter cut to me, and there was something about the sound that had me turning my head. Not too far away, Locke stood leaning against a wall, and he wasn't alone.

Lana stood with her hip jutted to one side and her shoulders back so far it made her breasts look as though they were practically falling out of the skimpy red dress she wore. I stared at them in annoyance, and Kade and the others followed my gaze.

Leaning down, Kade said in my ear, "Locke isn't looking for a mate, nor does he want to be alpha of the high house of vampires. The vampire newblood isn't going to make him change his mind."

I took a gulp of my wine just to have something to do as I watched Lana preen and laugh at whatever Locke had just said. I had to wonder what she was laughing at because nothing Locke ever said to me was fucking funny.

Lana was beautiful as a human, and now that she had been turned into a vampire, her dark eyes, ivory skin, and powerful monster body made her way more seductive than she had been before. I'd seen the way Locke's mother, Perene, and the other vampires treated her like a queen. Would Locke be able to resist that?

"I don't care what he does," I said to Kade before downing the rest of my drink. But even as I said it, I thought of the way Locke had pressed me against the wall in the tunnel, his fingers sinking into me as his wings curled around me like he was trying to shelter me from the world.

The next time I looked over, Lana was still busy chatting to Locke, but her delicate head was now tilted to one side as if she was purposely exposing her neck to him. I scowled at the sight, but when my gaze slid to Locke, I noticed his black eyes weren't focused on Lana. They were fixed on *me*.

A slow smirk pulled across his lips as if he knew exactly how much it irritated me to watch him with Lana, and he loved seeing me squirm.

I glared back at him, hoping that he could read the disgust and anger on my face, but as he stared at me, his face changed. One moment, he was cool, calculated, and smug as shit, and the next, he was frowning as if he was concentrating and listening to something only he could hear. His body hardened with rage, and claws peeked from his fingertips.

What the hell? I didn't know what was going on, but when Kade moved toward Locke, I followed after him. Asher and Darian weren't far behind. Lana, who was completely oblivious to whatever strange situation was happening, was still prattling on as if she thought Locke was listening. She continued talking about her fight against Nora and was saying something about the rush she felt when she brought Nora's huge bear down. Her words made me sick.

Lana noticed Kade and the rest of us as we neared, and she shot Kade and Darian appreciative looks. I could tell she wanted to admire Asher as well, but Perene must have been thorough in her education because somehow she managed to ignore him completely, a fact that had anger pulsing at my temples.

"Leave, Lana," I said harshly.

Narrowing her eyes at me, she smiled, showing her fangs. "I think you're the one who needs to leave, Raine. These guys are only interested in you because they haven't yet realized what a reject you are. You're a novelty for now, but they'll tire of you soon." She traced a finger down the center of Locke's chest, and my nostrils flared as I watched her. The urge to break that finger was so strong that I had to bite the inside of my cheek to control the impulse.

Kade growled and went to move toward Lana, but I placed a hand on his chest. I didn't need him to fight my battles. Lana had never been able to understand why I trained relentlessly in the forest while she and the other girls were busy making baskets and learning how to weave tapestries.

"I said *go*," I seethed between gritted teeth, and there must have been something in my eyes that made her pause.

Sneering at me, she dropped her hand to her side. "You'll see. After I tear you apart during the final fight tomorrow night and show everyone just what a pathetic shifter you are, you'll see just how powerful I've become. And Locky here won't be able to resist."

Locky? Seriously? I let out a deep breath through my nose and fought the impulse to smash my fist into her face. Would the fight still count if we went at it a night early?

To my surprise, I didn't have to answer because Locke stepped forward, getting right in Lana's face. Thinking he was about to kiss her, my heart lurched, but then he bared his teeth, his own fangs on full display.

His black eyes were filled with hate as he said to her, "My mother has this fantasy that we'll take over the House of Nesarin together, but you can tell her that nothing could compel me to go back there. I will never want you, vampire." Then he dismissed her completely and gestured for me and the others to follow him from the ballroom.

My jaw slackened, my mouth falling open as I let myself be led away by the others. When I peered back, Lana was still standing there, a hand to one of her cheeks as if Locke had slapped her in the face, but then her gaze met mine, and the hurt morphed to anger as she stared after me.

Of course, Locke's the one who tears her down, but I'm the one who'll suffer her wrath. Sometimes females made no sense.

When we were all in the tunnel, Locke whirled toward us, his hard mask still in place.

"What is it?" Darian asked, peering intently at the vampire.

When Locke didn't answer straightaway, Kade growled, "Locke."

Locke's body was stiff when he said, "That was Garan earlier. The fae are attacking."

"Where?" Kade practically shouted back at him.

"They've opened a portal on the southern end of the city. Near the markets. Garan didn't say how many warriors have come through, but I'm going to help."

"What?" Panic seized me at the idea that Locke was going to join the fight.

"I'm coming with you," Kade growled. Fury lit his golden eyes, and he rested his hand on the pommel of his sword.

I wanted to grab his shoulders and shake him. To tell him that fighting the fae wouldn't bring his family back, but I didn't. I wasn't one to judge because if I were in his shoes, I'd want to do the same thing.

"Asher. Darian. Head back to the party and pretend you know nothing. The last thing we need is a citywide panic," Locke said.

"We can't just drink wine and act like nothing is happening. I can help," I protested. I had no idea what the fae were like or how dangerous they were, but the idea of attending the party while I knew Kade and Locke were out there fighting for their lives didn't sit well with me.

Locke didn't even acknowledge me. "Make sure you don't let her out of your sight," he ordered Asher and Darian.

"You sure you don't need more backup? It's been a long time since we've had a fae attack, and you don't even know how many are down there," Asher said. I could tell he was about as happy as I was at the idea of going back to the party.

"A siren could be most useful," Darian added, lifting his chin.

Locke's gaze slid to Darian and Asher and then back to me. "Stay here. The last thing we need is someone taking out Raine. Then we'd all be fucked."

I understood then. Locke didn't want me to help because he thought I'd be a liability, and he needed Darian and Asher to stay and keep me in check. I mean, he wasn't wrong—I didn't know how much help I could even be—but it still irritated the hell out of me.

"We'd better go," Kade growled and swept me into his arms. I barely registered the press of his lips against mine before he placed me back on my feet. "I'll be back soon," he ground out.

"You'd better be," I said as my throat constricted.

The pair of them went to leave, but before Locke turned away, I stepped forward into him, my hands sliding beneath his long leather coat at the same moment that I kissed him on the cheek. He stiffened at the kiss, his eyes flaring with shock, but he said nothing as I pulled away from him.

Something like longing shone in his eyes, but then he gave me one last look and nodded again to Darian and Asher, and then Kade and he were striding away from us.

CHAPTER 26

~ Raine ~

Locke's folded map scratched against my boob as we walked back to the party. For nights, Locke had peered over the map, and each time he'd finished with it, he'd tucked it into the same spot on the inside of his coat. But finally, I had it. I wanted to grab it out and look at where Kade and Locke were headed, but I didn't reach for it.

Asher's thumbs fidgeted with the hilts of his axes, and Darian's brows were pulled low as if the siren was deep in thought.

"What are the fae like?" I asked Darian, and the siren blinked before turning to me.

"I was a boy the last time I saw one. I don't remember much except that they have pointed ears."

A boy? "Wait, but what about when they killed Kade's family? You weren't a boy then, were you?"

"No, but we didn't see the fae then. By the time we'd made it to the House of Worzel, the other wolves had driven the fae back into the portal they'd come through."

So Locke and Kade have no idea what they're facing. I tried imagining some alien race, but every time, I pictured some of the monsters I'd met over the past nights. The fae couldn't be any stranger than them.

We returned to the ballroom to find the party in full swing, just as when we'd left. Monsters laughed, danced, and drank wine by the gallons. None of them were aware of the fae and the battle going on in the city below.

"Here," said Asher as he held a goblet out to me.

"Not tonight," I said with a shake of my head. My stomach was churning, and wine was the last thing I needed.

"Dar?" Asher asked, holding the drink out to Darian instead. Frowning, Darian refused as well.

"Suit yourselves," Asher said, downing the contents of the goblet before starting on the other one he was holding. When both goblets were empty, he handed them to a satyr who was passing by with a tray.

"We're about to have company," I said to him as I noticed Losak approaching us from the right. Two members of Losak's house flanked him, and unlike Losak, who wore an easy smile, his friends stared at us with disdain. I recognized one of the companions from when I'd first met Losak nights ago. Quinn's dark hair was once again combed back neatly from his head, and his pale pink eyes bored into me as he sneered.

Asher lifted himself to his full height as he moved in front of me, and his hands dropped to his sides as if he was just itching for an excuse to grab his axes.

"What do you want, Losak?" Asher asked bluntly. It was the first time he'd acted overly aggressive during one of the parties, and I could only guess he was more on edge because the fae had attacked.

I stepped to the side, moving closer to where Darian stood so he wasn't covering me. Asher tensed as I moved, but he had to know I wasn't about to cower behind him. Besides, Losak hadn't tried to hurt me, and I had no reason to believe he would now. He thought I was a shifter like him, after all.

Losak's sharp gaze slid from Asher to me. "I'm here to offer my congratulations on yet another victory," he said, his voice almost coming out as a hiss and his lips curving upward. "Every night, you manage to surprise me."

Forcing a smile on my face, I nodded. "Uh, thanks. I'm glad you're finding the fights interesting."

"Indeed," Losak replied. "Win your fight against the vampire tomorrow night, and I would be happy to offer you a place with the House of Silat."

I blinked dumbly at the male as both Asher and Darian stiffened beside me. "I'm sorry, what?" I'd convinced myself that I wouldn't get any offers to join houses. I mean,

I hadn't even shifted or shown any display of real power. I'd merely beaten my opponents by sheer luck and skill with my blades.

"Presuming, of course, you show us your shifter side. I can't very well offer you to join us when I have no idea what you hide beneath that skin," Losak went on to add, and the way his gaze trailed over the bare curves of my shoulders had a chill snaking down my spine. It was almost as if he was imagining peeling back my skin to find out for himself.

Yeah, no thanks. There was no way I was joining the House of Silat. First, because I wasn't going to join any house, and second, because the male made me uneasy. Despite his cool exterior, there was a coldness to Losak that hinted that he wasn't the male he appeared to be. Something told me I didn't want to find out who he really was behind closed doors.

"Raine will shift when she's ready," Asher said, drawing Losak's attention to him. "No point shiftin' when the newbloods weren't givin' her much of a fight."

"That demon almost bested her tonight," said Losak's other companion. His round face had a ruddy complexion, and his brown gaze was anything but kind. "She's not shifting because her creature is pathetic. Why else would she keep from turning? There ain't room for weaklings in our house."

"Cassar," Losak said in warning and shot a glare at his companion before turning back to me. "Please, excuse him. Cassar isn't known for his patience. Though, it *would* be good if you could humor us and show us your creature."

"What, now?" I blurted in surprise, and when Losak just stared back at me expectantly, my pulse quickened. I'd known the monsters would be expecting me to shift during the last fight, but I hadn't thought they'd ask me to do it during the party. I mean, what the hell?

"She doesn't need to show you anything," Darian said, moving closer to me. "There's one more fight tomorrow night. You can wait like everyone else."

Quinn scoffed, and his upper lip curled. "Cassar's right, boss. Her creature must be weak. Why else would she keep staying with these rejects? She's crazier than Asher's mom was."

Anger rushed through me at his comment.

"You shouldn't have said that," Darian pointed out calmly right before Asher's fist connected with Quinn's face. The force of the blow had the male staggering backward, but Asher didn't relent. His face was the picture of fury, and as he lumbered toward Quinn, I wondered if the shifter was regretting saying something so vile.

Losak hissed with anger, and Cassar launched at Asher. Turning to his side, Asher kicked Cassar in the chest, sending him sprawling to the ground.

"Stop this," Losak shouted, but neither Asher nor Losak's companions were listening. Asher continued to throw punches at Quinn, while Cassar went on all fours.

I watched in horror as Cassar's skin began to change and shift, and an animalistic grunting sound came from his throat. In a matter of moments, Cassar had transformed into a giant boar with an enormous snout and massive tusks that were like small spears jutting from his mouth.

Oh shit.

"You'd best stay back," Darian said to me as he finished rolling up the sleeves of his shirt. Then he cracked his neck and stepped into the path of the giant boar.

Losak, who had initially tried to diffuse the fight, had managed to fight Asher away from Quinn. The pink-eyed shifter remained prone on the floor, blood oozing from his face. Asher and Losak stalked in a circle, both eyeing the other with hatred.

"You'll pay for what you've done to my second," Losak hissed, and then his body was shifting, rippling, and changing. Glossy black scales sprouted over his skin, and his body grew taller as it continued to morph.

Fuck. My gaze slid to where Darian was facing off against the huge boar. A crowd of monsters circled us now, all of them watching with interest. Cassar's boar charged forward, his massive hooves tapping on the marble floor as he picked up speed. Darian dodged to the side before the beast's tusks could connect with his chest, but instead of skidding to a halt, the beast continued charging right into the monsters on the other side of the circle.

Shrieks and cries filled the air as monsters scrambled to get out of the way, but one of the boar's tusks speared a satyr through the chest, and a succubus and wolf shifter were trampled and left bleeding on the floor. The boar grunted loudly and shook his head, and the satyr flew from his tusk and into the crowd.

Monsters howled in anger, and as the boar turned, charging toward Darian again, monsters from the crowd rushed after him. Shifters ripped at their clothes, shedding their skins to their creatures, while succubi and incubi leaped forward, brandishing their weapons. Even other satyrs came to avenge their wounded.

Before long, the ballroom was in chaos as monsters continued to join the fray, and I stepped back into the crowd, dodging swinging arms and gnashing teeth. In the midst of it all, Asher and Darian fought back-to-back, looking like a pair of fearless warriors. Darian's blue eyes were as hard as steel as he brought Cassar's boar down, using his song to daze the creature at the last second before smashing the hilt of his sword to the beast's head and rendering Cassar unconscious. When the beast stopped moving, Darian's gaze slid to me and he took a step in my direction, but more monsters rushed him. It was as if the monsters didn't care who they fought anymore. They were angry and wanted to cause pain.

I looked over at Asher in time to see him punch Losak's basilisk form in the side of the head. A wide grin stretched across Asher's face, and there was something wild and unrestrained in his gaze.

Fucking hell. What is happening? And then my gaze landed on *him*.

Warrick. The older vampire was watching the whole scene unfold from the back of the room with an amused gaze. His attention was on a troll who was busy fighting a vampire, and he sipped his drink, looking as though he was content to enjoy the show.

I dodged another flying fist, and the corner of Locke's map jabbed at my breast. With Warrick still in my line of sight, I knew what I had to do.

CHAPTER 27

~ **Raine** ~

My heart lurched as I moved further into the crowd, weaving and ducking to avoid the frenzied monsters around me. When I reached the double doors to the ballroom, I let out a relieved breath and slipped into the tunnel. The monsters' grunts and screams faded the further I fled down the tunnel, and I only allowed myself to stop when the noise ceased entirely. Peering around, I made sure no one had followed me before pulling Locke's map from my dress.

With shaky fingers, I unfolded the map and stretched it out on the wall of the tunnel, keeping close enough to a torch so I could make out the markings. The city of Katakin was inked in precise detail, from the winding waterways to the seven guard towers positioned around the city. Even the locations of the different high houses were depicted. Locke had left black crosses over the map, but they didn't appear to follow any specific pattern. Knowing I didn't have the time to figure it out, I traced my finger to where the markets were indicated on the southern end of the map. *The fae.*

My finger lingered on the spot before I turned the parchment over. On the other side, a map of the mountain was drawn with the same intricate detail. Many of the different tunnels and caverns were labeled, and I dropped my finger to the base of the mountain. *Warrick's lab.* The lab itself wasn't labeled on the map, but there was a clear path to reach down there.

I stared at the winding tunnels that led into the depths of the mountain and memorized the turns as I folded the map and tucked it back into the front of my dress. I hadn't seen Jarin at the party, and I was still going with the theory that Warrick had done something to silence him. If that was the case, Jarin wasn't going to be giving me any answers.

I was now convinced Warrick was hiding something, and it was clear the vampire wasn't someone willing to share his secrets. But if he had a lab, it was possible he might have documents that could give me information. It was my best hope. If I found nothing, I'd escape into the city and try to find Cara on my own. I couldn't go back to Asher and Darian and participate in my fight against Lana the next night. She was a vampire, and there was no way I'd be able to fight her without her spilling my blood.

And then everyone would know what I was. I'd thought Kade and the others might come up with a plan for me to avoid it, but if they had, they hadn't told me, and I couldn't take the risk.

Down, down, down I went as if I was climbing to the depths of hell itself. Slowly, the air grew stale, and the torches lining the tunnel dimmed as if they knew that deep down in the mountain, the monsters didn't like the light.

Soon I began passing rows of large iron doors, and my steps faltered as I took in the deep grooves and marks scratched into the thick iron. One door had grooves so deep I was surprised whatever was on the other side hadn't punctured through, and I shivered. As if whatever was in there sensed me, an ear-piercing screech sounded from the other side, and my heart jumped to my throat as I stumbled backward. Scrambling to my feet, I turned from the door and moved down the tunnel again, a trickle of fear sliding down the back of my neck.

I was beyond what was drawn on the map now, but I continued downward until I eventually reached two doors at the end of the tunnel. Neither of them had marks clawed into them, and I could only guess that one of them led to Warrick's lab.

Without letting myself hesitate, I stepped up to the door on the right. I had no idea how long the fight in the ballroom would last or how long Warrick would be distracted, but I didn't want him to find me down there.

Pressing my ear to the door, I ignored the cool bite of the iron against my skin and listened. When seconds passed and I heard nothing, I pulled back. Granted, the door was so thick I probably wouldn't have heard anything anyway, but it seemed like the smart thing to do.

With shaking fingers, I gripped the iron handle and twisted. The door didn't budge. *Damn it. Of course, it's locked.* I stepped over to the door on the left and groaned in disappointment when I found that one was locked as well.

If I can just get past these doors, I'm sure there has to be some answers. All right, so I wasn't really *sure*, but I had a feeling there had to be answers there. If not, then aside from Jarin I was back to having no leads.

I tried twisting the doorknob again but growled in frustration when it still wouldn't move. *Fuck. I've come all this way. I can't turn back now.*

I thought then of the way I'd turned the rocky ceiling to sand nights ago. Could I do it again? I ran my palms over the smooth rock to the right of the door. I had no idea what was on the other side, and if it worked, I risked someone seeing me, but I had to do *something*. Peering behind me, I checked the tunnel was still clear, and then I placed a palm on the wall and closed my eyes.

All right. Magic. I can do this. I tried not to think about how ridiculous I felt and instead focused on finding that energy inside myself. That spark that had seemed to explode inside me when I'd turned the rocky ceiling to sand and again when I'd conjured the wind in the rooms.

A moment passed, and I felt...nothing. It occurred to me that I was a human standing beside a wall, hoping to magically create an opening. Groaning, I opened my eyes and dropped my hand. *Goddess, this is stupid.*

I paced along the wall before reminding myself that, no, it wasn't stupid. Something was happening inside me, and whether I was turning into a monster or not, somehow I had done magic and I had no reason to believe I couldn't do it again.

Forcing myself to let out a long breath, I stopped before the wall and closed my eyes again. Gingerly, I placed my palm back on the cool rock. I thought of the times I'd felt the magic before and the sheer desperation that had every nerve in my body feeling as though they were on fire. Then I thought of Darian and Asher brawling with the monsters in the ballroom and Kade and Locke fighting the fae. Fear struck my heart, and a spark flared to life deep inside me. I focused on the spark, letting it burn hotter until warmth traveled from my chest to my fingertips.

Grains of sand fell between my fingers, and when I opened my eyes again, I had to take a step back and blink several times to believe what I was seeing. A section of the wall had fallen away, the rock transformed to sand that had fallen near my feet.

Mother Falia, I did it. I let out a cheer as I punched a triumphant hand into the air, but then, realizing what an idiot I was, I clamped a hand over my mouth and cursed internally. When the tunnel remained silent, I slowly crept forward, ducking my head as I stepped into the cavern.

Luckily, there mustn't have been anything on the other side of the wall. Blue torches around the cavern flared to life at my presence, and I let out a shaky breath when I saw no one else was in there. Glancing cautiously around, I took in the space. The small cavern, which wasn't much bigger than Kade's bedroom, had a simple design. Against the far wall, a wide, stained oak desk was the largest piece of furniture in the room. Sheets of loose paper covered the desk, and I couldn't read the writing from where I was. More papers covered the walls, all of them with scribbled writing and charcoal drawings of monsters I hadn't seen before.

Holy Goddess. Swallowing, I walked along the walls, scanning the pictures. There were beasts with crowns of horns, and others with massive fiery talons. The writing itself didn't mean much to me, but a chill raced over my skin as I stared at the illustrations. *All righty, some decorate their rooms with beautiful paintings, and others with horrifying illustrations of monsters. It's no big deal.*

Turning away, I moved over to the desk and instantly recognized the reports I had found in Kade's room nights ago, though there was more written on them now. Inked in black cursive were detailed observations regarding how each of the newbloods fought during the Week of Orash and who they fought against. My gaze fell on the report labeled *Subject 12*. A picture of me passed out on a cot and still in my tattered dress from the selection was at the bottom of the page. I scanned the writing.

My report was nowhere near as fleshed out as the other newbloods', but aside from a few question marks next to comments about what type of shifter I was and how powerful I was, there wasn't anything to indicate Warrick suspected I was still human.

I rifled through the other papers on the desk, but only the reports of the newbloods for the current round were there. Conscious that my time was running out, I turned my gaze back to the rest of the room.

Against the right wall sat a steel cabinet with multiple drawers, and I went over to it. Relief coursed through me when I found it wasn't locked, and I guessed Warrick wasn't usually worried about monsters breaking into his office. *Yeah, he's going to be rethinking that after finding the hole I've opened in the wall.*

Stealing another cautious glance through my makeshift door, I crouched and searched through the bottom drawer. Papers were filed neatly in separate folders, and I quickly flicked through them. *Are these reports of newbloods from previous years?* I frowned at the report I'd pulled out, and my throat went dry when I read the inked script. *Rory Finall. Aged 5 years.* Beneath the writing was the picture of a young boy with scraggly hair and small brown eyes. A childish grin stretched across the boy's face, and there was a twig in his hair as if he'd just been climbing a tree. Below the picture was the note: *Subject turned into a wendigo when the curse was created. Unlike a shifter, his antlers, claws, and teeth remain present at all times.*

My gaze trailed down then, jumping past the notes to where there was another drawing. This time, the picture was of a monster with an animal skull as a head and large deer antlers. Instead of warm brown eyes, empty sockets showed nothing but darkness. I shivered, knowing that I was looking at the same 5-year-old boy from the above picture.

My stomach also roiled at the thought that Warrick had observed the children who turned when the curse first happened. *Did he experiment on them as well?* Bile rose in my throat, and I slid the report back with the others. I couldn't imagine a child going through the ordeals I'd been through or worse.

My fingers trembled as I picked through more of the papers. There were dozens of them. Dozens of reports written for children aged between four and ten. When I came to the last two reports in the drawer, my heart nearly stopped. My gaze snagged on Locke's name, and my breath caught in my chest as I read. *Locke Hanmar. Aged 9 years.*

I stared disbelieving at the picture of a young boy with Locke's sharp jaw and sleek black hair. He wasn't smiling in the first picture, but his chin was held high, and a proud gleam shone in his eyes. My gaze slid to the second picture on the page. Membranous wings flared behind the young boy now, and his skin was a deathly pale white. Fangs protruded from his lips, and trails of blood dribbled from the sides of his mouth.

I forced myself to read sections of the report and tried to control my erratic breathing. *No.* My mind wanted to rebel as I read about the various trials Locke had been put through. All the words were written in a purely clinical way as if Locke had been nothing but another subject Warrick was determined to examine.

The report detailed how Locke was put through a multitude of tests that were designed to determine his pain threshold, instincts, the limits of his mortality, and the extent of his bloodlust. Locke's bones had been broken, he'd been starved, and he'd been drained of large amounts of blood.

There were also notes detailing emotional and mental tests placed upon him. Locke had been made to participate in a range of horrendous acts all so Warrick could measure his emotional and physical responses. After being starved of blood for nights, Warrick would place Locke in a room with other children to see how he would behave.

Goddess, I felt sick. In light of the report, everything Locke and the others had done to me seemed mild. I could see then why Locke was the way he was. The idea that his own father tested him in that way was unthinkable.

The next report was of a child called Garan, who had turned into a gargoyle. I didn't read any more of that report and slid it back with Locke's into the drawer. It occurred to me then that if Warrick was willing to do all that to his own son, I could only imagine what he would do to me if he found me trespassing in his space.

Self-preservation allowed me to mentally push the thought of the children from my mind, and I hastily searched through the next two drawers. Both of these contained reports of newbloods—girls who had been taken from my island—but Cara's report wasn't there. I even found all the reports for the newbloods of the previous round, and all twelve females were accounted for. There was no report of a girl with mousy brown hair and wide brown eyes.

I was about to close the cabinet when a handful of papers hidden at the far back of the top drawer snagged my attention. With shaking hands, I pulled them out.

As I stared at the first paper, I nearly dropped the stack. A nightmarish creature with thousands of beady eyes, a misshapen head, and six legs snarled at me. The charcoal drawing had been created with such detail that it almost looked lifelike, and I quickly moved onto the next page.

This drawing was of a monster with a skeletal body and pieces of flesh falling from its bones.

Each of the papers in the stack contained a drawing of a monster that was just as terrifying as the last, and I scanned them hastily. *They can't possibly be real.* As if in answer to my thought, my heart stuttered when I peered at the last drawing. It was the sea monster Darian, Locke, and I had faced when we were in the ocean. The beast was drawn in precise detail from the creature's spined back and fins jutting from its sides to its grotesque head with five bulging eyes and massive maw filled with needlelike teeth. *The outlier.* I took a step back, my gaze flitting from the papers in my hand to the charcoal drawings on the walls.

Are they all *outliers?* I swallowed as I stared at them all. If they were outliers, the monsters had once been animals. Animals that had been warped by the curse and transformed into horrifying creatures. All of a sudden, I felt uncomfortably warm, and I rubbed my sweaty palms on my dress. The words Locke had said not too long ago echoed in my head. *If all our animals start to turn, they will be like an army descending upon Katakin.*

If an army of the monsters swept through the city, I didn't think there would be any stopping them. I remembered the stench of rotting flesh from when I'd been in the sea creature's mouth, and I shuddered.

Hastily tucking the handful of drawings back into the drawer, I closed the cabinet. Seeing the drawing of the outlier was just another reminder that I needed to find Cara, but once again, I was empty-handed. *Her report isn't there because she's dead*, said a dark voice in my mind, but I pushed the thought away. I wouldn't believe it. Not unless I had proof.

Determined to keep searching, I left the office, climbing through the hole in the wall and striding to the room beside the one I was in. This time, I didn't hesitate to place my hand on the wall near the door and summon the energy that dwelled within me. Again, the rock dissolved into sand, creating an opening for me to walk through.

This time, the torches were already burning high up on the walls before I even crept through my new entrance. Clenching my jaw, I poked my head through the hole and gasped. In the middle of the room, a long form was spread out on a stone slab. Deep cuts and angry-purple bruises covered the male's naked body from his feet to his pointed ears, and his short azure-colored hair was coated in grime. *Pointed ears. He's one of the fae.* I thought about leaving. About pretending that I hadn't seen the captured male, but I knew my odds of ever being able to search Warrick's lab again would all but disappear once he realized someone had broken into them. He'd probably get monsters to guard his rooms from then on.

Slowly, I stepped closer to the male on the stone slab. The fae's long arms and legs were spread out, and iron cuffs were clasped around his wrists and ankles. With the treatment of his body, I would have guessed he was dead except for the almost imperceptible rise and fall of his chest.

A tube ran from one of the male's wrists, and my gaze followed it to where blue blood dripped from the tube into a steel tub on the ground. The tub was already half-filled, and nausea made me gag. Beside the stone slab, a small steel table held numerous knives and other medical instruments that were covered with black blood.

Goddess. How long has he been here? The male's eyes were closed, and he looked close to death. From what Kade had told me, the fae were as evil as Warrick was, but I still felt sympathy for him. From what I could see, Warrick had likely inflicted unimaginable pain on the male, and he had been tortured for a long while.

I tried not to give the fae my back as I picked my way through the room. Hundreds of glass vials covered the walls, most with black blood but some with blood that was different shades of red. There were also more charcoal drawings high up on the walls, depicting what I assumed were more outlier monsters.

I searched for anything that would give me some clue as to what had happened to my sister. There weren't any cabinets like the one I'd found in the previous room, but there was another, smaller table against one wall with a selection of papers on it. Again, I frantically rifled through them, hoping to find useful information, but the papers just held more notes on different outliers.

"You're not my usual tormentor," rasped a masculine voice, and I spun around, grabbing my dagger from my thigh in the process. Holding my blade before me, I prepared myself for a fight, but instead of Warrick standing in the doorway, the captured fae was staring at me. His emerald-green eyes watched me with interest.

"From that reaction, I'm guessing you're not meant to be here either," he said.

My heart pounded in my ears as I assessed the fae. His arms and legs were still shackled, so even if the male weren't bleeding out, he still wouldn't have been able to physically attack me.

"If you could do me a favor and go back to pretending to be dead, that would really help me out right now," I said as I returned my dagger to its position on my thigh.

I was aware that I was being a bitch to the male who was already near death, but he was evil, right? Besides, if he didn't shut up, I was going to be dead soon too.

The stranger just continued to stare at me curiously, his brow furrowed with concentration as if he was trying to figure me out. I realized he was probably confused, as I didn't have any obvious monster characteristics. He was likely trying to figure out what the hell I was.

"Shifter," I lied to put him out of his misery, then I cursed under my breath when I realized I should have said

I was something else. For all I knew, the fae would tell Warrick I'd been there, and it would have been better if the vampire thought a succubus or some other monster had intruded in his lab. "Just— Fuck," I said. "I'm leaving now. Please don't tell Warrick I was here." I had no reason to remain there. Every moment longer increased the chance Warrick would catch me, and there clearly wasn't any information about Cara's location. I started making my way back across the room

"Warrick?" the fae asked.

Despite his swollen left eye, his cracked lip, and the bruises around his face, he had a regal beauty and looked only a few years older than I was.

"Ah, I assume you mean my captor with the charming personality," the fae concluded. "Oh, you needn't worry. He doesn't seem to be interested in anything I say. I tried to explain to him that I was simply here to find and liberate some of our ancient texts that my aunt had brought to this world, but he doesn't listen. He's rather rude if I do say so."

I was almost at the hole I'd created in the wall when the fae stopped speaking, and I twisted toward him. "Wait. Your aunt?"

"Oh yes, she was the queen here once before she was murdered. Though, I suppose you would be well aware of who Queen Izla was, seeing as you monsters now live as long as us fae do."

Queen Izla is his aunt? I blinked, struggling to take in what he was saying. *This fae can't be for real.* "So...your people who are now attacking Katakin. You all came here for...*books*?"

The fae's eyes brightened. "They've come, have they? Oh, no, I came for the books. They're here for me. No doubt my father will never let me leave the kingdom again after this."

I rubbed at my head. I knew I should just leave the babbling fae. I'd been gone for too long, and the fight in the ballroom was surely over. But I couldn't help but say, "And they're here for you because you're..." I trailed off.

"Prince Azaren of the Kingdom of Zalei. Oh, my father, King Chalir, had forbidden any more portals to this world, and truthfully, no one had thought it was possible anymore. But I simply couldn't help myself when the old scholar told me about the ancient texts, could I? I thought I might be able to sneak in and find the texts using my magic, but I suppose I should have listened to the others. Sasha really did try to warn me. In any case, I can't turn back time. And I suspect the fae council will want to revisit the idea of war if I don't return promptly. Even if I do, I'm not sure it will deter them now."

War? He was talking as if it was no big deal, and I wanted to shake more information out of him. And who were the fae council? "So...your people aren't here to attack the city.

They're here to search for you, and if they don't find you, there'll be a war?" I said, dumbfounded.

"You are correct," the fae replied, and I still couldn't believe how chirpy he was considering he was still bleeding out into a freaking tub. "I tried to tell the other guy this, but he was too busy muttering about blood and magic and other such nonsense."

The other guy? I knew he had to be talking about Warrick. "How long have you been here?"

"About a day, I'd say, but it's hard to tell in this damned place. In any case, if you'd consider releasing me, I'd be most grateful. I mean, really, I'm your only chance of stopping the war, so you might want to do it before I bleed out altogether."

My attention went back to the wounds all over the fae's body. If he went back like that, I didn't think his father, King Chalir, or whoever he was, would be too happy. And did the male even have the strength to move? Not to mention the fact that releasing the fae seemed like a terrible idea. "How would you even get back?" I asked.

"Oh, that's easy. I'll go back through the portal I created to get here. It's in the forest near a waterfall and between two ancient oak trees." His face became thoughtful then, and he added, "You know, you should really come with me."

"I— what?" My brow creased, and I narrowed my eyes. "Why would I do that?"

"Well, because of your...affliction."

"My what?"

His expression was sympathetic as he said, "I can sense the magic on you. It's hard to tell exactly what it is, but I suspect some kind of curse?"

I took another step toward him. "Everyone here is cursed. Are you saying you can remove the curse from Katakin?" If the curse could be removed, it would mean Cara could be human again if she wanted. It would also mean no more humans would be taken from my island.

"Oh, right, yes, my aunt's curse. No, I'm not talking about that. I'm referring to the other spell that's been placed over you."

Curiosity drove me to step right up to the male. "What are you talking about?"

"I'm not sure exactly," he replied with a frown. "There's powerful magic surrounding you, and I can feel that parts of you have been bound to others. I've read tomes detailing ancient magic, and there's talk of curses that can bind your soul to other beings. I'm not certain that's what it is, but I'm sure I could figure it out if given time. Such magic has been forbidden for centuries, but I'm sure eventually, I could find a way to remove the spell. I tell you what, how about you free me from here, and in return, I'll remove whatever magic this is? I'm guessing one of your fellow pals has been experimenting and you're the one who's had to deal with the end result. Gods, I'd heard you monsters had inherited some of my aunt's fae magic, but it really is a wonder you haven't all killed one another by now."

Remove the magic? I thought of my bonds with Kade and the others, and my heart beat faster in my chest. I had been so certain once that I'd give anything to be free of them, but now—well, now I wasn't so sure. *But how can I ever escape if I'm tied to them? What if Cara wants to return to the island?* And not only that. I stared at the inside crook of my arm where I remembered waking to find a painful red dot. *Has Warrick been experimenting on me?* The thought of it made my blood boil. Was it why I hadn't changed into a monster? Because Warrick was turning me into something else?

Prince Azaren continued to stare at me, his intelligent green eyes watching as I processed the information he'd given me. "I hate to rush you, but I fear I might be incapable of moving if I lose any more blood. The fae are able to withstand a great many things, but we're not beyond death in the right circumstances."

I chewed on the inside of my cheek, but I still didn't move to help him.

"Perhaps you could at least remove the tube while you make up your mind?" he suggested.

"How do I know you won't use your fae magic to kill me?" I asked warily.

Prince Azaren started to chuckle, but it turned into a rasping cough. "If I had the strength to kill you, do you think I would still be here? I hadn't even seen the vampire you call Warrick, when he knocked me unconscious from behind. A fae's magic is tied to their blood. Clearly, I've lost enough of it that I'm not quite as able as I normally am. In any case, if I could, you wouldn't need to release me for my magic to work. If I'd been able, I could have killed you when you'd first entered the room."

Oh. Right. I figured he'd meant the knowledge to be a comfort, but it just made me feel ill. Still, if it was true, it meant it didn't really matter if I released him. I hesitated a moment longer. I couldn't be sure anything the fae told me was the truth, but if he had visited Katakin for what seemed like an innocent enough reason, it seemed wrong to leave him there to die. He was more of a prisoner than I was. Besides, if he really was a prince, it was possible he was the only one who could stop the fae from starting a war in their efforts to find him.

Eyeing the fae, I cursed under my breath and bent down as I slowly removed the tube. There was a disgusting pop as the tube came free, and I dropped it to the floor before quickly grabbing a nearby strip of cloth and wrapping his wrist to stop the blood flow.

"Thank you," Prince Azaren said with a grateful sigh. "I'd ask what your name is, but I have a feeling you wouldn't tell me."

I didn't answer as I grabbed a steel bar from the small table of medical instruments and used it to pry the shackle from his right wrist. I was about to move onto the shackle around his other wrist, but one of the drawings on the wall caught my attention. I stilled as I stared at the wolf-like monster with a single horn jutting from its head and multiple rows of sharp teeth visible in its open mouth. I'd never seen the monster before, but it triggered something in my mind.

Locke and the others had said they didn't know why the outliers were suddenly appearing. My gaze slid to the fae's face as understanding dawned on me. *What if the curse isn't changing, but the fae are infecting the animals?* My heart hammered again as I realized my mistake. *And I almost freed him.*

"You said your people hadn't thought it was possible to still come here," I said slowly, "but nothing else can explain why the animals in Katakin are only now turning into monsters. You say you'll try to stop the fae from declaring war again, but Katakin and the fae are already at war, aren't they?"

Prince Azaren looked shocked by my words, but this time, I wasn't falling for his act.

"The fae are infecting these lands with more magic, and you're making it seem like Queen Izla's curse is changing. This is all a planned attack," I accused.

"You're making no sense," the fae prince began, but I grabbed his free arm and pushed the steel bar to his delicate throat with my other hand, cutting his words off.

He's probably not even a prince. I didn't know why I bothered. Warrick had clearly been using way more persuasive methods than mine to get information out of the fae, but I did it anyway.

Prince Azaren's emerald-green eyes grew wider as he stared at me. "I-I promise, I really have no idea what you're talking about. My people haven't been here for years. I know nothing of these monsters, these animals that you speak of."

"Right," I said sarcastically, pressing the bar harder against his neck. "And let me guess, that's precisely what you've been telling Warrick this whole time he's been questioning you about it?"

"No. The vampire hasn't said anything about animals turning into monsters. He just keeps asking me about the fae kingdom and what defenses we have."

Defenses? I pushed the bar harder against his neck, and he coughed. "Tell me the truth. Did he ask you about the monsters? About the outliers?" I was practically shouting in his face now because it was all starting to make terrifying sense, and I was beginning to realize I'd been wrong yet again.

"No!" the fae spluttered. "As I said, he only asked about my homeworld. He wants to know the numbers of the fae army and what magic we wield."

A ringing started in my head, and I pulled the bar from his neck. *He only asked me about my homeworld.* I blinked as everything the fae had just said repeated in my head. I thought of the huge iron doors in the tunnel. Doors that held scratch marks so deep that there had to be something truly monstrous trapped inside. I then thought of the drawings I'd found hidden at the back of the cabinet, and in particular, the picture of the massive sea beast with five red eyes and needlelike teeth.

My body shook as the missing pieces finally settled into place. With a few swift movements, I freed the fae's other hand and passed him the bar. "If you are a prince, fuck, I'm sorry. If you can stop the war, do it. If not, well, at least I tried." Then I left him and strode toward the hole I'd made in the wall. Before I slipped through, I turned back one last time. The fae was sitting up now, but he was still staring at me with a bewildered expression. "I hope you find your books, Prince Azaren," I said, and then I was sprinting up the tunnel.

CHAPTER 28

~ **Raine** ~

My heart slammed wildly in my chest as I ran up the tunnel, pumping my legs as fast as they would go. The torches along the tunnel flickered as I flew past them, the flames casting distorted shadows on the massive iron doors as I passed them.

My toe clipped a small, jagged rock sticking out of the ground, and I stumbled before correcting myself. *Fuck.* I hoped I'd done the right thing by freeing the fae. *Prince Azaren.* I believed him now. His story was too ridiculous for it to be a lie. And even if he was deceiving me, I couldn't leave him there with Warrick. Not now that I knew what was going on.

Kade, Darian, Asher, and Locke. I had to warn them.

Fire burned in my lungs, and pain traveled up my legs as I continued climbing upward, but I didn't stop. *Goddess, how has everyone been so blind?*

Following the curve of the tunnel around a bend, I was so focused on putting one foot in front of the other that I didn't see Darian until it was too late. Before I could slam into his muscled body, the siren grabbed my shoulders, and my body jerked at the abrupt halt. *Oof.* The air whooshed out of me at the impact, and I scrunched my face in pain.

Darian quickly set me down on my feet and rubbed his hands up and down my shoulders. "Sorry, lovely, it was either that or let you give yourself a concussion when you ran into me." His body relaxed as he took me in, but his expression was troubled. He bowed his head closer to me. "Where the devil did you go, Raine? When I didn't find you in our rooms, I thought— Well, never mind that now. You need to go back there and stay out of sight."

"Where's Asher?" I gasped as I tried to get air back into my lungs. "I need to speak to you and Asher. To all of you. I was just at Warrick's lab."

Confusion and panic flashed across Darian's face, and he moved even more into my space. "What do you mean you were at his lab?"

"Just *listen*," I said, ignoring his question. "I found something out. It's Warrick, he—"

"You'll have to tell me later, lovely. Right now, you need to return to our rooms. Promise me you'll go there."

My brows lowered at Darian's steely expression, but then I noticed the fear shining in his crystal-blue eyes.

It wasn't fear for me. "Where's Asher?" I asked as I straightened, my voice becoming higher.

Darian's gaze flicked to the tunnel behind him, and that was all I needed to know. *Asher's still at the party.* I maneuvered around the siren and began running toward the ballroom again. Darian caught up to me in a few strides, his long legs easily keeping up with my pace.

"You can't go in there. The fight had barely ended when outliers crashed through the windows. The creatures must have climbed up the mountain. I didn't have time to count them all before I realized you were gone and went to search for you, but there must be around two dozen."

Two dozen outliers? I tried not to think about what I was running toward. Would Asher already be dead? "If it weren't for me, you'd still be fighting alongside Asher," I said between heaving breaths. "I'm not going back to the rooms."

Darian was quiet for a moment, and I felt his assessing gaze on the side of my face, but then he finally said, "Then, for the love of all that is good, try not to die." At that, he lifted his hands, drawing the swords at his sides and handing one of them to me, hilt first.

I wrapped my hand around the cool metal and gave him a sharp nod. *Right. Try not to die. How hard can that be?*

· · · · · **·** · **·** · · · ·

~ Darian ~

I heard the battle first—the grunts, snarls, pained cries, and clangs of steel on steel. Next came the scent of the smoke. The woody, earthy smell was mixed with the underlying tang of brimstone, and it tainted the musty mountain air the closer we ran to the ballroom. It wasn't the same smoke that fogged the air when monsters danced. No, this was something different. By the time we reached the double doors that marked the entrance, the scent of the smoke was strong enough that I could taste it at the back of my throat, and the magic in the air made my tongue tingle.

Raine's eyes were wide as she gripped the sword I'd given her, but I wasn't going to ask her to turn back again. I hated that she wasn't somewhere safe, but she'd made her choice. I'd do everything I could to protect her, but I wouldn't leave Asher there to fight the outliers without me.

Inside the ballroom, it was chaos beyond what I'd imagined. Many of the Katakin monsters had fled when the outliers first appeared, but some had been unable to escape or remained to fight the creatures. Most of the alphas from the high houses were there, and I was glad they'd stayed.

Twenty outliers were spread around the room, and the Katakin monsters battled them with deadly efficiency. Centaurs worked alongside shifters and vampires to bring down the creatures made of red fire. The outliers, who

were each the size of a bear, had bodies resembling those
of giant rats. Flames coated their wrinkled skin to the tips
of their long, wiry tails, and everywhere they moved their
unnatural red fire spread. Thankfully, because the fire was
caused by magic, the smoke wasn't overpowering, but the
few flammable items in the room were already burning.
Fire crackled and popped as it ate away at the long velvet
curtains hanging from the windows, and flames devoured
tables and settees.

The outliers made hissing and clicking noises as they
attacked the Katakin monsters in the ballroom, and a
bellowing howl rose over the din as an ogre accidentally
stepped into one of the unnatural fires and caught alight.

My own skin felt uncomfortably tight at the heat of the
fire, and I focused on the feel of my sword in my grasp.

"Over there," Raine said behind me, and she pointed
her sword to the opposite side of the room, where Asher
was fighting two outliers. My demon brother was covered
in sweat and blood, but he appeared unharmed as he
fought with terrifying precision against the creatures.
Relief rushed through me at the sight of him, and I sent
a silent thank you to the Devil Enzal for keeping him safe.

With a roar, Asher's powerful arms lowered as he sank
an ax into the first outlier's head, then he pivoted in time
to throw his other ax at the next outlier that charged
him. The weapon buried between the creature's red eyes,

the metal instantly catching fire as the outlier fell to the ground.

"Stay on my heels," I said to Raine as I indicated with my head for her to follow me. Then I jogged forward, moving around my fellow monsters and picking what I deemed to be the safest path through the room. While constantly scanning the area around me, I listened to the sound of Raine's breathing and turned my head every so often to check she wasn't falling behind. I wasn't willing to lose Asher or Raine to these beasts.

My demon brother spotted me when we were halfway across the room, and he dropped low to grab the discarded sword of a fallen Minotaur before running over to meet us.

"Why didn't you take her to our rooms?" Asher shouted when he caught sight of Raine behind me.

"Given your delicate nature, Raine thought you might require her assistance," I said.

Sweat streamed from his face, and his lips quirked to the side. "Delicate, hey." His gaze slid back to Raine, and his body tightened as he flexed his massive muscles.

She looked unimpressed, but some light returned to her panicked eyes. "Admit it, you're glad to see me," she said, though her gaze moved from him to swipe around the ballroom as she tracked the outliers.

"While I always enjoy seeing you, sweetheart, Dar should've made sure you stayed in our rooms. Even if he had to stay there with you." He gave me a hard look then, and all amusement was gone from his face.

"And listen to you boast for the next century about your victory against the outliers?" I drawled. "That wasn't happening."

Raine coughed, and her grip tightened on her sword. "Shouldn't we stop talking and do more stabbing?"

Asher's face became grim then, and with his free hand, he wiped sweat away from his eyes. He shook his head. "Everything that touches these beasts catches fucking fire. I enjoy a good joke, but this is bad. At first, I grabbed weapons from the fallen and used a few of the bigger shards of glass from the broken windows to kill the creatures, but as you can see, I just lost my axes, and most of the glass is now covered by fire. There aren't many weapons left."

Scratching and clicking sounded high above us, and I pushed Raine to the side as an outlier fell from the ceiling. The creature landed on its feet before me, and I wasted no time before slicing the outlier's head off in one clean swipe. When I lifted my sword, red fire raced up the blade, and I dropped the weapon seconds before the fire reached my hands.

"Cruel seven devils," I cursed. "And that's one less weapon we have." Lifting my hands, I grabbed the five metal stars hidden in the belt crossing my chest and let out a long breath. "We'll have to make sure they count."

· · · ●·●· · · ·

~ Raine ~

I watched as Darian's last star sliced across an outlier's eyes, blinding the beast. The creature shrieked and shook its head from side to side, and I threw my sword to Asher. He sliced the outlier's head off and promptly dropped the sword before fire consumed it.

"So that's it, then," Asher said grimly as he wiped his sweaty palms on his chest. "We're outta weapons."

"Not quite," I said, reaching at my thigh and grabbing out my hidden dagger.

Asher raised a brow, and a grin stretched across his face. "Of course, you had that up there."

"Isn't that what dresses are for? To hide weapons?" I said with a shrug.

"Not exactly," Darian said with an approving smile. "But it should be."

Many of the outliers had now been taken care of, but there were still a number of the creatures around the room. The Katakin monsters had joined to form bigger groups as they ran out of weapons, and against the far wall was a large group of ogres, satyrs, goblins, and shifters. An ogre stood at the head of the group, wielding a small table before her as she faced off an outlier that snapped and clawed the air in front of her.

Goddess, they're going to die. "We have to help them," I said, swallowing against the grit coating the back of my throat from the thin layer of smoke in the air. "That table won't do anything to protect against the outlier."

"Neither will your dagger, unfortunately," Darian said, moving closer to me as if he was afraid I would sprint to their aid.

On the other side of the room, two more groups were bunched together with their backs pressed to the walls. Losak and a few of his monsters stood with at least fifty others. Losak faced off three outliers, holding a single sword, while Cassar, the boar shifter, stood at his side shouting obscenities at the creatures and making animalistic grunting sounds.

The other group had Kenric, the alpha of the House of Axeran, and Drustan, the alpha from the House of Nesarin, along with at least thirty others. An outlier bared its teeth at Drustan as its tail flicked from side to side, and the vampire held his sword preternaturally still as he waited for the creature to attack. Kenric had a broad grin on his face as he threw an ax that sank into an outlier's neck, and then he took a sword offered by a goblin behind him.

Most of the newbloods weren't in the ballroom, and I assumed they'd fled when the outliers first appeared, but

Lana stood huddled behind Drustan with a handful of other vampires. Her round eyes frantically darted to the four outliers surrounding them.

A hiss sounded from above, and Asher grabbed me around the waist, jumping forward with me in his grasp as a burning section of curtain fell and landed on the floor in the spot I'd just been standing in. Burning embers rained down on us, but thankfully, none of them landed on our skin.

"Thanks," I gasped, and his hands lingered on me before he released me. A ring of fire surrounded us now, the flames crackling and popping as they rose into the air.

I ducked lower, where the air was cooler, but I kept my dagger before me.

"This isn't lookin' good, Dar," Asher said as two outliers crossed the room, moving toward us. "If we can't find a way to stop that fire, we're as good as roasted. You shouldn't have come back for me."

Darian licked his cracked lips and rested a hand on Asher's shoulder. "I have no regrets."

The siren pulled his hand back and took an offensive stance as an outlier neared on our right. The creature scurried through the flames as though it was walking through blades of grass, and my dagger felt pathetic in my grasp. Straightening, I took a steadying breath and let the blade loose. It spun through the air until it landed with a sickening thud into one of the outlier's red eyes. For a moment, the creature's clicking sound faltered, but then the clicking started up again, even louder than before. The outlier shook its head, and its remaining good eye fixed on me.

Well, shit. All I'd done was anger the thing.

Asher pulled me back behind him protectively. "I don't suppose you have anything else under that dress of yours?" he asked.

"When I dressed for this party, I didn't exactly know I would be fighting giant, wrinkly fire rats," I responded, stretching out my empty hands.

He was silent for a moment, but then he pulled off his shirt and wrapped it around one of his fists. "You did good, Sharachi."

Darian moved closer on my other side, and the pair of them stood as if they thought they could protect me from the two outliers coming at us from both sides.

"What are you doing? You don't have any weapons left. If you touch them, you'll burn!" I shoved at their bodies, but the pair of them stood like immovable statues.

Asher rubbed a hand across his chest. "There aren't many outliers left. If we take these two down, you might survive until Kade or Locke finds you. With this damn throbbing pain in our chests now, our brothers must know you're in danger. Let's just hope they've finished up with the fae."

My throat tightened at his words, and I turned to Darian, hoping he had a plan that was better than the ridiculous nonsense coming out of Asher's mouth. Darian's beautiful jaw was set, and his blue eyes shone with resolve. "If you die, we all die, and there's no sense in Kade and Locke dying as well. It's been a pleasure, lovely."

Anger spiked within me, and I wanted to kill them. I was no one and they had no right to act like my life was worth more than theirs, but...even the fae had detected that I was bonded to them. I knew it wasn't all about me. They were also hoping to save Kade and Locke.

I clenched and unclenched my fists at my sides and tried to swallow against the razor-sharp pain in my throat, but my mouth was too dry. I scanned the floor desperately for anything that could be turned into a weapon, but there was nothing but smeared black blood, the smooth marble floor, and the circle of red fire that held us captive.

"Assholes!" I cursed, my voice cracking, and I shoved at their backs again. I knew I shouldn't have cared. They were fucking monsters, and I'd grown up hating the beings who took my sister, but fear clawed at me, and my heart throbbed with pain.

Movement from my left drew my attention, and I shouted as an outlier sprang at us.

Asher was ready for the creature and didn't hesitate to shoot forward into the outlier's path. Panic seized me as his wrapped hand connected forcefully with the side of the outlier's head. A disgusting crack sounded, and the beast flew backward, sprawling to the floor on its side a few yards away.

For a moment, hope sparked in my chest at Asher's victory, but then my eyes widened in horror as he grunted in pain and began shaking his arm. His shirt caught fire where it connected with the outlier, and the fire moved faster than he could remove the burning clothing.

"Asher!" I cried, and my eyes began to water as the fire ate further up his arm.

Darian's muscles tensed as he prepared to fight the outlier approaching from the other side, but Asher moved past him.

"No, brother," Asher gritted out, though his face was contorted with agony. "I've got this one too. Protect Raine."

Darian's expression hardened at Asher's words, and I could see the reluctance on his face as he stepped back, but he nodded at the demon. *No. No. No. No.* Asher was too kind. Too fucking good to be sacrificing himself for me.

The skin tightened around Darian's eyes, and his lips thinned. "I'll see you where the air burns red and the earth is black," he said as some kind of strange goodbye.

Twisting his head, Asher replied with a weak grin, "See you in hell, brother." He looked as though he wanted to say more, but as the flames traveled up over his shoulder, the outlier stopped scratching at the floor and charged.

Asher turned his back to us and dodged to the side. Spinning around, he grabbed the outlier in midair with his powerful arms, jolting it to a halt. His hands moved to grip the top and bottom of the outlier's mouth, and then he pulled, his biceps flexing as he tore the creature's lower jaw off with a sickening ripping sound. I winced but kept watching as he shifted his arms and then ripped off the creature's entire head before dropping the outlier's body to the ground.

Asher took a step toward us, but he stopped as the flames burning both his arms licked across his bare chest. The skin touched by the fire looked as though it was trying to heal, and I guessed that was what was slowing the spread, but his demon healing ability wasn't fast enough.

Darian let out a pained noise beside me, and I fidgeted with my trembling hands. Not far from Asher, the outlier Asher had punched in the head slowly lifted to its feet. It blinked its beady red eyes at Asher, then launched toward Darian and me. Darian dropped into an offensive stance, but Asher clumsily moved toward the creature and jumped onto the creature's back before it could pass him.

With a pained roar, he wrapped an arm around the creature's head. The outlier screeched, trying to buck from side to side, but Asher held on. His arm around the outlier's head tightened, and the creature's bones cracked before the skin and muscle tore, the outlier's head ripping clean from its grotesque body. Asher stood as the outlier's body crashed downward, and I choked back a cry as flames engulfed Asher's entire body, racing over his legs, torso, and head. He took two steps away from the outlier before falling to his knees. His violet eyes peered at Darian, then fixed on me.

I couldn't do anything but stare back as the flames burned away his shaggy hair and ran up his beautiful, curved horns. *Beautiful.* Because even though Asher was a monster, he *was* beautiful. Goddess, I'd never felt so useless. The bond between us sent a wave of pain through me, but it wasn't physical pain. It was a throbbing agony in my heart that told me if Asher was taken from me, I'd never be whole again. A stream of curses went through my mind.

A shadow fell from above, and I prepared myself to fight the outlier with my bare hands like Asher had, but as I peered up, it was Locke who'd flown through one of the high windows. His black wings folded behind his back as he landed silently before Darian and me, and his dark gaze quickly swept over my body before he turned his attention to Asher.

Locke's body hardened as he watched the burning demon, and he clenched his jaw so forcefully it looked painful. Blue blood was splattered on his face and along his arms, and I frowned at the sight of it.

"Why isn't he fucking healing, Dar? Fire can't kill demons. Not with their healing ability," Locke ground out. "And why the fuck didn't you get Raine out of here?"

"It's not a natural fire. Anything the outliers touch ignites into flame," Darian replied, stepping up beside the vampire.

"And it's not Darian's fault I'm here," I added. "*You* should have taken us with you to fight the fae. Then Asher wouldn't be on the floor fucking dying."

Locke's cold gaze slid to my face. He didn't respond, but something like regret briefly shone in his eyes before it was gone again. A part of me knew it was wrong to make it sound like the whole situation was Locke's fault. Fighting the fae could have been just as dangerous, and he hadn't known outliers were going to attack the party. But the part of me that was hurting and confused, that part wanted someone to blame.

Asher remained on his knees with his head hung low. His healing power was still trying to heal the damage the fire was creating, but it wasn't fast enough, and his skin had begun peeling away.

"Kade's on his way. I would have carried him, but I feared I wouldn't make it here in time," Locke said as his gaze roved over the other monsters around the room, then returned to Asher. "And it looks like I haven't." He stepped forward then as if he intended to try to walk to the demon, but Darian gripped his arm. "If you touch the fire, you'll burn as well."

Locke cursed, but when Darian released his arm, he remained where he was.

I was still staring at Asher when Darian shifted.

"What the fuck?" Locke said under his breath, and I lifted my head to follow his gaze.

A dark figure dressed all in black strode toward us from across the room, and I squinted to try and make them out through the flames and haze of smoke. The figure walked through the red fire as though the flames were as cool as the mountain wind, and when I made out Warrick's cruel face, I wasn't surprised. Around the ballroom, the remaining outliers stopped attacking and all stared at him as if he was their god.

Warrick's clothes burned away as he walked, and by the time he stopped a short distance from us, he was completely naked. However, unlike Asher, the vampire was unharmed.

"Locke, my son. I was starting to think you might miss the demonstration. It has been most successful, as you can see," Warrick said and opened his arms wide, gesturing to the chaos of the room as if he was proud of the destruction.

"Demonstration?" Locke asked, his face an emotionless mask. "What is this?"

Warrick smiled, baring his long white fangs, and it was then as I stared at his self-satisfied expression, that I knew

I'd been right. I resisted the urge to grab Locke's sword. "Warrick is the one creating the outliers. It was never the fae," I said as I stared down the monster.

Darian and Locke stiffened on either side of me, and delight filled Warrick's eyes as his gaze locked on my face. The vampire flicked his wrist so fast I didn't see him move. Locke and Darian each caught a tiny blade that had been aimed at my face, but a third blade carved a shallow cut into my left cheek. Warmth dripped down the side of my face, and when I touched it with my hand, red blood covered my fingertips.

Locke drew his sword and stepped in front of me, and Darian swore as he turned my face to him to inspect the wound.

Warrick's lips widened into a gleeful smile. "I wondered if someone would figure it out, but I must say, I never thought it would be a newblood. Or should I say, *human.*"

Even through the fire and the strange clicking sound of the outliers, I could feel the tension rise in the room as the monsters who were still standing all turned to stare at me in shock. Locke and Darian angled their bodies as if they could shield me from view, but I simply lifted my chin as I glared daggers at the vampire.

"Oh yes," Warrick continued enthusiastically. "I figured out your little secret too. I became suspicious when Locke didn't immediately hand you over to the Taratun, but when I saw you with my own eyes, I could believe he simply wanted to toy with you. However, when I realized he was giving me shifter blood that didn't belong to a newblood, and you refused to change during the Week of Orash..." He trailed off. "Well now, fitting the pieces together wasn't that hard. It does amuse me, though, that the human without powers or monster abilities was the one to uncover my involvement with the outliers."

"You won't get away with what you've done," I said, stepping out from behind Locke so I could see the male. I hoped to keep him talking about the outliers rather than the fact I was still human. "Your role with the outliers became obvious after I visited your lab. How else would you have a detailed drawing of the outlier in the ocean? Its head exploded when the gargoyles destroyed it, but you had carefully depicted every detail of the monster as if you'd seen it with your own eyes. The only rational explanation was that you *had* indeed seen it before. You had because you created it."

Locke's hands gripped tighter on his sword. "You told me you needed the outliers to determine why our animals were turning into monsters. You didn't say you were the one creating the fucking beasts," he spat.

"Oh, don't act so surprised," Warrick said, waving his hand at Locke as if he was a petulant child. "You've merely been helping me collect my specimens. And, you're missing the point. Just look at this destruction," he said, opening his arms and spinning in a slow circle as if he wanted to take in every detail of the room around him. "This is but a show of what my monsters will be able to do against the fae. Oh yes, the Week of Orash was such a perfect distraction for me to finally test my work on a greater scale. By experimenting on the animals and adding an amount of my blood, the monsters answer my commands and I'm immune to their magic. By the time I've finished, we'll have an army to not only protect Katakin but take over the fae world!"

"You said you were searching for a fucking cure!" Locke shouted as he took a step toward Warrick. "A way to break the damn curse."

Warrick sighed heavily. "Why would I want a cure for immortality and power? No, I'm not going to take away the greatest gift the people of Katakin were ever given. No, these monsters," he said, gesturing to the outliers with a fond expression on his face, "they will be our weapon to rid ourselves of the fae and finally take what's theirs."

Locke's jaw ticked, but he let his father continue speaking.

"But first, I must rid us of this...nuisance," Warrick said, sneering in my direction. "The last thing I need is for the citizens of Katakin to start thinking they could be human again. Not when we're finally close to getting it all. I'm doing this for them as much as I'm doing it for me."

I scoffed, surprised that Warrick was able to believe his own bullshit.

"Raine has nothing to do with this," Locke said coldly as he moved to block Warrick's view of me.

"She has everything to do with this!" Warrick bellowed, spittle flying from his mouth. "Now move aside, or you can join her just like your..." He looked down at Asher writhing on the ground as the fire continued to burn him. "...friend," he finished with disgust.

Warrick narrowed his eyes in challenge at Locke. "I'll give you a moment to decide. I trust you'll make the right decision. And don't even think of trying to fly off with your little human toy. If you do, I'll make sure the entire city suffers." His lips stretched into a sadistic smile then, as if he was challenging Locke to disobey him.

Locke's nostrils flared, and the male radiated anger. For a moment, I thought he was going to launch himself at Warrick, but instead, he took a few deep breaths and turned stiffly to Darian and me.

"Fly her out of here, Locke. We're not getting out of this," Darian said calmly, and his defeated gaze lingered on where Asher still burned.

Locke's temple pulsed, and his dark gaze peered at the other monsters in the room. "Warrick will unleash his outliers on the entire city. I can't let that happen."

I thought of how Cara was likely living somewhere in the city. I didn't want Locke to save me if it meant condemning others. Still, it wasn't easy facing the idea of death. Though, you'd think I'd be used to it by now. "Looks like you put me through all those trials for nothing," I said with a weak smile, trying to lighten the mood even though a heaviness had settled over me.

Turning me toward him, Locke lifted my chin with his clawed fingers, and I expected him to say something about me being their downfall, but instead, he pressed a kiss to my lips. It was rough and punishing but also full of longing, and it wasn't long before he pulled away again.

"I wouldn't say that, *beautiful*," he said with a small smile and released me. Rolling his shoulders, he tightened his grip on his sword and turned to face Warrick again.

I blinked, still reeling from Locke's kiss. It became clear then that Locke wasn't choosing his father's side. I knew he was likely staying because he thought if I died, he and his brothers would die as well, but something still made me ache at the thought that he might be staying because of me.

"So that's your decision?" Warrick said, looking both disappointed and disgusted. "Your mother is going to be quite forlorn, but I suppose I'm not too surprised. I'll collect your ashes for her when it's done." With that, he turned and clapped his hands together as he strode away from us across the ballroom.

The clicking sound of the remaining five outliers rose as they all turned to us, their red eyes fixing on our location. As the creatures started forward, their wrinkled bodies scampering toward us, I dropped into a crouch and steeled myself for their attack.

"Stay behind us," Locke ordered, but I moved to the side so he wasn't blocking my view. I wasn't going to spend my last moments cowering behind monsters. At most, Locke would be able to take out two outliers with his sword before the weapon burst into flame. That would still leave three for us to fight off.

I peered at Asher on the ground. He was hardly moving now, and the gaping cavern inside my chest felt as though it'd swallow me whole. I clenched my jaw as I turned my attention back to the gnashing teeth of the outliers and their snarling, fanged mouths.

Fuck this. I'd fought too damn hard and trained for too many years for it to end like this. Deep down, I knew I wasn't just angry at the idea of my own death. I'd faced the idea of death so many times over the last few nights it was almost like a common occurrence. But seeing Asher burning had me filling with rage, and knowing that Locke and Darian were still there because of me made me sick.

It was then that I thought of how I'd opened a hole in Warrick's lab using magic. *If I create a hole in the floor, there must be a cavern below us, right?* Another cavern meant possibly more weapons or at least, an escape from the fire and the outliers. It was worth a shot.

Squeezing my eyes shut, I focused on finding that spark of energy inside myself. It was easier to find this time, probably because I had used the magic not too long ago, and I unearthed it from where it was hidden deep inside me. Wasting no time, I let my desperation and anger fuel the spark into a raging inferno, and my eyes popped open as power rushed through me, burning in my veins.

Whoa. I didn't have time to be shocked that I had been able to summon the magic again. The first outlier attacked, jumping at Locke with its jaws outstretched, and Locke's muscles bunched as he maneuvered his body, slicing the beast in two. Instantly, the blade caught fire, and Locke dropped the weapon to the ground.

The other four outliers neared us, and I squatted to the floor, placing my palms on the cool marble stone of the ballroom. The red fire burned around us, and sweat slid down my face into my eyes, blurring my vision. Goddess, it was so hot.

The clicking of the outliers sounded in my ears, and I focused on releasing the power inside me. *Come on, turn to sand.*

When nothing happened, I cracked open an eye. Power still pulsed from me, but the floor was still intact. I cursed under my breath when a deep groan came from deep in the mountain. The floor shuddered beneath our feet, and the walls trembled around us.

"What are you doing?" Locke barked.

I pulled my hands away from the floor, but energy still zapped from me. "Nothing. I'm not doing anything," I said, standing again.

Darian cocked his head. "I can hear water! It's about to get bumpy!"

Water? Before I could try and understand what was happening, clicking sounded to my left.

"Raine!" Locke shouted as an outlier lunged at me, snapping its teeth at my torso.

In a blur, Locke reached out, pulling me with brutal force into his muscly arms. I cried out as black wings stretched above our heads, and Locke lifted me into the air. My first thought was of Warrick and whether the vampire would punish Locke for saving me, but as the ballroom cracked and groaned around us, all I could think about was Darian and Asher below us and the power still pulsing from my fingertips.

The walls shuddered again, and a deafening roar sounded as glowing blue water crashed through the double doors of the ballroom and gushed through the high-arched windows.

The red fire hissed as the water flooded the ballroom, and steam filled the air, the warm mist brushing over my face. Monsters cried out, and panic went through me as I imagined them being swept up in the torrent, but Locke held me tight. I couldn't see what was happening.

"You're using too much magic!" Locke yelled in my face, but I couldn't stop.

The air squeezed from my lungs as the energy drained from me, and all I could do was focus on the fear in his onyx eyes and the drops of water spraying on my feet. Then the world went black.

CHAPTER 29

~ Raine ~

My eyes fluttered open, and I awoke to find Kade's stubbled chin above me. Closing my eyes, I groaned as memories came back to me in flashes. I remembered the sensation of my magic flowing out of me, the rush of the water as it had spilled through the high windows, and the screams of monsters from below us in the ballroom. I remembered...

"The outliers!" I gasped, my eyes snapping open again as I jolted upright.

"You're all right," Kade said calmly as he wrapped an arm around my belly and tried to force me to relax against him again. "You were out for a day, but you're going to be fine. We're at one of our houses in the city."

I tried to resist him, but I stopped squirming when I took in my surroundings. *One of their houses?* Kade and I were on a large four-poster bed that had an absurd number of downy pillows and satin sheets that were pleasantly cool. Beautiful paintings of what I guessed was scenery from around Katakin decorated the walls, and to the right sat a long wood-carved wardrobe and full-length mirror. To the left, a small table held a jug of pink liquid and various alcoholic bottles.

Locke stood in front of the large window not far from the table. The curtains were pulled back, and the moonlight cast his shadow across the floor. The vampire was facing me rather than peering outside, and it was hard to make out his face.

"Are— Are we dead?" I croaked.

Locke's chuckle was low and devoid of genuine humor. "You saved us," he said quietly, and I didn't miss the strange softness of his voice.

"You gave us a scare, but no, we're not dead, Mahare," Kade said as he nuzzled the side of my neck.

I breathed in deeply, taking in his scents of sandalwood and coffee. The faint scent of smoke also lingered on his skin, and I frowned. Had he made it to the ballroom?

Kade brushed my hair away from my eyes, and I swallowed. There was a dull ache throbbing throughout my whole body, but nothing too painful. *You saved us.* Locke's words repeated in my ears, and I struggled to believe them.

"Asher and Darian," I said, my voice tight. "Did they—?" Darian, I hoped, was alive, but I knew Asher was too much to hope for. The fire had consumed him. There was no way he could have lived, but still, I had to ask. My heart pounded faster, and my breath caught in my throat as I waited for one of them to answer me.

Before either Kade or Locke could speak, the door to the room opened, and Darian entered the room, carrying a stack of plates and cutlery, followed by a grinning Asher, who held a large silver tray laden with food. He was wearing a clean shirt and trousers, the kind he usually wore when he was relaxing in the rooms, and he was completely healed, from his violet horns to his forked tail.

My mouth dropped open, and for a moment, I couldn't speak. I had to be dreaming. *Please tell me I'm not dreaming.* Tears welled in my eyes, and when Asher peered over at me and gave me a lopsided smile, I scrambled from the bed and barreled into him. He barely had time to drop the tray onto the bed before I was in his arms, running my hands over his face and body.

"You fucker!" I growled. "How dare you!"

Before I could say anything more, he lifted me into the air and smashed his lips against mine.

The anger fizzed out of me as I kissed him back, and he held me like he was never planning to let me go again. When I finally pulled back, he set me down on my feet again reluctantly.

"Now *that's* a greetin' I could get used to. I should almost die all the time," Asher said with a massive grin, and I punched his arm.

"Do it again, and next time I'll be the one that kills you," I threatened.

The others chuckled behind us, but Asher's cocky grin just grew wider.

He's alive. I repeated the words in my head as my hands ran up and down his arms over and over. The skin was as smooth as I remembered, without a single scar or mark to show he'd been burned.

"How?" I asked in disbelief.

Asher's expression sobered, and he stared at me intensely. "Well, that would be because of you, sweetheart."

"But you were on *fire*," I said. "*Magic fire.* I watched you burn."

Asher cringed as if remembering the pain of the fire, but then he said, "I passed out before your chat with Warrick, so Locke and Darian will have to explain."

Nodding, I turned my attention to where Darian stood near the table. He'd placed the plates down and stood watching me with a relieved smile.

"Same goes for you, you know," I said, my expression becoming serious. "Try to sacrifice yourself for me again, and you'll regret it."

Darian simply arched a brow as if he had no intention of listening to me. "You aren't one to talk, lovely. And it's a good thing you finally woke up. Locke has barely left this room since we brought you here, and he's been more irritable than usual."

I snorted and choked on a laugh at Darian's insinuation. *Locke?* When no one else laughed with me, I frowned at the vampire. He was still watching me with an intense expression, and he said nothing. I found it hard to believe that he had been worried about me, but then I thought of how he'd lifted me into the air, saving me from the outlier. I could still hear him shouting in my face before the world went dark.

I was suddenly not sure what to say to Darian's comment, and I climbed onto the bed again and settled back into Kade's arms. A part of me wanted to go to Locke instead. To have his cold palms resting on my skin, and his steady presence next to me. *Did he really stay in the room the whole time while he waited for me to wake?*

"I remember you lifting me into the air," I said slowly as I kept watching Locke's face. "And there was water."

Asher moved the tray of food from the bed to the table and began loading up a plate.

Locke's expression remained neutral. "You must have used a significant amount of magic," he said with a dip of his head. "You flooded the ballroom, and I could feel the magic radiating from you."

"Flooded?" I asked, my brows shooting upward. I remembered the water streaming through the windows and the shuddering of the mountain, but had I really *flooded* it?

"You must have called upon all the water sources in and around the mountain that still had traces of magic, and the water combined with the magic was able to douse the fires of the outliers," Locke added.

I stared in disbelief. "*I did that?*" I had felt the energy and magic leaving my body, but it was still hard to grasp. I tried to think back to the fight with the outliers. I'd intended to turn the floor to sand, but the stifling heat kept making me think of the red fire. I vaguely remembered wishing I had something to douse the flames. *All right, that's great. First, I could turn rock to sand, then I created a vortex of wind, and now I'm flooding caverns.*

"Yes, it was quite the sight," Darian said as he poured himself a drink from the jug on the table. "The Katakin monsters were tossed around rather brutally, but they all obtained injuries they could heal from. I don't think anyone was complaining."

I scrunched my face as I thought of how badly some of the alphas and other monsters were likely hurt.

At that moment, Asher strode over and handed me the plate piled high with different cheeses and meats, then he stretched out on the bed beside Kade and me. "And when I was no longer on fuckin' fire, my body was finally able to heal. I'm lucky I'm a demon. None of the other monsters who caught fire had my healing ability and were able to survive."

I swallowed then as I pictured Asher's burning body, and my stomach roiled, but I forced myself to nibble on a hunk of cheese. Eating was the last thing on my mind, but my body felt weak, and I knew I had to get some food into me.

Darian swirled the wine in his goblet. "Thankfully, there was only enough water to extinguish the fire, and then when you passed out, the water started flowing back to where it had come from. The outliers were weakened by then and tried to escape, but we finished them off with a little help from the other alphas."

"And Warrick?" I asked apprehensively.

"He wasn't there when I arrived," Kade answered as he grabbed a rolled up piece of meat from the plate and popped it into his mouth.

I turned to look at Locke sympathetically then. For all his faults, I couldn't imagine my own father trying to kill me. "We'll find him," Locke ground out, and his eyes blazed with fury. "But first," he said to me, "you need to tell us what you were doing in Warrick's lab."

"Oh, that." I placed my half-eaten hunk of cheese on the plate and cleared my throat. I'd been waiting for them to ask. Letting out a long breath, I went on to tell them all about the drawings of the outliers I'd seen in Warrick's lab. I didn't mention that I'd seen Locke's report, nor did I explain about my sister. I simply told them I was desperate to know if Warrick had information about what I was or why I hadn't changed into a monster. I also explained all about the fae male who'd been tortured and why he said he was there. Finally, I spoke about the portal the fae said he'd created. When I finished, everyone was silent for a beat before Kade growled, "You shouldn't have gone down there. There's a reason Warrick's lab is so deep beneath the mountain."

I prepared myself to argue, but Locke spoke up, his brow wrinkled in thought. "When we fought the fae in the city, they were shouting about a prince. There were only around twenty fae warriors, and when Kade and I joined the gargoyles and other monsters who were already fighting, I thought they'd flee back into the portal when they realized they were outnumbered. But they didn't. Some of them used magic, but it wasn't enough to overpower us. It wasn't until there were only two fae left that one of them went back through the portal. It closed soon after, but it's possible this Prince Azaren is who he says he is."

"If he's a prince, why would only twenty soldiers come through?" Asher asked.

Darian placed his goblet on the table and strolled over, dropping down on the bed near my legs. "It's been a while since the fae have attacked. They might have been hoping to create a portal in the forest like Prince Azaren and thought they could scout the area in smaller numbers to find him."

"Do you think he's found the books?" Kade asked Locke.

I jerked my head back so I could look at the wolf shifter. "Wait. So the books are real?"

"Very," Kade growled. "Locke and I have been searching them to try to find information about the curse or whatever bond this is. I'm not sure why we bothered when they're all damned fairy tales."

Fairy tales? I thought of Locke and Kade reading fairy tales together, and my lip quirked up, but then I thought of what Prince Azaren had said about me. "So about the bond...," I began.

"What about it?" Asher asked, and one of his large hands casually flopped onto my thigh. "It's turned out to be useful. Locke wouldn't have known about you being in danger without it."

I tried not to think about how both Kade and Asher were touching me now, and I said, "Well, Prince Azaren said he could tell I was cursed."

"Cursed?" Darian asked, his blue eyes sparking with interest. "Aren't we all? You're obviously turning into something powerful."

I wiggled uneasily against Kade's body.

Kade sucked in a sharp breath, and I realized I'd rubbed against his growing erection that had begun to poke into my back. An erection that I'd been trying desperately to ignore. "Sorry," I muttered, then turned my attention back to the others. "He said he could feel strange magic around me. Magic that's different from the curse Queen Izla placed on Katakin. Magic that has bound my soul to others. He suggested that maybe someone has experimented on me."

"Your soul? What the fuck," Asher spat out.

Kade growled, and Darian cursed.

"Warrick," Locke bit out, and his lip curled to reveal fangs.

"So you think he did something to me too?" I asked, a little deflated.

No one answered, but their silence told me that they did. *Well, fuck.* So I was another of Warrick's experiments. I sighed heavily. "Well, Prince Azaren said if I went with him to the fae realm, he would be able to remove the curse."

Kade's body stiffened behind me, and the others tensed as well.

"We're not removing the bonds," Kade growled, and I was surprised at the anger rolling off him. *Didn't he want to be free of me?*

Darian and Asher muttered their agreement, but Locke was the one to say, "If Warrick has experimented on her, there's no telling what he's done or whether Raine's life is in danger. We should try to remove the magic he's placed over her."

Asher and Kade went to protest, but I held up my hands. "If there's a way to remove the curse on me, there must also be a way to break the curse on Katakin. I intend to find it. You heard Warrick. His 'demonstration' went well. He intends to create an army of the creatures and doesn't care if any of the monsters of Katakin are killed along the way. We *need* to find that cure. Besides, I won't be responsible for getting you all killed. I want to try to find the portal and go to the fae world."

The idea of going to yet another strange world made my stomach churn, but I had to do it. If the curse was removed from Katakin, Warrick would no longer have magic and could no longer create outliers. I might not have found my sister yet, but Warrick was still alive, and if she was in Katakin she was in danger. I didn't know how long Prince Azaren's portal would stay open, and it could be my only chance.

"The fae would kill you," Kade snarled, his body rigid.

"And who's to say where this prince is now? Not to mention, even if you did find him in the fae realm, why would he help us?" Darian asked.

It was Locke who answered. "If there's a cure, we must find it. Warrick wants war. If we break the curse, we destroy the outliers."

"And who's to say the fae won't wipe us out when we've been turned human again?" Kade growled, challenging Locke.

"I'd rather die a human than remain a fucking monster," Locke replied calmly. "And, if we're human, maybe we can stop the war."

Asher pulled his hand from my leg and sat up straighter. "So you're just goin' to waltz into the fae realm and find it? I'm down for an adventure, but that's madness."

"It does sound rather risky," Darian added. "You know we can't be far from Katakin or we'll die."

I whipped my head in Darian's direction. "Wait, what? Did you just say *die*?"

"Oh yes, when we try to go too far from the mountain where Queen Izla initiated the curse, we grow weaker and die within nights. It's why we never stay long when we visit your island," Darian explained. "There's no telling what will happen if we go to the fae realm."

"That's it, then," I said, throwing my hands in the air. "I'm going alone."

Locke didn't seem at all concerned with the idea of death. "We die because we're away from the queen's fae magic. If we go to the fae realm, I imagine we'll be surrounded by fae magic. And even if it doesn't work in the same way, we'll have four nights before we have to return."

"And what if we're captured?" Darian asked.

"Then I'll kill them," Kade growled viciously.

Asher chuckled at that. "You and me both, brother."

Darian shook his head at the pair of them. "Well, that's obvious, but in the case we can't? The fae have powerful magic. Or have you forgotten how the queen cursed us all?"

Kade growled again in response to Darian's sarcasm.

"We'll deal with that problem if it comes to it," Locke said.

I wanted to tell them they couldn't risk it, but as much as I didn't want them to get hurt, as long as we were bonded, their lives were tied to mine. I'd have a better chance of surviving the fae realm with them by my side.

"If Prince Azaren has escaped through the portal, it could be closed by now," I pointed out. "Not to mention, we still have to find it."

"I think I know where it might be," Kade said.

"Then there's only one way to find out if it's still there," Asher said with an eager grin.

CHAPTER 30

~ Raine ~

I rested my hand on the pommel of my sword, letting my thumb rub circles over the fine steel. Kade had insisted that we all arm ourselves before leaving the house, and I'd been downright ecstatic when Asher had pulled out a trunk of weapons and handed me several throwing knives and a sword.

The moon was high by the time we trekked through the forest and Kade led us to the portal. The large circle of blue fire was still burning near a waterfall and between two ancient oak trees, just as Prince Azaren had described. The gnarled roots of the trees sprang out of the ground like wooden fingers, as if the trees were trying to drag us toward the portal, and the thought had unease slithering through me. The last time I'd gone through a portal, it had brought me to Katakin and the monster trials. This time? Well, this time, it would bring me to the fae, and once again, I wasn't exactly sure what I would find on the other side.

"I can't believe it's still here," I mused aloud as I stared at the doorway to another world. "Does that mean Prince Azaren is still somewhere in Katakin? But if he didn't make it back, that means the fae will keep attacking." A part of me had hoped we wouldn't find the portal. That the fae prince had just returned home, and by some miracle, the fae wouldn't return for war.

Locke had been silent the entire time we made our way through the forest, and his face was unreadable now as he said, "It's only been one day. If he was as determined to get those books as he said, it would have taken him some time, but we should get moving. He might not be too far behind us."

Kade was rigid beside me, and I brushed my shoulder against his arm, sensing the storm of emotions going through him. "You don't have to come, you know," I said quietly to him. Kade hated the fae for what they did to his family, and I wasn't sure how he would handle being in their world.

Kade's golden eyes fixed on my face, and his brows lowered as if the mere suggestion of him staying behind was a personal insult to him. "I'm not letting you out of my sight, Mahare. What makes you think I'd let you go to the fae realm alone?" he growled softly. The intense look he gave me was equal parts terrifying and reassuring.

"We'll face the fae together, lovely," Darian said with a smile, pulling my attention to him. His white teeth and silver hair gleamed in the moonlight, making the moment seem way more like a dream than the strange reality I found myself in.

Asher stepped forward beside the siren, crossed his arms over his broad chest, and grinned. "Don't even think about asking me to stay. Life is way more interestin' with you around, Sharachi," he said.

I grinned back at him, but then I noticed Locke's sharp onyx eyes were studying my face. "While our lives have been bound to yours, we should all remain together," Locke said, his dark gaze not leaving me.

I didn't miss his choice of words. *While our lives...* He made it sound like we'd be breaking the bond soon, and I forced myself not to react. I shouldn't have been surprised. It was what I said I wanted. Wasn't it?

"Then let's go," I said coldly and turned back toward the portal. Before I could step forward, Kade's hand gripped my waist, and his body tensed.

"What is it?" Locke asked as Kade cocked his head to the side.

Kade's nostrils flared as he scented the air. "Zacal's wolves. Several of them are headed our way."

He'd barely finished speaking when a howl cut through the air, followed by another and then a third.

Asher drew his axes and rolled his shoulders as if he was readying himself for a fight. "Sounds like they're huntin'."

"Hunting? Is it Prince Azaren?" I asked, suddenly irrationally worried for the fae. I knew the fae were murderers, but the male had such a friendly attitude that the thought of him being torn to shreds by Zacal's wolves didn't sit right with me.

"See for yourself," Kade growled as a tall, slender male with short azure-colored hair ran into view, appearing from between the trees at the bottom of the hill we were standing on. The prince held a tall stack of books in front of him as he ran, and his muscled arms strained to hold them as he staggered forward. Twice when the books swayed to one side, I thought he would drop them. A bandage wound around Prince Azaren's right wrist, the one that Warrick had cut and used to bleed him, and he now wore a black shirt and pants that I could only imagine he'd managed to steal from a monster on his way out of the mountain.

"Well, would you look at that. The royal fucker found the books," Asher commented, grinning at the sight of the prince running toward us.

Kade didn't look amused. He still hadn't released my waist, and he took another deep inhale, his nostrils flaring as he scented the air. "He's not going to make it. The wolves will be on him before he sets foot through that portal."

"What? But if they kill him, then there'll definitely be a war. You need to save him," I said as I stared at the prince.

A low growl started in Kade's chest, but Locke's voice cut through the sound. "She's right. The prince needs to live, and he must get back through that portal. Kade, you and I are the fastest. We'll grab the books and the prince. Asher and Darian, you wait with Raine beside the portal. When Kade and I return with the prince, we go through together."

Kade's eyes darkened, his growl growing louder, but he nodded and released me. Lifting me off my feet, he literally placed me into Darian's arms. I barely had time to splutter a protest before he said, "I'll be back with the fae," and was sprinting away from us, shifting into his wolf form as he went.

Locke's wings speared from his back, and the vampire flew after Kade, the pair of them heading toward the prince. Prince Azaren's eyes widened at the sight of them, but then my view of the prince was cut off. Darian had turned around, and he was carrying me toward the portal. His strides were confident and graceful, almost as if he was gliding over the ground, but his body was hard, his muscles tense as if he was readying himself for battle.

"Hey!" I complained, but he held me tight. It wasn't until we were right next to the portal that he set me down. By the time I spun around, Locke was flying back with the books stacked in his arms, and Kade had shifted back to his human form and had an unconscious Prince Azaren bent over his shoulder. Asher stood next to us, but his axes were back at his sides, and he was holding the clothes and weapons Kade had shed when he'd shifted into his wolf form.

Locke landed near us a short while later and placed the books on the ground, but I kept my eyes trained on Kade and the prince. Kade was halfway up the hill when Zacal's wolves burst from the trees at the bottom. At first, I could only see two of them, but soon there were five wolves running after Kade and the fae, their large paws flying over the ground.

Darian grabbed two of the throwing stars pinned to the leather pouches on his chest, but Locke shook his head. "Don't hurt them. It's bad enough they'll see us leaving with the fae. We don't need to wound them as well."

Shit. I hadn't thought about what the other monsters in Katakin would think of Locke, Kade, and the others if they left for the fae world. No one else knew the fae was a prince or that there was the possibility of a cure. Would they think Locke and the others were traitors? I couldn't dwell on it now. Reaching down, I picked up three books from the stack and piled them onto my other arm. I didn't know why Prince Azaren was so desperate to save the fairy tales, but I had a feeling we'd need his goodwill when we were on the other side of the portal. Saving the books seemed like a good way to start building some.

Locke frowned at me, and I thought he was going to snatch them back, but instead, he picked up the rest before I could grab more. To my surprise, he held the books carefully, as though he was worried about destroying the leather hardcovers or aged pages within.

Howls broke out across the forest, and I looked up as Kade barreled toward us, grunting as he ran.

"Get ready," Locke shouted. "We go through together."

When Kade reached us, I frowned at the prince's unconscious form. No doubt, Kade had used his fist to persuade the prince to go with him. Before I could comment, Darian scooped me into his arms, taking me into the portal with him. Light sparked in my eyes, blinding me, and I couldn't tell if Locke and the others were with us. The three fae books dug painfully into my chest as Darian gripped me tightly, and all I saw was the endless blue that spiraled in my vision. *Well, fuck.*

TO BE CONTINUED IN BOOK 3:
THE CURSE OF MONSTERS

LET'S BE FRIENDS!

Thank you so much for reading book 2 in my *Her Cursed Protectors* series! If you enjoyed the story, please consider leaving me a review on Amazon or Goodreads. As an indie author, it's hard for me to get eyes on my books and every review or rating helps.

Want to be friends? Join my newsletter via *www.miahartson.com*. You'll receive writing updates, teasers, and giveaways.

Not a fan of email? You can also find me on Facebook at www.facebook.com/AuthorMiaHartson, Goodreads or Bookbub. I look forward to getting to know you!

HER CURSED PROTECTORS READING ORDER

Shadow Shifter (prequel)
The Blood of Monsters
The Cries of Monsters
The Curse of Monsters
The Wars of Monsters

ABOUT THE AUTHOR

Mia Hartson is an Australian fantasy and paranormal romance author who enjoys writing stories about badass heroines who have multiple partners. (Because the only thing better than one mate is four, right?)

Mia particularly enjoys writing stories with a heavy dose of fantasy, adventure, and spice that keeps you up at night. When she's not writing, Mia's going on adventures with her husband and two girls, decorating cakes, singing her heart out, or devouring another book.

For more information about Mia Hartson, her books, and upcoming releases, visit her website www.miahartson.com, Facebook page, Goodreads page or Bookbub.